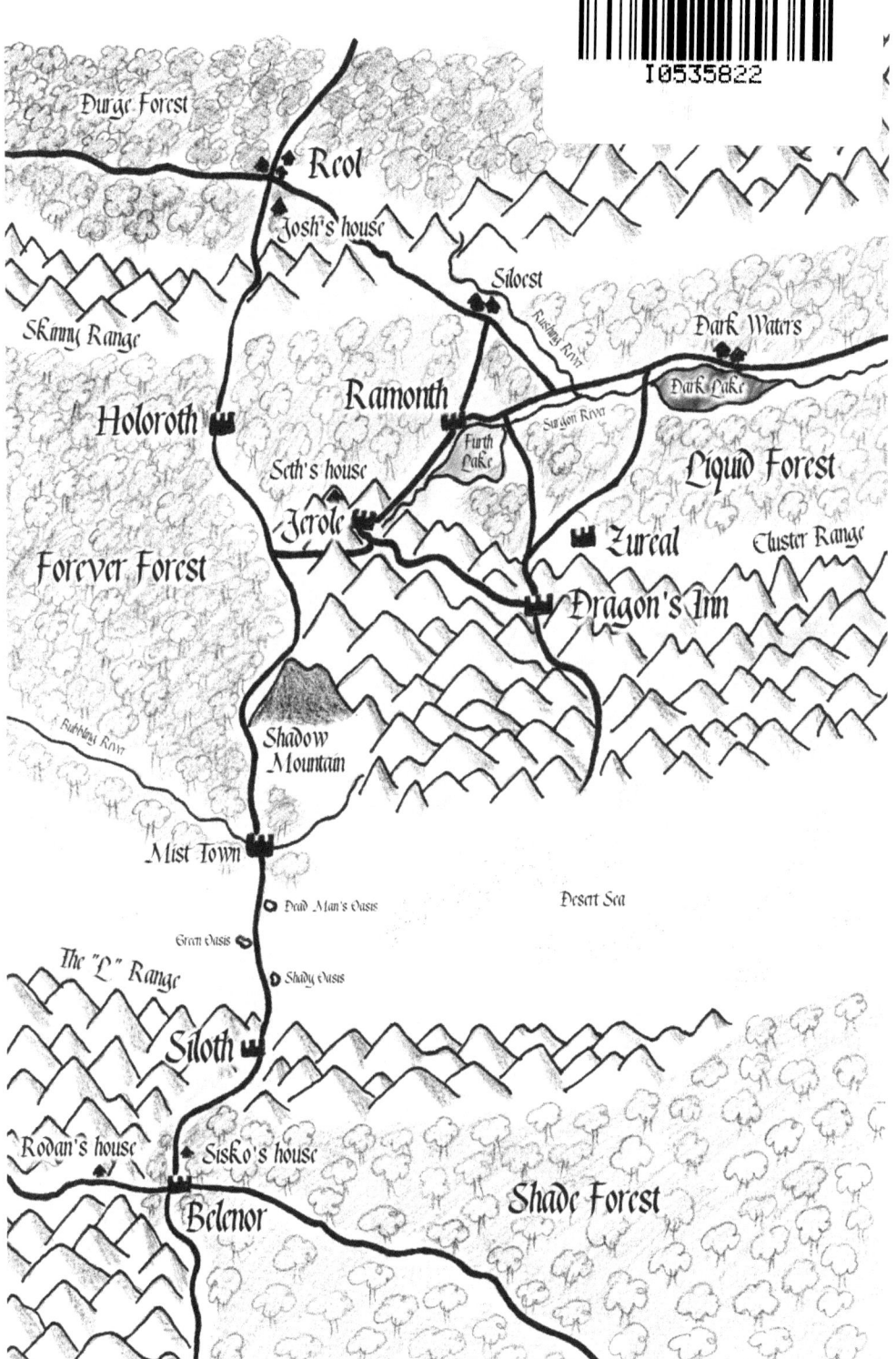

Reality's Ascent

R. L. Copple

ISBN: 978-0-9864517-9-9
Splashdown Books, New Zealand
http://www.splashdownbooks.com

Acknowledgments

I'm in deep gratitude to many people who helped me with this project. Several have provided in-depth critiques and input, including Selena Thomason, Boris and J. B. Skaggs at Notebored.com, and proofing help from several at the Lost Genre Guild. Without their valuable help in catching things I missed and helping me to see issues I'm blind to, this story wouldn't have the same punch and smoothness it does now. Thanks to every one of you who have helped.

I also would be amiss if I didn't thank my dear wife and kids, who are not only the first beta readers of my rough drafts, but also give me the space and time to write.

I thank Bill Snodgrass and Cameron Walker, who first published this book as *Transforming Realities* under the banner of Double-Edged Publishing, Inc. Their support is priceless and I pray they are richly rewarded for their efforts.

And many thanks to Splashdown Books, not only for a willingness to republish this edition when DEP could no longer do so, but for the invaluable help in improving it in quality and content.

There are many others who touched the work in one way or another that I could list. I'm grateful for all the input and support.

But most of all, I thank God for providing the story. I pray Reality's Ascent will encourage each of us to discover God's reality rising in our hearts.

R. L. Copple

This book is dedicated to my wife, Lenita Copple,
who has given me a taste of Paradise in this life.

Part One

S i s k o

1

The stars winked through my bedroom window. I winked back. Anytime I gazed upon them, they always transported me back to the day I had died and visited Paradise far beyond any of the twinkling lights I could now see. A memory that would always stay with me. A memory I looked forward to renewing someday when my life cast its last rays of energy in this world.

Did I want this life to end? Yes and no. I had carried the memory of Paradise with me for twenty years. But the reason I had returned to this world lay beside me. I glanced at Gabrielle's sleeping form. She shifted, and her golden hair, now a dull yellow in the dim light, fell from her face.

I brushed the remaining hairs back. My ring reflected the night lights against her delicate skin. The ring that led me to Gabrielle. As well as my death, but then to Paradise. Yet He gave me a choice to stay in Paradise or return to marry Gabrielle. Despite the pull to stay, I chose to return because I loved her that much.

My hand rested against her cheek. A gust of wind blew into the room; her hair waved in the wind and her sweet scent wafted across my nose. Yes, I could still taste Paradise in her. It never failed.

Her eyes cracked open and turned my direction. "Are you still awake?" She yawned.

"Not feeling too sleepy."

She rolled over, placed her hand on my shoulder, and glanced at the ring on my finger. "You're thinking about the ring, aren't you?"

I smiled. She knew me too well. "The ring, Paradise, the steam house. You."

She chuckled. "Glad I'm in there somewhere." She rolled onto her back and stared out the window with me. "All these years you've spoken of the steam house but you've never taken me there to see it. Or your parents. Remember ten years ago? You promised we would make the trip someday. Someday's flown past into yesterday and I fear any-day-now will, too. Take me to see the steam house as you promised."

"It's just an old, wooden building."

"Yes, one that turns people into animals and trees if they're evil. Or gives good fourteen-year-old boys magic rings to heal people with."

I shook my head. "No, not specifically evil people. It brings out character flaws and attempts to make people deal with them, or enables good traits."

She giggled and fell back on her pillow. "Well, excuse me for not getting it just right! I say if they're evil it will change them for the worse."

"Have it your way then." I chuckled. "But I have to say, if you went into the steam house in order to see everyone turn into something bad, you're not likely to come out in good shape yourself."

She laughed. "I suppose not. Still, I would like to go." She propped her head onto her hand and stared at me. "All we've heard are your stories. We need to go there. Can't we plan on it? Kaylee and Nathan are nearly grown and haven't once seen their grandparents or uncle. We're running out of time. You said we're going to do it. So do it now."

I sighed in mock exasperation. "I don't know. I have so much to do tomorrow."

She grabbed the pillow from behind her and swung it onto my head. "I demand you take me there!" She giggled as her blows landed on my upraised arms.

"All right! All right! I give! We'll go. I'll plan the trip tomorrow!"

She landed one more swing against my stomach, fell over on me, and wrapped her arms around my waist. Her smile hinted at victory. She lowered her lips to mine. Her hair caressed the sides of my cheeks as her soft skin melded into my lips. Her soul burst through me, as it always had from our first meeting. It ended way too soon.

She rolled back onto her side of the bed. "I've done all I needed to do for one night. I have a full day tomorrow and need my sleep. I leave you to your thoughts of the ring, the steam house, and Paradise."

"And you. Don't forget you."

She laughed, a tinge of impishness hung on the end of it. But within moments, she had settled down and snored softly into the breeze. I marveled how she could fall asleep so quickly. I, on the other hand—

Sisko?

I jumped. Then realized Josh, my best friend from Reol, must be trying to reach me. He had learned the craft of magic and had become quite the wizard. Before I left on my journeys, he'd created a link between us so we could keep in touch, and he'd promised to watch over my parents and brother. He would occasionally contact me to keep me updated on happenings in Reol.

I settled onto my pillow and closed my eyes. *Yes, Josh?*

I have some bad news, I'm afraid. I'm not sure what to make of it.

Are my parents all right?

For the moment. A demon named Beltrid attempted to kill them with a sickness and almost did. I nearly exhausted myself keeping them alive. They're bedridden, but still very much alive.

Josh, you have my eternal gratitude, but did you discover why?

I'm not sure, but when he realized he couldn't do any more against them, he made a comment about you. I believe he is trying to get to you through your loved ones. And he…interested…ring…playing into…hands…

The link stayed, but no further words arrived. *Josh! Are you there?*

Another voice broke through. *Sisko, I must speak with you.*

Who is this?

The darkness behind my eyelids deepened and I could feel a pull. I couldn't tell if my body remained on my bed or not. A moment passed before I felt a solid floor under my feet. A ray of light penetrated a dark void; I could only see a few feet away. The darkness hung heavy all around me.

"Hello, who has called me?"

Seconds passed before a form appeared. A pale face hung on a thin skull; eyes of fire blazed from a bald head. Long black robes sank over his frame, and a parched smile spread across his face.

"Sisko, my name is Beltrid. We must talk."

I stepped back. "What are you?"

"You already know. But what I am is not the issue. I'm here concerning the ring."

I raised my hand and gazed at it. "What about the ring? You could not use it."

A dry laugh echoed from him. "You think not, do you? Maybe He hasn't told you as much of its history as I thought." He studied me while he circled. "Sisko, you have much power. Power to heal and to kill. The ring grants that. Why don't you use it?"

Didn't he know I couldn't use it? I hadn't been able to since I used it for myself twenty years ago. "I've never used it to kill."

His eyes widened. "Really?"

Images swirled about and then rushed past me as if I flew through the air at great speeds. I tried to break out of the link, to open my eyes, but I couldn't budge them. He had trapped me in Josh's own magic.

When I landed to a stop, the view gelled into a familiar scene. I watched Jack holding my younger self, twenty years earlier, in front of his wagon. Sir Edward came forward asking Jack what he accused me of. "I

3

brought him to heal my wife, but when he placed his hands on her and prayed, she died. He must have prayed for her death!" His face burned red. Grief and anger poured from him as a fountain.

"You see..." Beltrid's voice rose to a high pitch of excitement. "You have killed with the ring!"

"But no...I didn't." My voice trailed off. "I didn't."

"Oh yes, you did kill her. For once you used it to punish. But why you held back after that is a mystery to me." He moved toward my face. "Did you not have the stomach for its proper use?"

I had always taken comfort that her death had been a coincidence. That my power to heal had stopped working because of the curse. But could it be as he said? Could the curse have caused my prayer to kill her? I couldn't accept that.

I fixed my eyes on him. "I didn't pray for her death."

Beltrid shook his head and stepped closer. "You didn't have to. You used the ring to feed yourself. You even brought yourself back to life when they killed you. Three times you used it for yourself, yet you have refused to use the ring all these years since. Why?"

He thought he knew how the ring worked, yet he assumed I had killed her and brought myself back to life. I had indeed fed myself and brought the curse of the ring upon me, stopping any further miracles. Yet, as long as he thought I had power, he would be unlikely to attack me. "The ring can only be used to bless others."

Beltrid threw his hands up and groaned. "You heard the words your priest said! You're blinded by your religion's propaganda."

The world blurred into a stream of colors until a new scene formed. A priest focused on a young boy's ring. I heard him say words that I had heard thirty-one years ago. "The steam revealed you have a heart for helping people. So He gave you the means to do so in greater ways." The priest straightened. "The inscription God wrote in Hebrew says, 'It is more blessed to give than to receive.' If you use the ring to help others, it will be a blessing to you. But if you use it for your own benefit, it will be a curse. So don't use it without careful thought, or you will wish you had never been in the steam house."

Those last words echoed in my mind. Wish I had never been in the steam house? Well, yes and no. It did lead me through some horrible experiences, but it also led me to Gabrielle.

"Did you hear what he said?" Beltrid interrupted my thoughts. "It can be a curse. That's the way religion talks about your rightful power. A Curse? Maybe for Him, but for you and me, it is the beginning of equality with Him." The demon thrust a pointy finger into the void. "He knows you could be his equal and wishes to prevent you from having it. But it's yours for the taking. Just reach out and ask, not for Him, but for yourself!"

The surroundings vanished into a puff of smoke. I stood before Beltrid in the dark room again.

"You have much power, Sisko. Use the ring again!"

Truly, demons weren't omniscient. Whether he knew truths about the ring that I didn't, or he had been deceived by his own evil I didn't know. But either way, I had but one answer. "I'll use it only to bless those around me, but never again for myself."

He shook his head. "Foolish idiot! If you'll not use it, then I'll find someone who will. I want the ring!"

Now he revealed his true intentions. "I can't take it off and God would prevent me or you from doing so."

"I know the history of the ring—better than you!" He spat on the ground by my feet. "If you'll not hand its power over to me, I'll find someone who will." A smile cracked across his face. "And that process is well underway, even as we speak."

A sick feeling arose in my gut. "What have you done?"

Smugness covered him. "My servant Rodan has met with your wife."

I trembled like a geyser ready to blow. "What have you done!" I struggled to move toward him, but my feet remained fixed to the floor.

His eyes narrowed. "The ring. I want the ring."

"I can't give it to you! Why attack my wife?" I pulled at my leg with all I had, but nothing would move. I screamed. The whole scene fractured into tiny pieces like glass breaking apart.

Sisko, are you there? Josh's voice pushed through the fog of debris.

Yes. My chest rose and fell rapidly.

He breathed hard, as if he had finished a sprint. *What happened? Someone took over our connection, and I struggled hard to get it back.*

Gabrielle! Beltrid has done something to her. I have to go.

Yes, of course. But we should avoid using this link for now. Not until we can ensure he won't take it over again.

Yes. Thank you, Josh.

I opened my eyes and immediately turned to where Gabrielle had lain. "Gabrielle?" I jumped from bed and threw on my tunic. I rushed through the cloth hanging over our doorway. The moon cast ghostly shadows through the windows as smoldering coals glowed from the fireplace.

Then I noticed the front door hanging open on the frame. "Gabrielle!" I rushed outside and scanned the area. "Gabrielle! Where are you?" Tears welled up in my eyes and a knot formed in my stomach.

I heard Kaylee and Nathan exit the house and I turned toward them. Kaylee's face fell upon seeing my expression. "Dad, what's happened? Is Amma—"

"I don't know. She's been taken, and I don't know what they've done to her." Kaylee's nickname for her mother reminded me how painful this would be for her. As a child she heard Nathan call her "mamma." She pronounced it "amma" and it stuck as she grew older.

Nathan's jaw tightened. "Who took her? I'll go after them myself."

"Someone I've never heard of before. A wizard named Rodan, a servant of the one I talked to in a vision tonight named Beltrid. I believe he is a demon of Hell."

Nathan wrinkled his brow. "A demon? Beltrid, Rodan? I've not heard of them before." He stared at Kaylee.

She shook her head as it sank. "I've never heard of them either."

Nathan squatted to scan the ground in the moonlight. "Here's her tracks." He crawled along the ground as Kaylee and I followed him.

He stopped about twenty feet from the front door and swung back and forth. "Her tracks stop here, as if she disappeared." He pounded his fist on the ground. "Now what are we going to do?"

I breathed deep, trying to keep the fear from my voice. "We'll all go find her. In the morning, we'll go into town and see if we can find any information on this Rodan. We'll get her back."

We moved toward the house. Kaylee opened the door. "Tell us about this vision. Maybe we can help you find out what happened."

I nodded, and they entered the house. I scanned the area one more time, hoping the nightmare would end. But I knew it wouldn't. Why Beltrid thought kidnapping Gabrielle would help him get the ring, I couldn't imagine, but he obviously wouldn't give up easily.

I stepped inside, and I felt as I shut the door that I had shut the door on my former life of bliss with Gabrielle. Now the curse had returned in full force. Now I did wish I had never entered the steam house. Not if it would end this way.

Once inside, Nathan and Kaylee demanded I tell them everything that had happened. I hadn't ever mentioned Josh's link before; it was our secret. So I related that I had closed my eyes, and then Beltrid invaded my thoughts. I explained to them how Beltrid had tried to get me to use the ring for myself.

"And when he couldn't get me to use it, he said he would get another. That's when he mentioned Rodan meeting your mother, and I panicked."

No one said anything for a few moments. I watched them both. Kaylee, with her mother's golden hair brushing just past her shoulders, stared at the table top. Then she shifted her gaze to me. "Can you use it?" Hope danced in her blue eyes.

"I don't believe so. It's never worked other than to protect me from harm since I abused it in the desert."

Nathan banged his fist on the table. "Then why does it still cling to your finger? What good is it?" His blue-green eyes, full of energy, peered at me from under his sandy locks of hair.

My head sunk. "It represents my marriage. First to God, then to your mother."

Nathan groaned. "I'm sorry. I just hate feeling like I can't do anything to save her." He plopped his elbows on the table and rested his chin in his hands. "Aren't you afraid Beltrid will do something, you know, to violate your marriage vows?"

I winced inside and turned to see Kaylee's reaction.

She rose from her chair and stepped to the wall. She pulled her sword from its sheath hanging on the wall and caressed the flat of the blade.

At twelve years of age, a drunkard from one of the local taverns had found her alone in the streets. He pulled her into an alley and attempted to rape her, but some locals happened by and she escaped. However, she hadn't escaped the experience, which still surfaced after four years had passed.

Nathan's eyes widened, then dropped in realization of his mistake. He turned to Kaylee. "I'm sorry, Sis. I wasn't thinking."

Without turning she said, "When do you ever think?"

She had isolated herself for several months after that event. Then her Uncle Seth visited and gave both her and Nathan swords he had forged. Training with it had given her the control she needed to return to her former self. But times like this reminded us of its lurking presence.

I rose and cradled Kaylee's arm in mine while I answered Nathan's question. "I don't think we need to worry. Beltrid doesn't have any interest in such matters. Nor can demons force us to do anything. Only trick us into thinking we want something." Though I couldn't be so sure about Rodan. "He's after the ring, that's his only focus."

She lifted her eyes to mine. Tears rolled down her soft cheeks. "Dad, what if she's…dead?"

I pulled her into my chest. "I doubt it. Beltrid is using her for bait. I don't know what the trap is, but to kill her would defeat his purpose." I rubbed her back. "He wants us to visit this Rodan, and I don't see we have any choice. I only hope we can free her and be done with this."

Nathan stood. "It won't be long before first light. Another hour perhaps. We should prepare to leave."

I nodded. "Yes, let's prepare for the trip. I don't know how far away he is, so pack for at least a week. Change into traveling clothes, and we can get Homer down the lane to watch the farm for us."

Nathan stepped toward his room. "I'll go tell Homer and then get Crystal."

I sighed. I didn't feel like having this confrontation, but she didn't need to go with us. While eighteen years old, his immaturity still required a father's wisdom. "Crystal? Why would she come?"

Nathan froze and turned around. "She's my girlfriend, the one I intend to marry, your future daughter-in-law."

"Not if I have anything to say about it!"

His face reddened and he moved toward me. "Maybe you don't have anything to say about it! Apparently not anything good. Why don't you like her?"

"Same as I told you last time, I can read people, and she's not good for you."

He stared at me for a second. "I don't trust your ability or your supposedly magical ring, because you obviously aren't reading me very well!" He jerked his head around and stomped into his room to pack.

I glanced at Kaylee. She stood, her back against the wall, her eyes wet. She hadn't revealed too much of her tomboyish manner tonight. I didn't blame her, though.

"I'm sorry, Kaylee." I hung my head.

She wiped her eyes with her sleeve and proceeded to the fireplace. "Did you roast any coffee?"

"Yes, yesterday."

"Good. You need some. I need some." She proceeded to stoke the fire and put a kettle of water over it.

"You know me too well." Like Gabrielle. I breathed deep and headed to pack.

The sun dove toward the hills as we prepared to mount our horses. It had taken nearly all day to prepare for the trip. Nathan still hadn't returned from Belenor with Crystal in tow. My heart ached to get underway. Not knowing Gabrielle's fate ate at me like a cancerous depression.

Kaylee fed Rain a carrot and patted her neck. "Good girl. You'll be fine. We'll watch out for each other."

Nathan rounded the corner at a gallop, pulled to a stop in front of us, and leaned over his saddle. "Homer will send his two sons to feed the animals till we get back."

While relieved I didn't see Crystal, I had to ask, "And where's Crystal?"

Nathan raised an eyebrow. "I didn't find her at home."

I couldn't help but breathe a sigh of relief. That explained why he'd taken so long returning. No telling how long he'd searched for her. However, that proved to be short lived. A horse rounded the bend in the lane. Crystal halted before us but stayed on her horse.

I let slip, "Well, speak of the devil."

Nathan glared my direction.

Crystal's eyes widened for a moment before speaking. "I came as fast as I could. I heard in town what happened."

I sat up straighter. "You did? How? We've told no one yet."

"I couldn't sleep last night, so I strolled the empty streets. Then I heard a horse galloping to the gates. The gatekeeper had fallen asleep, so I asked the man who he was and what he wanted at that hour. He said he was Rodan, and wanted to water his horse."

Kaylee broke in with hope in her voice. "Did you see our mother?"

Crystal shook her head. "No. I let him in. He rode alone. I did get from him that he headed home, a house in the mountains about ten or fifteen miles west of Belenor. He left and I thought no more about it until I received word from my friends that Nathan had been asking for me, and left the names of Rodan and Beltrid. I immediately rode here to tell you."

I couldn't deny she had helped save us valuable time finding information on him. "Thank you, Crystal. The trip should take about a day there and back."

Kaylee pointed at the sinking sun. "Perhaps we should wait until morning. There's only a couple hours of light left."

I frowned and shook my head. "We've taken too long as it is. That will be two hours more trimmed off our trip if we leave now."

Nathan swung steady eyes toward me. "And Crystal can come, right?"

I'd started to open my mouth when Crystal interrupted. "Nathan, this is a family matter. I would be in the way. Besides, within a week you'll be back. Go without me."

Nathan's shoulders sank, but he nodded his head.

She blew him a kiss, then flipped her reins and the horse responded by trotting down the path.

I shook my head. She had diffused that situation. I should have felt relief, but instead I wondered about her motivation. I had prepared for a fight about it, but received the olive branch instead. Yet, the bigger question might very well be, why did I feel this way about her? I couldn't point to anything specific. She acted kind and courteous enough. Still, I couldn't shake the feeling that she hid her true motivations from us. Something wasn't right about her.

I took a deep breath. "Let's get going."

The weather cooperated. A cool breeze flowed crisp and clean, keeping the sun bearable. Trees lined the road to Belenor, filled with green leaves dancing with the wind.

It felt good to encounter nature on the road again. So many years had passed since my days of traveling from place to place. I didn't realize how much I had missed the road after twenty years of living in one place.

Still, I would give anything if I didn't have to make this trip, if I could live out my days in peace with Gabrielle into old age. But the ring and its curse upon me ensured that would never happen.

Kaylee and Nathan hadn't said anything since we left. None of us felt much like talking. Worried thoughts for Gabrielle consumed all speech.

Birds sang as we crossed a babbling brook. The sun dove behind mountains in the west, casting a reddish glow across the horizon after three miles had crawled under our feet.

My eyelids felt like lead weights after missing a night of sleep. "We'd better find a place to settle until morning." I pointed to a clearing just off the road. "How about that one over there?"

They both turned without a word toward my suggested spot. I followed them. We set up the shelter and started a small fire. No one felt like hunting for fresh meat, so we made do with cuts of cheese and bread we had packed.

We pulled an old log from the edge of the clearing and used it to sit. We munched on our small meal, feeling the warmth of the fire against the cool of the evening.

"Dad?" Kaylee gazed into the dark forest.

"Yes?"

"When did you know you loved Amma?"

I remembered the first time I spotted her, rounding the corner of their mountain cabin. "Well, when I first left home to fulfill my call to seek out those God wanted me to help, I encountered a bunch of thieves—"

"Dad! I didn't mean to tell us the whole story again." Kaylee cracked a smile. "But when did you know you loved her? When you touched her and felt her love for you?"

"That's a good question." I cleared my throat. "I think I knew it in my heart before I admitted it, to tell the truth. But it really hit me when I ran her through with a sword."

Kaylee laughed. "Dad, do you know how silly that sounds?"

Nathan's lips turned up slightly.

"Yeah, but it was true." Thoughts of the events flooded my mind. "Though the rage drove me and I couldn't stop myself, when I thought she would die, that's when I knew for sure I didn't want to lose her. Ever."

"But how did you know?" Nathan stared into my eyes.

I met his gaze. While he asked about his mother, I had a sense his feelings for Crystal lay at the heart of his query. "People talk about falling in love, as if they couldn't help it. Truth is, they can. Love is ultimately an intellectual and emotional decision to unite to another. A sacrifice of self to gain what you cannot be alone. Someone who will complement you, enrich you, make you a better person, and you can make them a better person."

I stared into the fire. I hoped she lived, and her captor treated her well. "I knew I could help her to grow, and she could enrich me. And she did. I wouldn't be here if it were not for her."

Nathan rose from his seat and paced around the flames.

I bit off a piece of bread, chewed, and swallowed before asking, "What about Crystal? Do you feel that way about her?"

"I love her."

"Like I just said?"

"I think so."

"You don't sound sure."

He stopped and faced me. "What do you have against her?"

I met his eyes and gazed into them for a moment. "I want nothing more than to confess that you will both live a long and wonderful life together. I want that for you." I absentmindedly played with the bread in my hands. "I can't point to anything specific, but one gift God has given me all my life, ring or no ring, is a heart that can read people. Sometimes it's like I can see what's in their soul. I would be lying to you if I told you otherwise, but I don't see her making you a better person."

He continued to pace back and forth, avoiding my gaze, but did appear to consider what I had said.

I ventured a risky question. "Did she do or say something that is bothering you?"

He stopped and sighed. "No. Your words are bothering me. I think I'll go to sleep." He lay in the shelter and wrapped himself in blankets.

I sighed. At least he considered my words this time and didn't blow up. Then I noticed Kaylee watching me. "I'll go to bed. You take the first watch."

She rose and hugged me. Then whispered, "He'll be all right. I can read that in him."

I shook my head as I crawled into the shelter. The only people I couldn't read well were my own kids.

Despite my tired body, I listened to the forest noises. An occasional hoot of an owl or the call of a bird off in the distance sang in the night. At one point, a wolf howled through the night air, and others answered it.

A twig snapped. I jumped to my feet, ready to react. Nathan also flew out and stood by Kaylee's side, drawing his sword to team with hers.

"Who's there?" I called out.

3

Gusts of wind rustled the trees as we all three stood poised to act, waiting for some indication of who spied on us. After a few seconds passed, footsteps rushed further into the forest. Nathan and Kaylee both bolted for the sound.

"Wait," I said. "It could be a trap to draw us away."

Kaylee paused, but Nathan dove into the forest.

I sighed. *The impulsive son does it again!* "You better go after him. No telling what he might get himself into. I'll stay here in case someone is attempting to empty the camp to loot us."

Her eyes paused in indecision. She didn't want to leave me either. She frowned and then sped after him, disappearing into the night.

I sat down by the fire again, but kept a good-sized-log close by. Better than nothing.

The fire crackled as I shoved the wood around and put another log on. A disturbing voice interrupted.

"Sisko."

I spun around to see Beltrid standing on the edge of the clearing.

"Sisko, you're a smart one, you are. Too bad Nathan isn't quite so bright."

My jaw tightened. "Why are you doing this? What do you want?"

"I told you already. The ring."

"You know I can't give it to you. What purpose could capturing my wife have?"

"Maybe I'm just cruel that way. If I can't have it, then I'll make life miserable for the one who does." A deathly smile creased his face. "But I wanted to make it clear to you that I'm watching, and I can get to you or your family anytime I desire. You can pick up your son in Belenor." The last words echoed into the night and he disappeared.

"Nathan!" I had often wondered in what manner I would have to deal with my sin of breaking the vow of the ring twenty years ago. When anything bad happened, I wondered if that had been it, if the curse had ended. But the bad thing about sin is it's never over, at least on this side of life. Forgiven, yes. Consequences, however, don't always disappear so easily.

If I could still do miracles, I could save her. What if I could? Maybe I should try? I watched the ring, seeking a sign. The firelight danced upon it. What could it hurt? She benefited, so I wouldn't do it for myself. I had to try.

"Father, free Gabrielle from this wizard's prison and return her to me."

Nothing happened. Maybe she had been freed and sought to find me? Or, maybe God waited to use me to get her out. I felt my eyes water. Now, when I most wished I could still do miracles, I couldn't.

A few seconds passed before Kaylee returned, and found me with my head between my knees.

"So what did you find?" I asked after regaining my composure.

Kaylee paced around the fire so that I had to keep turning my head to watch her. "A girl, I think."

"A girl? Out here?"

"Yes, for a brief moment, I thought…"

"You thought what?"

"Oh, nothing. It couldn't be."

I sighed. "Couldn't be what?"

Kaylee stopped her pacing and met my eyes. "I thought I saw Crystal. But she and Nathan disappeared before I could get a good look at her. I found no further signs of them."

"Perhaps magic?" I offered.

Her eyes caught my stare. "Could be. But why do you suspect that?"

"Beltrid appeared and told me he took Nathan."

She sank onto the log beside me and covered her eyes with her hands. Her voice cracked. "He's going to die, isn't he?"

I swallowed back a lump in my throat. "He said we could pick him up in Belenor. Let's pray it is to his advantage right now to keep his word."

We sat in silence for a few moments.

"You best be off to bed."

She nodded and arose. Kaylee bent down and asked, "Are you going to be all right? You were crying when I came back. Is anything wrong?"

I stared at her. "There's plenty wrong. But no, nothing extra. Just the stress of your mother's disappearance and now Nathan's."

She kissed me on the forehead. "Goodnight."

"Goodnight."

14

She settled into her bedding while I watched the fire and contemplated what Beltrid had said. If he knew I couldn't give him the ring, why did he think he could get it? What could it benefit him? No one could use it for selfish reasons without being cursed. And why this game? It didn't make sense. He knew something I didn't. Something about the ring I had never been told.

The next day we kept a good pace and arrived in Belenor before the sun had reached its peak. After obtaining a room at the inn, Kaylee and I asked around the city about Nathan. No one knew anything about him, nor could we find any trace of his presence. I began to fear Beltrid might not have kept his word.

As the sun disappeared behind the mountains, and shadows grew into night, Kaylee and I returned to the inn. We'd not eaten all day, and though our hearts sank into despair, our bodies demanded energy. So we bought food and returned to our room.

We didn't talk much. Occasionally a topic would come up, but for the most part talk felt cheap. Cheap when the lives of your loved ones weighed upon your mind. It's amazing what frivolous banter most of our conversations are filled with. I had never noticed until a topic of great importance and weight stood next to them, leaving little else to care or think about.

Kaylee finished her meal, then arose. She unsheathed her sword and froze into an attack stance. She glided her sword through a series of moves and footwork. Her steps and swings balanced each other in a perfect symphony. I had noticed her practicing before, but I hadn't realized the skills she had mastered. I could have been watching a professional dancer.

A knock echoed through the room. Kaylee froze, then leaped with me toward the door. I swung it open. Footsteps echoed down the hall as Nathan stood before the door as if in a trance.

"Nathan!" Relief flooded over me as I threw myself into a hug around his neck.

His eyes blinked rapidly, he jumped back with a grunt and breathed heavily. He focused on me. "Dad? Kaylee? Where am I?"

I stared into his eyes. "You don't remember anything?"

"Last I recall is chasing the spy through the woods. As I drew close, I realized it was a woman, and from the back she resembled Crystal."

Kaylee caught my eyes. "That's the same thought that had crossed my mind."

Nathan nodded. "But when I reached out to grab her shoulder to get a look at her face, I suddenly appeared here." He breathed in deep. "Wherever here is."

"You're in Belenor, at the inn. We've spent all day searching for you. Come, sit. You must be hungry."

He nodded. "I do feel like I've not eaten for a long time."

As he ate, I caught him up on what Beltrid had done. I now wondered if Beltrid did this to delay us for another day. If so, why would be a mystery.

Nathan finished eating. He strolled to a window and gazed at the shadow of the mountains silhouetted by the moonlight. Gabrielle lay up there somewhere, hopefully alive and no doubt he worried about her as we all did.

I stepped up beside him. "She has to be alive. Beltrid would have nothing to lead us on if she wasn't."

Nathan nodded. He continued to stare at the mountains. "Why does he want that ring? I don't."

"I'm not sure. As far as I know, it would be useless to him. He must know something I don't. But I did plan on giving it to you someday, when the ring allowed it."

"I wouldn't put it on, I'd sell it."

"Nathan! Don't even think that!"

He turned to face me. "I don't want a ring I can never take off. And if your stories are true, I don't want the life you've led."

I sighed. "True, mine isn't a life I would suggest you take up. But when the time is right, we'll know and you'll be ready." Though, I admit, he had a lot of growing to do before that day arrived. "But my 'stories,' as you call them, are true."

"We've never seen you do anything with the ring. To me, they're stories. Maybe stories that happened, but still just stories. It would be real if you could save Mother—"

"Don't you think I've tried!" My face grew hot.

Nathan pulled away. "I'm…sorry. I didn't mean—"

I breathed deep and place a hand on his shoulder. "I know, Son. We're all on edge. We're all worried."

I peered over my shoulder; Kaylee watched us with wet eyes. She turned away and sheathed her sword, set it by her bed, and crawled under the covers without a word.

I rubbed Nathan's back. "She has the right idea. Tomorrow may be a long day."

He nodded, and we both settled down for the night. Thoughts of Gabrielle haunted my half-awake dreams, punctuated by visions of Beltrid yanking her away each time I tried to grab her.

The next morning, we arose, packed our belongings, ate breakfast at the inn, paid our debt, and left on the road headed west. Today, we would confront the wizard who held my wife. Hopefully free her, at least find out if she lived or not.

Or die trying.

I expected a castle or large house to loom from the woods as we approached. But nothing stood above the trees save for birds fluttering and chirping about. We had come a full ten miles into the hills and had not found a house of any kind. Then a small cottage broke into view just off the road, and I decided to ask for directions.

A green gate attached to a white fence bordered the yard. Flowers grew in beds along the window sills, displaying reds, yellows, blues and violets. Smoke drifted lazily from a chimney. I knocked at the door.

Soon, a bald man opened it. "Ah, you are here. The master has been expecting you."

"You don't even know who we are."

"Come, come. Don't argue."

No sense in arguing with the help. Best to meet the master of the house. We entered.

I froze and stared. A high vaulted ceiling and a vast expansive room built of rock indicated we stood inside a castle. I poked my head back out the door; a small cottage still sat nestled among the trees. Nathan and Kaylee both stood gazing around as well. This had to be the wizard's house.

"I like my space, but prefer to keep a low profile," an older voice echoed from across the room. A white haired man, clean shaven and dressed in a white shirt, a brown vest, and britches, sat at a table. He motioned for us to sit as well.

"Are you Rodan?" I asked as we approached.

"Yes. I am."

Nathan drew his sword. "Release our mother, scum of the toilet!"

Kaylee followed with her sword.

He waved his hand and the blades fell limp as if Nathan and Kaylee held giant noodles.

Kaylee gasped. "My sword!"

"They will return to their former state once you have left my premises."

"Who needs a sword when I have my fist?" Nathan tensed his arms and moved toward the wizard.

I grabbed his shoulder. "No, Nathan. It will do no good."

Rodan smiled. "Smart man, your father. I would listen to him."

I locked eyes with Rodan's. "Do you hold my wife, and if so, why and what are the conditions of her release?"

He motioned again for us to sit. I nodded to Nathan and Kaylee. I sat, and they followed.

The servant placed glasses filled with an unknown liquid before us. But I didn't feel much like drinking. I only wanted answers.

"As to the why, all I know is this." Rodan sipped his drink and took his time swallowing. "Beltrid asked me to capture her. He didn't tell me his purpose. I didn't ask. He paid me handsomely; a wizard must make a living.

"The how is a bit more tricky. We knew of your ability to do miracles with your ring, so I had to use a conditional spell. A spell that could not be undone by any other spell, but only by meeting certain conditions."

I knew there would be a catch. There always is. "And those are?"

"The spell imprisons one in the Crystal of Virtues. It takes seven keys to unlock its magical gate. To find those keys, find seven persons who accomplish each of the seven virtues: humility, honesty, generosity, hospitality, contentment, purity, and love."

"You've got to be kidding." Nathan rose from his seat but sat down when the wizard raised his hand.

I ran fingers through my hair. "Can I see her?"

"See her? You can have her." He reached into his pocket and placed a crystal, the size of a small ball, upon the center of the table.

I carefully lifted it to my eyes and gazed into it. Through light fractured by the crystal, I could make out Gabrielle's form, as if frozen in time. She held her arms up as if fending off an attack. Then my eyes focused beyond her; my ring flashed through the crystal, magnified by the rock. My own prison had resulted in her prison. Perhaps she would have been better off if I had stayed in Paradise.

I sighed. "Is she in danger?"

"She'll be fine, as long as you don't break it."

I stared at him. "Why?"

"If you break it, she will shatter into as many pieces as the crystal. That's why I'm giving her to you. Though she would be safer here, if anything happened to her, you would lay the blame on me."

My stare turned to a glare. "You're already to blame, though not the only one. Whether by us or by God, you'll eventually answer for this deed."

"Nevertheless, she is in your hands now. Find the keys and you can unlock her from this prison. You'll see in the crystal small holes, in various shapes. Each key will have a crystal protrusion that fits in those holes. Insert it and break it off."

He took another drink. "And only one key can come from any one person, including yourselves."

Nathan leaned forward. "What do these keys look like? How will we get them?"

Rodan laughed. "You think I'm here to make this easy? I've given you all the information you'll need. You're on your own from here."

He rose from the table. "Mr. Tomolin, please show our guests to the door." He left, leaving us sitting, and me holding Gabrielle in the palm of my hand.

We left the castle, or house if you will. Upon crossing over the threshold, Nathan and Kaylee's swords returned to normal as he promised. We stood on the road outside the gate and stared at the crystal ball.

Nathan shook his head. "How are we going to find people who can do those seven things?"

"Sadly, it won't be easy." I pulled a cloth from my pack, wrapped the crystal in it, and placed it close to my body. "But I don't see we have much of an option but to try. While the wizard is a bad sort, I didn't sense any lies. He told us what he knew and how to free her. What I don't get is why? What could Beltrid hope to gain from this game of his?"

"If I had my way he would be chopped into little pieces by now." Nathan huffed.

"If I could still do miracles, I would say, 'Father, send this wizard to the steam house in my hometown.'"

Nathan and Kaylee smiled, recalling the stories I had told about how the steam house brought the inner flaws of the soul to the surface.

A swoosh sounded and we turned. The house had disappeared. Wind whipped through an empty clearing. We stared at each other. Could the ring have really worked again?

"Nah, couldn't be," I said.

Kaylee nodded. "Yeah, probably Rodan is keeping a low profile like he said, and moves the house every so often."

I gazed at where the house had been and wondered.

We had to eat, so we started a fire. Kaylee took her bow and hunted a few small animals to cook. We took our time, because we had to plan how to find the keys. We discussed it as we ate.

Kaylee stopped chewing long enough to say, "The first one he mentioned was humility."

"And how do you find that?" Nathan waved his hand at her.

The fire blurred in my mind and transported me back twenty years ago, roasting birds God had provided at my request. The meat then had tasted extra good, and so had the pride. Pride that ended my days as a miracle worker.

"You won't find it in me." I slumped my head.

"That's just it." Nathan placed his hand on my back. "How can we find humility? If you ask someone, 'Are you humble?' they'll either say yes in which case they obviously aren't, or no—"

"In which case we've found our honest person." Kaylee smiled.

Nathan rolled his eyes.

"You're right, Son," I said. "It will do us no good to ask people about it."

"Finally, you admit I'm right about something." He smiled.

It felt good to see him express some joviality. He had been so serious lately.

I winked at him. "We'll have to catch people in the act of being humble, honest, and so on."

He stared into the fire with a far away look. "We'll never get Mother out of the crystal."

I patted Nathan on the shoulder. "We have to hope and have faith. God wouldn't allow this if it weren't possible to achieve."

"It makes no sense that God would allow this."

"It usually doesn't, Son." I thought back to an invisible dragon I had faced many years ago. "But somehow, He works things out for the best. We simply don't see it. Sometimes may never see it. Not until it's breathing right in our face."

Kaylee sighed. "But where do we find someone with humility?"

An idea grew in my mind. Gabrielle had wanted Nathan and Kaylee to visit the steam house of my youth. "Perhaps it's time we paid your Uncle Jake a visit."

"Dad, that's a long ways."

I smiled. "Yes, and maybe along the way we will find some of these keys. They'll be harder to find limiting ourselves to those who live around us. Anyone have a better idea?"

"I've always wanted to see your side of the family. I'm for going." Kaylee dipped some meat wrapped in bread into the sauce.

"Then it's settled. Let's finish our meal, and head back home so we can prepare for the trip."

A note of happiness surfaced at the idea. It would be good to see my brother and parents again. I hadn't been back home since I left on my travels at nineteen years of age. I had always intended to take the trip, but something always prevented it. It would take several weeks of traveling to get there. Yet that sounded exciting more than dreadful.

But I noticed Nathan had said nothing, and his expression indicated he didn't like the idea, probably due to Crystal. He would want her to come and dreaded facing me about it. I dreaded it as well.

We finished our meal, cleaned up, and headed home. A long trip lay before us, along with its unknowns. Deep inside, I sensed I wouldn't be returning, either. I hoped that feeling proved wrong.

We arrived home within two days. I spent a day making arrangements for the place to be taken care of while we were gone, the animals cared for, and the weeds hacked down. I tried to think of everything we might need for our long journey. We prepared four horses, one for each of us and one to carry the supplies.

After a good night's rest, we ate breakfast and packed for the road. Kaylee led the horses, saddled and loaded, into the yard. Nathan and I swung onto our mounts.

She caressed her horse. "Don't worry, Rain. This is a long journey, but we'll watch out for each other." The horse neighed and nudged her face. She fed her a carrot, and I noticed Kaylee wore her mail vest under the leather one. No doubt a good precaution.

Hoof-beats grew down the road. I raised my eyes to see Crystal riding up on her horse, packed and ready to go. I sighed and stared into the sky.

Nathan smiled, hopped off his horse, helped her off hers, and into his arms.

I frowned. "It appears you want to come on this trip with us."

She smiled with a twinkle in her eye. "I do. And if you do not permit it, I will simply ride on my own a few feet behind you, and camp by myself a stone's throw from you. It's one thing to have Nathan gone for less than a week, but another when we're talking weeks or months."

"You would not be alone in your camp," Nathan said. "I would be with you."

I could see this would be a losing battle. Better to keep them under my eye than off in their own camp. "Very well. But beware, Crystal. People who take journeys rarely return the same." I held her gaze.

She nodded. "Indeed, they do not." She climbed back on her mount.

"I'm ready when you are."

Nathan slid into his saddle. I nudged the horse and with a huff and neigh, we moved out. The clopping of their hooves on the ground, the breeze in my face, the smell of the cool night air warmed by the sun—it all rejuvenated my energy.

I could hardly wait to see my family again. Josh's last contact had indicated my father and mother lay sick in bed. But there were many miles to go before I would hear their stories.

And, though I had not mentioned it to either Nathan or Kaylee, I hoped to take them through the steam house, though I feared most for Nathan. But often seeing the reality of what dwelt in one's soul brought about repentance and healing, once the shock had worn off.

I glanced at Crystal riding next to Nathan. They chatted together, staring into each other's eyes. She glanced in my direction. I still felt no good in her soul. She hid her purpose in attracting him. I couldn't help but feel she had ulterior motives and he would end up hurt in the end. But I had warned Nathan, and now God would have to bring about the right thing.

I admit, though, staring down the dragon took less faith than watching my child walk into a trap he couldn't see.

A couple days had passed when we came upon a path leading off the main road. A wooden plank, jagged edges on both sides, had been affixed to a tree and read, "Mystic Monastery" in blue lettering.

"What better place to find humility," I said.

"Maybe we can catch a service too," Kaylee added.

We directed our horses down the path, though Crystal hung toward the back. Her lips curled downwards, which I took as not being comfortable with our decision. Nathan must have sensed it too, because he rode close beside her.

The path led two miles up a hill. Brilliant green branches towered over us, waving gently in the wind upon the canvas of a deep blue sky. A sense of peace filled the air as if even the birds hushed this close to the monastery. Then a walled enclosure, embedded with a large door, emerged around a corner. We dismounted, and I banged upon the wooden door-frame.

After a moment, a small window opened and a face peered out. "What may we do for you?"

"We seek a place of prayer, and perhaps your blessing. Do you have a service soon?"

He nodded. "We do, when the sun hangs low in the sky it will be

24

time." His eyes darted around. "But the weapons will have to stay outside these walls. Such items are not allowed in here."

"I'll take care of them," Crystal said. "I didn't plan on going in anyway. I'm not particularly religious. I'll camp out here until you return."

Somehow I wasn't surprised.

"And I'll stay with her," Nathan said.

Now I was surprised. "Nathan, we need your help finding what we seek." And I knew the service wouldn't be bad for him either.

"I can't leave Crystal out here by herself. She needs…" He glanced her direction. "She needs protection. Besides, I'm sure you and Kaylee will do fine." He dismounted.

While his explanation made little sense, it would be rude to leave her out here alone. I dismounted and drew near to him. "Just be careful. I get the sense not everything is as it appears with her."

"Father!" His face grew red as if holding back a dam of emotions, but then his jaw and shoulders relaxed. He sucked in a deep breath. "All right, I'll be careful. Don't worry."

I hugged him and he hugged back.

Kaylee and Crystal dismounted. Kaylee placed her sword and bow in Nathan's hands; her eyes pleaded with him.

"Don't worry little sister, I'll take care of your sword."

She smiled and hugged him.

The monk knocked on the door to get our attention. "And the girl, she will need a skirt."

"I'm sorry," she said. "I forgot I wore my traveling clothes." She dug in her pack and pulled out a light skirt, which she wrapped around herself. Though it appeared odd for her pants legs to stick out below it, it would do.

I nodded to Nathan. "You two can take care of the horses as well, so we don't burden our host with the cost of their care. You ready, Kaylee?"

She nodded and we entered through the gate, following the monk as he led us to the chapel. Rock buildings, well-groomed gardens, and several benches filled the grounds.

He pointed to the tower. "Moments before the service starts, the bell will ring. Until then, feel free to enjoy the gardens and peace. We will have a meal after the service, if you would like to join us."

I bowed. "Thank you. Your hospitality is commendable."

He bowed back. "Now, if you will pardon me, I have duties to attend to, but if you need anything, I'll be in the cell by the gate." He bowed again and departed.

Kaylee scanned the area. "I don't see a key. Not even sure where such a thing will appear, or what it will look like."

"A key for what?"

"Hospitality. He performed an act of hospitality."

I patted her on the back. "Not all acts come from the heart. If his statement arose merely from duty, he may not have had it within himself."

She lowered her head.

"But it certainly doesn't hurt to check." I smiled and her face lit up.

The bell rang over and over amidst the peaceful setting, breaking me from my wandering thoughts. Kaylee and I arose and headed toward the chapel.

Stepping through the old mahogany doors, intricately carved with vines and scenes from the Bible, I felt like I had entered another world. A sweet scent filled my nose as incense hung in the air over our heads in lazy clouds. A couple of monks chanted text in one corner of the small room. Others moved behind a wall, their heads bobbing over the gate in the middle.

As the service progressed, a peace flooded over me. Time slowed to a crawl, and my senses dulled to the point of sharpness; little details stood out while all else faded to the background. The chanting reverberated in my mind, and grew into an echo. The room pulled back and sank into a distant view as if no longer important.

Then they flung open the gates, and a blazing light burst forth, filling my vision until I could see nothing else. As the light vanished, however, the chanting disappeared, the lingering smell dimmed, and a blast of cold air flowed over my body.

A new scene focused into view. Kaylee and I stood atop a mountain, many feet into the air. I gulped for breath and stepped back a couple steps. The side of the mountain dropped straight down for miles, and other peaks, arising from valleys, filled the horizon. The wind bit into my skin with gusty blasts. My fingers already grew numb. Snow swirled around us, piled up to our knees.

"Where are we?" Kaylee chattered.

"I don't know." I turned from the ledge and saw a cave behind us. "Over here. Let's get out of the cold."

We plowed through the snow into the cave entrance. It helped to get out of the wind, but still the air seeped into my pores and chilled me. We would need to get a fire going.

Strange how one moment peace and contentment rule, and the next moment your focus is on surviving. My eyes searched further into the cave. It would be warmer further in, but we needed light, and we had nothing with us. Then I noticed a soft, flickering glow of firelight, playing across the wall a ways in.

I motioned to Kaylee, and she followed me as I worked my way along the cave floor. The firelight provided a beacon, and as it grew, the way brightened and warmth enveloped our bodies.

We entered the cavern. A small girl sat by a fire, her back to us. Then I heard a growl to our side. I jerked my head around to see a bear hovering over us, up on its hind legs.

"Hold still," I said to Kaylee.

6

"Sisko, what do you seek?" the child said, but with a confident voice I didn't expect in one so small. She remained seated and kept her back to us.

"I seek someone who is humble." My legs quaked in the presence of the bear. One move and he could end my life.

"Then why do you not demonstrate humility?"

"How do I do that?"

The bear growled again, baring its teeth.

"You are seeking someone who is humble, but you don't know what it looks like?"

The little girl's words cast a light upon truth I had ignored. I wouldn't know humility if it stared me in the eyes.

She lifted her head, causing long, brown hair to shift further down her back. "I see you don't. Humility is lowering yourself in relation to another. The bear does not see you as humble."

Another growl echoed against the cave walls.

The bear? Its eyes glared upon me a few inches above eye-level. "Oh, I see. Kaylee, sink to the floor very slowly."

We both lowered ourselves to the floor until we lay prostrate before the furry beast. I peeked and watched it drop to all fours and saunter into another cavern.

"At least you learn fast. You may join me around the fire."

We found a seat across from her. The fire's heat enlivened my spirit and reminded me of a place far away that I had once visited. As I studied the flames closer, I noticed no wood fueled it. Rather, a pure, refined flame glowed before her.

Paradise? Couldn't be. The freezing cold and gloom outside the cave felt nothing like what I had experienced when I had died twenty years ago, and God had sent me back to live again. Yet I felt the same feeling from the fire and the little girl.

"Did we die?"

She giggled. "No, Sisko. You know what that's like."

I nodded. I didn't think so, but had to ask. After all, I'd only died once. "Then, where are we and who are you?"

"We are in the monastery. But you have been put into a trance-like state by the monks. We're taking advantage of it to guide you."

"But where is this place? What am I seeing now?"

She stared into my eyes—pierced into them. "Your soul, Sisko. This is your soul."

My jaw dropped. "My soul?"

Kaylee placed her hand on my shoulder. "Dad, why is your soul so cold?"

"I…I don't know."

The little girl nodded. "I think you do. What have you been carrying around with you for the last twenty years?"

Could this little girl really know? "My curse."

She shook her head. "Deeper. The curse had been removed when you returned to this life."

"Who are you?"

"That's not important now. Dealing with your pride is."

I ran my fingers through my hair. "My pride? I know I have it, but what do you mean?"

Kaylee remained quiet, listening with rapt attention.

"What have you carried with you these past years?" Her piercing stare searched my heart with divine light.

I tried to figure out what she wanted me to see. Then I recalled what I had thought earlier: the curse lay behind every bad event in my life, even our current situation.

I shook my head. "But I have to deal with the consequences of my failure to keep the vow of the ring."

She sighed. "Consequences? Not every bad thing that happens to you is a consequence of your failure."

"But some of it is. How can I know what is and isn't?"

"Why do you need to know? What is, is. Does it matter after the fact why something bad happened? Even evil can be used for good if you deal with it in God's grace. And that's what your pride has prevented."

I hung my head. "But I failed."

"God has forgiven you, why do you continue to punish yourself? Because you are not humble enough to accept His decision, so you take His place, judge yourself unworthy, and continue whipping yourself for sins God no longer recalls."

Tears flowed from my eyes. Kaylee put her arms around me and rubbed my shoulders. We all three sat there for several moments as dark shadows I had ignored, residing deep within, flew to the surface and out with the tears. After a few moments had passed, my tears dried up along with the guilt. I gazed at the little girl who patiently waited.

"But who are you? You have such a deep wisdom and knowledge for one so young. How would you know of evil and pain?"

She stared into the fire. "My name is Love. My sisters are Faith and Hope." She paused, waiting for me to acknowledge her. "We were martyred as children by the Emperor of Rome for our faith in Christ."

I gasped. I recalled hearing her story, long ago in my youth. Sophia, and her children: Faith, Hope, and Love. The Emperor had done unimaginable horrors to the three girls and finally killed them for confessing Christ.

"I'm so sorry."

Her gentle smile cast joy upon me. "Don't be. I would gladly die for Him again. As a result, many were brought to Him, and we entered Paradise. For no man can truly take your life, only send you to the next."

A smile lifted my spirits, recalling the pure joy pouring from that world. The same joy I now felt from her. "I see what you mean." I sighed. "And you're right. I've failed to let go and have allowed my failure to color everything since. But how do I fix it? I'm sure changing twenty years of seeing everything through those eyes won't be easy."

"No, it won't. But now you know what to search for. If you find the person who exhibits humility, it will go a long ways to accepting it yourself."

She stood, and we did too.

"I must go now. I think you can leave the cave in safety."

Kaylee shuddered. "But it's so cold out there."

She smiled. "Go and see." Then she vanished. However, The fire continued and followed us as we worked out way toward the cave entrance.

When we exited, warm air greeted my face. Birds flew through the air, crisp and clean. The mountains wore green foliage decorated with many varied colors of flowers. Brightly colored butterflies fluttered everywhere. Pure joy radiated from every blade of grass and drip of water flowing among rocks. Paradise had returned to me.

Kaylee breathed deep. "It's so beautiful."

"Yes, it is." And to think, I had kept it covered in guilt for all these years. We sat on the edge of the cliff, dangling our feet over miles of air as we soaked in the glory.

"Father! Wake up!" Nathan's voice sounded distant, but grew as the moments passed. "Father!"

I cracked my eyes open. I couldn't focus, but could see enough to tell Nathan's form hovered over me.

"Father, are you all right? Say something."

"I'n finth." I shook my head, trying to get the cobwebs out. Nathan's features grew sharper. "Where aum I?"

A smile of relief grew over him. "We're outside the monastery."

He helped me sit up and gave me water to drink, which helped.

"And Kaylee, is she all right?" I asked after I finished swallowing.

"I'm over here, Dad." Crystal helped her drink water as she sat against a tree.

"What happened?" I asked.

Nathan glanced at the monastery walls. "Let's just say, these monks have a very unusual system of getting donations."

I rubbed my forehead. "The last thing I recall before the vision, was standing in the service, smelling the incense, and listening to the chanting."

"Vision?"

"Yes." My ring finger throbbed, and I winced. Apparently those nerves had woken up. I lifted my hand. A red and slightly swollen finger bulged around the ring.

"Appears the incense caused you to fall asleep. They must have some way to not be affected by it themselves. Once visitors pass out, they rob them and throw them outside the gate.

"When they couldn't get your ring off, which appeared to be the only thing of worth you had, they threatened to hold you forever unless we gave them a ransom."

"And so you gave it to them? How much?"

"A week's wages." He set his jaw. "As soon as Kaylee is back to normal, we'll raid the place and get our money back. Such thieves give the Church a bad name."

I placed my hand on his shoulder. "No more than our sins do. We have more important tasks to attend to. Remember your mother?"

He sighed. "Yeah."

I stood and Nathan steadied me as I gained my balance. "God will deal with them in due time. Besides, I would have given them all we had for the vision I experienced while in there."

Kaylee stepped carefully to me and fell into my arms. "Oh Dad, I had no idea what you had gone through." A tear fell down her cheek.

"So you were there with me?"

She hugged me tight and smiled. "I was there. And you're so beautiful inside. Like I would imagine Paradise being."

Yes, like a corner of Paradise in my soul. And I had shared an

31

intimate part of me with her. That would stand as a special connection between us.

I saw Nathan glance at Crystal and shrug. "Sounds like I did miss something special."

Crystal didn't smile or frown. She stared at us, as if wishing she could ask a question, but not knowing what question to ask.

My balance had returned, so I mounted my horse. "We still have to find a humble person. There are none here, maybe we can reach Siloth before nightfall."

The name hit me like a knife. I hadn't thought about the connection until now. I had been executed in Siloth twenty years ago for killing a girl. At least, that's what they charged me with. I had tried to heal her, and she had died instead. Her husband blamed me for it.

Now I know why little Love wanted me to deal with the guilt of my failure. Still, I feared what I might face in Siloth. Memories can be pesky things.

7

As Siloth's city gates drew near, I couldn't help but recall the first time I came through them. I had been taken prisoner, so I could be put on trial by the king. When they executed me and I came back to life, they had taken it as a sign that they had judged incorrectly, and they released me. But I wondered how many would remember me, and what feelings they would have if they did?

Gabrielle and I had joined in matrimony in that city as well. We didn't waste any time after my return from Paradise. A priest married us, then we left and settled in the valley where we currently live. I never returned, not until now. I hoped to keep a low profile. Creating a stir would make our task much harder to accomplish.

A steady stream of carts, horses, and foot travelers entered and left through the gates. Siloth boasted a vast merchant market, so many traveled here to find goods not readily available elsewhere. The crowds would make it easier for us to blend in. But it might also mean space at an inn would be difficult to find.

We dismounted our horses and led them through the city streets. Various people bumped into me regularly, and I wondered if any were on purpose, to pickpocket me. But my pockets carried little of value. I noticed Nathan and Kaylee both kept their hands on the hilts of their swords.

"Over there." I pointed at a sign hanging from a mounted, iron bar, which said, "Hill's Inn."

We pulled our horses to the front. Nathan agreed to hold the horses while I checked for rooms. Crystal stayed with him. Kaylee and I entered the rustic, wood building. Windows allowed the sunlight in, giving the place a cheery feel. I approached the counter and rang the bell.

A man entered from a room behind the counter. I froze. The innkeeper was Jack, the man whose wife I had failed to heal and who had demanded my death. When I returned to this life, he had argued against releasing me, but failed. Would he recognize me now?

His eyes locked on mine. "Can I help…" He stared hard at me, his mouth frozen open, then slowly closed. I felt the same way—very uncomfortable.

"Mister?" A young voice said off to my side.

I bent my head down and around to see a five-year-old boy at my feet.

"Do you have any bags to carry or horses needing tended?"

I glanced up at Jack.

He let out a breath. "I've a room for you if you need one."

"There are four of us."

"We have one big enough."

The boy watched me intently.

I smiled at him, glad to focus on someone else. "Outside, we have five horses. Take care of them and the bags, and I will pay you well. Tell my son Nathan I sent you."

He bowed. "Oh, thank you, Sir." Then he rushed out.

I turned back to Jack. "How much for a night?"

He cast his gaze at the counter. "I, well, you know, I owe you enough as it is. No charge."

I faltered. "Owe me?" I stared into his eyes and could tell he wasn't the same man I had left twenty years ago.

He smiled, still looking uncomfortable. He continued talking as he reached below the counter. "Yes. I know we didn't leave each other on good terms. Long story, but I realized I had wronged you something fierce."

He reached out and placed a key into my hand. "The room is down the right hall toward the end, on the left."

I checked my palm. The key appeared to be an unusual sort. An iron grip, decorated with vines narrowed to a point. But on the end, instead of the normal wrought design to match a lock, a thin crystal protrusion about a quarter inch long glistened in the sunlight.

A flash of joy struck me; the first of the keys lay in my hand!

Jack followed my eyes to the key. "What? Where did that come from? I could have sworn I had given you a key to the room." He stuck his head under the counter.

I slipped the key into my pocket and glanced at Kaylee. She grinned while rocking back and forth on her feet.

"Here we are. Sorry about that." He handed me a key.

"No problem. And Jack?"

He sunk his shoulders and stepped back. His eyes drooped as if expecting the worst. "Yes?"

"Have no fear. All is forgiven." I smiled.

His face melted into peace. He stood taller as if a heavy weight had lifted from his shoulders. He dashed around the counter and wrapped me in his arms. His voice cracked as tears glistened in his eyes. "You don't know how long I've desired to hear those words."

I hesitated at the unexpected display of affection but hugged him back and felt my own eyes watering. I also noticed several staring at us. They had probably never seen Jack crying before. This could be causing a scene, and I didn't want to draw attention.

"Jack." I pulled him back to stare him in the face. "We all have our sins to deal with, me included. But I'm here for an important reason. My wife is in danger. I cannot tell you more, but the last thing I need is for crowds to gather around if people recognize me."

He wiped his eyes. "I understand. We can talk later, in your room."

The door opened and the boy entered pulling three packs across the floor. One of them held Gabrielle. My heart jumped. "I'll take that one, my boy. There's something breakable in it I need to protect."

Jack pointed down the right hallway. "Dan, take those to the last room on the left, that way."

"Yes, Father."

I stared at Jack. "Father?"

He beamed and nodded.

"You have a fine son there. I'm sure he'll make you proud."

"He already has. And is this one of yours?" He pointed at Kaylee.

"Oh, yes. Forgive me. This is my daughter, Kaylee."

She bowed.

Jack grinned. "I'll bet that sword is to keep the boys away."

She giggled. "They do think twice before messing with me."

"And my son Nathan is outside tending the horses, along with his girlfriend."

"And your wife? You said she was in danger. Gabrielle, if I recall correctly."

I nodded. "Yes. Another long story."

"Go and settle in, but I have more to share with you later."

I bowed. "I look forward to it."

Nathan and Crystal entered in and we left for the room.

No sooner had the door to our room closed when Kaylee jumped up and down. "Hurry Dad! Nathan, we got a key for the crystal!"

His eyes perked up. "Really? What for."

Crystal peered over Nathan's shoulder.

"Humility, I think."

I took the crystal out of my pack and unwrapped it, then pulled the key from my pocket. The protrusion formed the shaped of a star on its end, so I checked the crystal for a star-shaped hole. When I found it, the letters "hos" sat over it.

"'Hos,' the first three letters for 'hospitality.' Appears that's what we've got, not humility."

"That makes sense, I guess. He did give you a free room out of the goodness of his heart." Kaylee stared at the crystal. "Are you going to insert it?"

"Yes, hold on." Everyone watched as I slid the key in, then broke it off. The spot on the crystal glowed for a moment before fading away. The hole disappeared into a smooth, clean surface.

It felt good to have taken the first step toward our goal. Still, hospitality would be one of the easier to find. We didn't even try. Finding someone truly humble loomed as the bigger hurdle. But it did prove one thing: Jack was sincere in what he had said. Having the relationship between us healed felt good.

Nathan plopped down into a chair. "There're a lot of people here. Maybe we should stay. We're more likely to find people with virtues in a bigger town like this."

Kaylee jabbed him on the shoulder. "What? You don't want to see Dad's hometown? And our grandparents we've never met?"

"Of course, but it is logical, is it not?"

I nodded my head. "Yes, you're probably right. However, we can't impose upon Jack's hospitality for an indefinite period of time, and the longer I stay here, the more likely I'll be recognized. I simply don't know what people's reactions will be if that happens."

"If it's anything like Jack's, maybe it would be a good thing," Kaylee said.

I shook my head. "I don't think so. If word gets around that I'm here, we won't be able to get anything done. Remember, to these people, I came back from the dead after being shot with arrows. That kind of story only grows with the telling. No doubt, I'm now depicted as a messiah or god in some stories. We'll have crowds lined up outside wanting me to do miracles. Miracles I can't do and they won't understand why."

I met Kaylee's eyes. "However, it would be good to get some local news and such. Perhaps you and Nathan can check around. No one would know you."

Nathan jumped up. "I'll go into the streets and see what I can find. Split up, we might get the keys faster." He turned to Crystal. "You coming?"

She nodded. "Sure." She followed Nathan out the door, casting a glance my direction as she disappeared into the hallway.

I noticed she had been pretty quiet through all this. Hardly even acted excited about finding a key. More like an observer, watching as if she would report the events to someone.

A sinking feeling hit my gut. What if she's a spy? Maybe that's why I had felt bad feelings from her. What if she used Nathan simply to be with us and keep her superiors advised of our progress? Maybe even attempt to thwart it at the right time? Or my imagination could be running wild too.

"Dad, what's wrong?"

I blinked. "Oh, nothing. Just deep in thought is all."

"Don't go so deep I have to jump in after you." She winked. "Guess I'll go listen to conversations in the main room."

"Very good. I'll stay here for now."

She rose and left. I paced the floor and stared out the window, watching the crowds of people trading and moving about. I wondered how many of them ever received visions, or was I simply one of God's special cases. I smiled at the thought.

A knock at the door brought me out of my thoughts. I answered it to find Jack standing there, with a woman I recognized, but couldn't place.

"You might remember Helen. She tended you when I first approached you at the oasis."

"Oh yes, I remember." I shook her hand. "Come in, both of you."

They seated themselves at the small table in the room.

I glanced between them. "Let me guess. You're married?"

Jack nodded. "About a year after you left here. It took me a while to get over Mary's death."

"Understandable. That was a difficult time for you."

He stared at the table. "Yes, and I took it out on you. I wanted someone to blame, someone to take out my frustration on, and you neatly fell into that role. But that was no excuse. I'm very sorry for all the pain I caused you."

"Jack, what you did was wrong, yes. But I dealt with my own sins at that time as well, sins that caused me to lose the ability to heal people. If not for that, I probably could have healed your wife. And that's a guilt I've only recently released. Don't hold onto it like I did for so long."

He gazed into my eyes and nodded. "You're right." He placed an arm around Helen who patted his hand on her shoulder. "If not for her patient care, both as a friend and later a wife, I would not have come as far as I have. But I'm truly grateful that you have forgiven me."

I smiled.

He leaned forward. "But what of your wife? You said she is in danger?"

"I wish I could tell you everything, but it wouldn't be prudent. I'll just say, we're on a quest to find the keys to release her from a wizard's spell."

"A spell!" He leaned back and glanced at Helen.

She responded with wide eyes and then asked me, "Is there anything we can do?"

"I think we may want to stay an extra night, but I'm willing to pay for it."

Jack waved his palm toward me. "I wouldn't think of it. Stay as long as you like."

I leaned forward. "Thank you. You're both so very kind. But one extra night will be all we need. I'm afraid if I stay too long, I'll be recognized and you'll have a crowd pressing in, chasing your paying customers away."

I checked the room, to make sure no one had dropped in without me hearing it. "There is one other thing you might be able to help me with."

"Sure. Name it."

"My son Nathan has a girlfriend with him. Her name is Crystal. At least that's what we've been told. But I know nothing about her. She appeared in our village, and Nathan fell in love with her. If you could find out any information on her, if anyone recognizes her, that would be great."

He nodded. "I've not seen her before. Though I doubt I'll learn anything, there are some customers here who have traveled widely. I'll see if any of them recognize her."

"Thank you for trying."

We chatted a while longer. Then they left. I rocked in the chair, contemplating our situation when Kaylee burst through the door.

"Dad, Nathan's been arrested!"

8

I raced out of the room, Kaylee followed close behind. As we left the inn, I noticed Jack watching us.

I pushed through the busy streets until the prison loomed ahead. A dread came over me. This place brought back memories I would rather not recall. But concern for Nathan drew me on and into the building.

I burst into the reception room. A man at a counter lifted his head. His eyebrows raised. Did he recognize me?

He rose from his chair. "What can I do fer ya?"

"My son's been arrested, his name is Nathan. Is he in here?" I breathed in hard gasps.

"Aye, we did bring in a boy with that name."

"What is he charged with?"

"Stealing from a local vendor."

I held back a gasp. I found it hard to believe he would steal. "Can I see him?"

"Being yer his father, I suppose so." He grabbed a set of keys and headed down a hall. "This way."

Kaylee and I followed him. The dark, dank feel of the place came rushing back as we sank under the ground. Loud echoing clanks of metal rang as doors opened and closed, just as it had many years ago. Not much had changed, except the place smelled dirtier and older, if that were possible. I realized I had grabbed Kaylee's hand and held on tightly. She squeezed back as if she understood my thoughts.

When Nathan saw us, he sprang from his bed and thrust himself against the cell door. "Father, I didn't do anything. They tricked me!"

"Calm down and tell me what happened."

He let out a breath. "Crystal and I were checking out some shops along the main street. I came across one, and the man acted nice enough. We chatted for a while, and then he said, 'Here, have a sample on the house.' I thought, maybe this will..." He glanced at the guard standing close by. "Maybe it would be an example of honesty or humility or something, so I accepted his offer. But no sooner had we stepped away than he called out 'thieves,' and guards appeared from nowhere and grabbed us."

I scanned the cell. "Where's Crystal?"

"Oh, I mean grabbed *me*. She got away. Ran into an alley, and the guards lost her."

"I see." I thought for a moment. While Nathan had an impulsive nature, I'd never known him to lie. Not about anything like this. "Let me see what I can do." I nodded, and the jailer led us back out.

Once back in the reception area, I asked, "How do I get him out?"

"Well, there's the matter of paying for what he stole. And by law, he pays three times more and takes a flogging."

"Three times more? I've not heard that law before."

"Ya can go to the king's lawyers and have 'em pull it up for ya. Then ya can file a protest. Should take a few days. Or, ya can pay the fine and be on your way."

I realized the racket they had going: he and the vendor trapped travelers who wouldn't take the time to fight it in the king's court and charge them way more than the law allowed. "And what's your cut?"

His eyes narrowed. "Cut? Look, fella. He broke the law, he pays by the law, or he stays down there."

"What law, when you and your merchant friend so flagrantly break it? Does the king know about this?"

He spit on the floor. "The king? Who's he gonna trust? A thief and his father who weren't there, or me and my guards who saw him take it?"

I knew he had me. There's nothing I could do other than pay the fine or spend days I didn't have in court and most likely lose. I heard the front door open, and then a voice:

"I would like to file my own charges of theft, and I'll testify to the king."

I swung my head around to see Jack standing in the doorway. My heart leaped at the sight.

The jailer eyed him closely. "What do ya mean?"

Jack took a breath. "I've seen this charade go on for far too long without standing up to you. You've cheated many out of their money, and it's time it stopped. Starting with these visitors to our fair city. If you persist in this, I intend to bring charges of theft to the king against you and the merchant."

He grumbled. "You have no cause to be doing this. Stay to yer own business."

Jack's jaw set. I recognized his expression from way back, when he directed it against me.

He put his face into the jailer's. "It is my business. My customers are the visitors to our city that you have defrauded. You have stolen from several of them, and none have returned. If I hear of one more such incident, you will be in jail instead of putting people into it. Do I make myself clear?"

The jailer grumbled under his breath as he stared at the floor. Then he said, "No sense in getting all huffy about it. I'll investigate your claims and if this vendor is falsely accusing people, I'll put a stop to it meself."

He pulled the keys off his belt and headed back into the prison. As soon as the door closed, I grabbed Jack and hugged him tight.

"Thank you, Jack."

He patted me on the back. "No problem. Everything I said is true. It has been going on for far too long and it has hurt my business. But ever since what happened with you, I've always feared to accuse anyone of anything like that again. I couldn't stand if more innocent blood dripped from my hands because of my temper. But you helped heal me of those past hurts and I couldn't bear to see him do this to you."

Soon, the jailer led Nathan out of the cell. Kaylee, who had been silent, jumped to Nathan and hugged him. "Oh, thank goodness you didn't have to stay down there as long as Dad did." As soon as she said it, she froze and turned to the guard.

The jailer eyed me. "I thought ya looked familiar. You're that Sisko feller, aren't ya? The one who came back to life after gettin' shot with five arrows?"

I gulped. "You know, I've heard that story too. Sorry I don't have time to hear your version of it, but I doubt it's true."

The jailer moved closer to me. "Oh, it's true all right. I saw it happen before me own eyes. And they say the five archers died horrible deaths for shooten ya too."

"That can't be right! Killing me couldn't have—" I swallowed.

A grin creased his face. "Ah, I figured I was right! Well, what do ya know, the living legend himself, standing right here in my jail once again!"

"Sorry, we really need to go." I opened the door and exited. I noticed him follow us out and wave some men and ladies around him. I leaned over to Jack. "I think we'll have to get out of town now."

He nodded. "I'll see that your horses are packed and ready, with plenty of food." He paused. "And I'll bring them to your back window."

I glanced at Nathan. His mouth hung open in a half-frown and his eyes darted around, as if thinking. I realized he feared we might have to leave Crystal behind.

At least she'd be able to make her way back to our village from here with some traveling group. If we didn't find her at the inn, we certainly couldn't wait for her.

When we entered our room, I spotted Crystal sitting in a chair.

"What happened to you?" Nathan sat beside her with his arm around her.

She smiled. "I got away. I don't think they saw me come here."

"It's all right now. Father and Jack got the charges dropped."

"Really?" She furrowed her brow.

"You're not happy we're cleared?"

"Oh, no. It's not that. Just, I didn't expect you would get off so easy."

I broke in. "Get packed now. Word is getting around that I'm here, and crowds will be trying to get in soon. We can't move around freely here anymore, so we'll need to slip out."

Everyone busied packing. As promised, our horses appeared out the back window. We lugged our packs out while Jack and his son Dan loaded them onto the horses. Lastly, we each slipped into the alley.

Jack hugged me. "I'm so glad you came, and I'm sorry to see you go so soon."

"Thanks for all your help, Jack. I'm glad to have a friend like you."

"Oh, and I didn't have time to find out much about the information you wanted." He whispered into my ear, "I can tell you she's not from around here anywhere. No one I talked to had ever seen her or her family."

I nodded. "Thanks." I paused. "One other thing. Did those five archers really die horrible deaths because of me?"

He smiled and shook his head. "You know how it is. A couple of them died horrible deaths, and stories circulated that it was because they shot the man who came back to life. Soon, the whole group had been included."

I smiled and mounted the horse. "Not like I would feel guilty about it or anything, you understand." But I felt better knowing it wasn't true.

"Of course not." Jack winked and then pointed down an alley. "I would go that way. At the end of the alley, take a right. It will lead you back to the city gate."

"Thanks again." I nudged the horse and led the rest down the alley. After getting onto the street, we followed it until we entered the main road to the gate. People rushed down it toward the front of the inn. Already a large crowd had gathered there.

"Trot easily, don't draw attention to yourselves," I warned.

The gate drew near. We pushed our way through the flow of people.

I heard snippets of talk. "The miracle worker who came back from the dead is in town? Where?" "I can hardly wait, I've suffered with this ailment for so long."

My heart wept for them. I felt a surge of guilt. I couldn't stay and heal them, because of my failure. But I recalled what Love had said, and reminded myself God would take care of them. The struggle must have shown on my face, because Kaylee rode up beside me.

"Dad, they'll be all right, but what about you?"

We passed through the gates and into the open countryside. "It hurts not being able to do anything. It always has." I nodded. "But I'll deal with it. It's my lot, it seems."

The memories of Siloth had been hard to face, but it turned out for the best, especially concerning Jack. A heavy weight I had carried for a long time no longer pushed me down. In its place, a gentle peace ruled.

Now another bad memory loomed ahead: the desert. How would we get across that?

In no time at all, the forest faded away into the packed sands of the desert. Trees shrunk into shrubs, and shrubs into weeds as we descended the hills and onto the parched plain. It stretched out wide before us, no end in sight. The sandy loam had broken its crust where many wagons had traversed the area, leaving a trail leading over the horizon.

I shuddered. I hadn't thought facing the desert would be this hard. But now, standing on the edge of it, I knew I didn't want to cross it. I feared the same madness would take hold of me and drive me to do something else to ruin my life.

I reminded myself the desert only cast the background upon which my pride, already formed, had a chance to manifest itself. I had grown since then, even recently. Besides, I had no power to lose, no pride to cast an angry shadow over my life like I did then. Did I?

I watched as Kaylee and Nathan dismounted. Nathan helped Crystal to the ground and they both stretched. Nathan paced around the horse.

He stood, staring over the desert. "How do we get across this?"

"Not the way I came the first time, that's for sure." I pointed at the ruts in the sand. "This trail I know leads to an oasis. Beyond that, I'm not sure where it goes, but it is a route traveled by caravans, so I'm sure it leads somewhere."

Kaylee patted Rain who neighed in response. "Maybe we should wait till a caravan comes through we can join?"

That did sound appealing, but perhaps not practical. "I'm afraid the news of my appearance would be too fresh from Siloth, and they may be watching for me." I smiled at her. "I think if we stick to the trail, we'll be all right."

She smiled back and remounted her horse. "Then I'm ready."

Nathan helped Crystal back onto her horse. "Don't worry Father, this time you're not alone."

That's right, I'm not alone. I breathed deeper and relaxed. I nudged my horse on, and we struck out over the desert. Still, an uneasiness clung to me like a vulture over a carcass.

We met no one on the trail, other than birds flying overhead and a few desert animals scurrying away as we approached. Within a few hours, the trees of the oasis blossomed over the horizon. Soon, we rode up to the water's edge as the sun set and a cool wind offset the heat of the day.

No one camped at the oasis though I could see evidence of recent fires. We set up our shelters and prepared our meal. As the sun sank, the stars in a dense and vast array broke through the sky. It struck a sense of awe in me. I recalled my trip from this world to Paradise, how I had traversed untold distances in a brief instant, past any stars I could now see. I longed to be there again, and someday I would. I knew that.

"On guard, evil maiden!" Nathan held up his sword.

Kaylee raised hers. "Evil, eh? We'll see about that."

"No hits to the face, you two." I sat on a rock to watch. They liked to keep in practice by fighting each other but, of course, not pushing through, though nicks and cuts were common.

Nathan thrust forward, and Kaylee parried it to the side and swung back in to point him on the chest. "Ah, now ye be dead, brother. What say ye now?"

"I say, Ahhhhh." He dropped to the ground.

Kaylee laughed. Nathan swung his feet around, knocking her to the ground. He leaped to his feet and landed his point to her stomach. "Ah, thou shouldst never assume, evil demon, that the dead don't live!"

Crystal rose and strolled to the water's edge, staring over the night horizon rimmed by moonlight.

I would have loved to know what churned in her mind.

"We're even now. Let's go again." Kaylee rose to her feet and held her sword in position.

Nathan thrust with a twist of his wrist. Kaylee attempted to dodge, but the point landed on her shoulder.

"Where did you learn that? Not from our teacher."

"No." He stood tall. "I invented the move myself. If all I ever use is what I'm taught, that means others know it too. This is something only I know."

"It's very effective." She contemplated the move. "Try it again."

They took their stands. Nathan thrust again as before. She attempted a parry, but the point landed on her chest.

"Again."

Nathan jabbed five times before she figured out how to parry the blow successfully. "Ah! This is one evil demon who won't get caught with that move again!" She smiled.

"Maybe," he said. "But you'll notice your parry takes more energy than most to execute. My opponents will tire faster, and my sword is left in position to attack again or parry."

"You'll have to teach me that."

I rose to leave them to their practice and strolled around the water's edge till I came to the dunes on the far side. After climbing to the top and sitting down, I stared over the vast horizon. The desert glowed dimly in the moonlight. In my mind's eye, a young man struggled to push on, dehydrated and near death. This would be the worst day of his life. Not because he nearly died, but because he…that is, I had used the ring to feed myself. Yet just beyond these dunes lay water and food. I had been so blind to what churned inside me then and failed to trust that God would provide.

Despite the uneasiness, a burning desire to see the rock where I had broken the vow of the ring sprang up within me. It lay a few yards away. I stepped lazily through the night, retracing steps in my mind. In a few moments, I came upon it, split down the middle. The rock that gave me water still glistened wet in the dim light.

I saw a bone sticking out of the ground. I dug down and found several more bones. The bones of the birds I had eaten, still here after twenty years. A tear dripped down my cheek as I held the evidence of my sin.

"What happened to you here?"

I spun around to see Crystal standing behind me. The moonlight played upon her hair as it swayed in the gentle breeze.

"It's personal." I clamped the bones into my hands.

"I'm sorry. I didn't mean to intrude." She sighed.

"I don't mean to be short with you."

"I know you don't like me. Nathan has said as much."

Now I sighed and turned to face her. "That isn't true." How do I put this? "I simply know nothing about you. Where you are from, who you are, your history." I hoped knowing her better would dissipate the bad feelings I received from her.

"That's a little personal for me too." She met my eyes. "But you deserve to know if Nathan and I continue down the path we are on." She strolled aimlessly as if thinking. "My history, as you put it, is in a land far from here. It is long and involved, but what you need to know is that my parents wished to sell me into slavery. Said they could spare a girl like me."

Shadows from the moonlight danced through her hair and over her face, casting an eerie stare into her eyes. "So I ran away, seeking someone who wanted me. I traveled far. But when I entered your town, Nathan bowed and asked what a fair maiden, as he put it, was doing, wandering alone."

I smiled. That sounded like something Nathan would say.

"Your son was the first, and so far, the only person to show me any kindness. And I've learned that he loves me for who I am, not what some might perceive me to be at first glance. For that, I love him."

Guilt flooded over me, and the bones in my hand stung, I held them so hard. Have I judged so wrongly? Can I no longer trust the sense in my heart that had always guided me so willingly?

I swallowed. "Thank you for sharing." I stood up and put the bones into my pocket. "Now I'll share with you."

Her eyes froze on mine.

"I was given an ability to perform miracles by God when I was fourteen."

She nodded. "Yes, the ring. Nathan told me about it."

I frowned. I rarely told anyone about the ring. Though people knew I performed miracles, I'd always been too afraid they would seek after the ring itself, like Beltrid. I would have to talk with Nathan.

"On this spot, I abused that power. I misused it. And I've suffered ever since. Now, on this very same spot, I realize that I've again abused an ability I have. I can usually read people pretty well. I can sense motivations for good or for bad, even hidden character traits."

Her eyes grew wide.

"No, I can't read minds or anything." I smiled.

She relaxed some, but her guard remained up.

"I feel an evil emanating from you. While I can't say it's gone, now I know in part where it comes from. You've experienced some nasty things in your life. I've judged you wrongly, and so I ask your forgiveness."

I thought I saw a frown crease her face, but she quickly smiled, even if half-heartedly, and simply nodded. "I appreciate your candor. Thank you."

She turned and walked back to the oasis, leaving me standing by the split rock.

I watched as her form receded—a mystery on two legs. I still felt like she hid something. But perhaps she hid other horrors from her past too painful to reveal. Growing up in a family as she described, devoid of love, could grow evil in anyone's heart. She would need to deal with them before she could be healthy. I knew that much. And while I felt better about her and Nathan, I still worried that those issues would hurt him in the end.

After thinking and praying for a while longer, I returned to the oasis. The night had grown old; we needed to sleep.

I awoke with a kick to my gut.

"Wake up, dog!"

I opened my eyes to see a sword pointed at my neck. A young man stared down at me. At first, I smiled because he reminded me of Seth, but I realized a different face stood over me.

I peered into the man's eyes. "What is this about?"

He laughed. "Why, we're robbing you and taking you as slaves. And a fine bunch you'll make, too."

I glanced to see Kaylee and Crystal also with swords to their necks. Crystal, surprisingly, didn't act afraid. Nathan, who had been on watch, stood with a man behind his back who held a blade against the back of his head.

I should have waited for a caravan. My decisions hadn't proven the best, so far.

The stubble-faced man narrowed one eye and held out his hand. "Don't try anything you'll regret."

Did I have a choice with his sword trained on my neck? I grabbed his hand and he pulled me up. When he let go, I felt something in my palm, but I didn't dare peek. It felt like a key, but what key would I have received from a thief?

While he said something to the others, I discreetly slipped the key into my pocket. Though he would search those, maybe he wouldn't consider it anything important.

"Let's chain 'em up. We can inventory their goods once we're home." He grabbed my hands and noticed the ring. "Well, this looks like pure gold."

I nodded. "Oh yes, it is. Pure gold. Worth a fortune I would think."

Kaylee shot a what-are-you-doing expression at me. Nathan jerked against the arms holding him.

The thief pulled at the ring but it didn't budge.

"That's never come off in years. If you want it, you'll have to cut it off, I'm afraid."

"Dad!" Kaylee yelled out.

The young man looked at me, then at Kaylee, and then back to the ring. He chuckled. "What's the catch?"

"Well, I'm not sure exactly what happens, but usually it isn't good."

"Aw, I get it. You think you can scare me, eh?" He pulled a dagger from the side of his pants and waved the knife at my face. "Well, let me tell you. Ol' Billy of the Desert didn't get this far by not seeing when people tried to fool him."

I gazed around nonchalantly. "Well, don't say I didn't warn you."

He shook his head and put the blade to my finger.

"No!" Kaylee jerked at the arms of her captor.

A rushing wind broke through the stillness and slammed into the thief, knocking him off his feet. He flew through the air and banged against a tree, before sliding down into the water, unconscious. I stood where he had left me, gazing at the other two men.

They stared at their comrade, and then back at me. One of the men widened their eyes. "You're that Sisko fellow they were talking about in town!" His legs and arms shook. "Please, don't do anything to us." They backed away from Nathan, Kaylee, and Crystal. One of them threw their friend over his horse and they galloped away, glancing over their shoulders to see if I would come after them.

Nathan and Kaylee dashed to me and wrapped me in their arms. Nathan laughed and said, "Wow. It really is true what you've said about the ring."

"You didn't believe me?" I gave him my best incredulous face.

"Well, yeah, but I'd never seen you do anything."

Crystal raised an eyebrow.

I dug in my pocket. "Oh, I almost forgot. I received another key."

Kaylee's jaw dropped open. "A key? Here? From whom?"

"From that thief."

"You've got to be kidding."

I opened my palm. Another iron-wrought key like the first, but this time the crystal attached to it formed the shape of a moon on the end. I took out Gabriel's crystal prison and found the moon shaped design. Over it the letters "hon" sparkled in the sunlight.

"Honesty," I said.

Nathan wrinkled his nose. "Honesty?"

I nodded my head. "Makes sense. He honestly told me what he intended to do to us. He was pretty straight up about it all."

Kaylee nodded. "Hum, guess so."

"'Man looks on the outward appearance, but the Lord looks on the heart.'" I met Kaylee's eyes.

They widened in realization of the truth as she nodded her head. "Sometimes virtue pops up in the strangest places."

I slid the crystal in and broke it off. As the last time, it glowed and then died off, leaving the hole invisible.

"Two down, five to go." I scanned our camp. "I'm hungry. How about some breakfast before we head out?"

The desert sun rose high in the sky, pulling the moisture from our bodies. Despite having filled the flasks with water, I wondered if we would have enough to make it to the next oasis. The frequent drinks didn't satisfy the demand of our bodies.

Thinking about it forced me to take another swig. I wiped my mouth and focused on the long desert road ahead of us. But my mind kept returning to the thief. Not so much him, but how I had tricked him into attacking me and the ring.

On one hand, it had been so long since I had felt the ring do anything, so it left me with a feeling of power and confidence to know it still worked in the background—even if I couldn't actively use it to heal. On the other hand, it didn't feel right. I had forced God's hand, like someone using faith to get what they want. I recalled people who would attempt to manipulate me and the ring for their own selfish purposes after my popularity had grown, and it disgusted me. Had I now done the same thing? Had I once again abused the ring as I had twenty years ago in this same desert?

Kaylee pulled up beside me. "You look deep in thought."

I nodded. "I was."

She wiped her forehead. "Anything you can share? This never-ending desert doesn't provide much distracting scenery."

I sighed. I didn't want to dump on her what she couldn't do anything about. "I was thinking about the thief."

She giggled. "That was so amazing!"

Crystal looked over her shoulder at us.

I smiled. "That was nothing compared to the time Josh and I broke out of—"

"The Ball of Desires. You've told us that one many times, Dad."

"But you said you're bored, don't you want to hear it again?"

A grin spread across her face as she nodded. "Sure. It's a good story."

I welcomed the distraction, and besides, it was one of my favorites to tell. "One day when I was a teen in Reol, I spotted a young girl on the edge of the forest—"

A gust of wind circled around us. I froze, wondering if God might now punish me for my manipulation with the thief.

The sand rose into a wall, enclosing us in its grip. The sand-wall grew denser, darker, and taller until it met over our heads, blocking the sunlight from our eyes.

"Dad, what's happening?" Kaylee cried out.

"I don't know."

The horses bucked wildly, sending us to the ground as sand bit into our skin and mouths. They galloped through the walls of sand flying around us. I covered my eyes with my arm. The wind died down and the sand no longer pelted against me, yet the world remained dark.

Then a reddish glow rose in the distance, then another close by, and another, until the scene burst into flames around us. We lay on what appeared to be the flat top of a big rock jutting amidst volcanic flames. The edges dropped straight down into a fire that filled the air with caustic fumes. Breathing the heated and smoky air proved difficult.

Nathan lifted himself to his feet. "Where are we?"

I coughed, gasped for air and croaked out, "I would say we're in the opposite of Paradise. My guess would be Hades."

Beltrid's voice rang through the air as if broadcasting from every corner of the cavern. "You're correct, Sisko. Welcome to my domain."

My eyes locked onto Nathan and Kaylee's in succession. Both were wide in surprise. I'd almost forgotten about Beltrid. Did he intend to trap us here forever?

Two beasts crawled onto the plateau. Both wore rags upon bodies that bulged with muscles. Their heads resembled that of a snake, but their bodies, that of an ape. Each held a sword of black fire.

The beast lunged toward Crystal and me. I pushed myself up against the edge as it raced toward me, but Kaylee jumped between us, swinging her sword to get its attention. It worked.

The creature attacked Kaylee, who ducked, then swung to the side, avoiding the smoldering blade. When it hit the ground, sparks burst forth and smoke filled the air. She planted her blade in its side. It let out a screech, but the snake head extended from its body and attempted to bite her. She pulled the weapon out and it bit her blade instead. Black blood flowed from its mouth.

But the pain infuriated the creature, and it attacked her with a new vengeance. She dodged its blows, occasionally parrying a shot, but it clearly had the offensive. Kaylee backed closer and closer to the edge.

I checked the other one. Nathan had also engaged the beast to prevent it from attacking Crystal. Yet he appeared to be getting the upper hand with his opponent.

Crystal had drawn herself closer to me. "Can't you use the ring? Nathan may die." She watched Nathan as he dodged a thrust to his mid-section.

"I can't use it to attack."

"But the thief, you used it with him."

"Only because I got him to attack me."

"Well, why not the same thing here?"

I stared into her eyes, they bore a remarkable calmness considering the situation. She was right; I could get one of them to attack me, but I didn't feel right about it the first time.

I checked Kaylee's progress. She now held her ground because she had no more ground to give up. Her heels nearly hung off the side of the precipice. Fire leaped up behind her.

Nathan had struck a fatal blow to his adversary, but by the time he finished, it would be too late for him to help Kaylee. No time to trick the creature into an attack; I had only one course of action left. Whether the ring would protect such foolishness, I didn't know and didn't care.

I leaped to my feet and hurried to her. The creature had knocked the sword from her hand, and she stood helpless before him. He raised his blade of death and began the plunge into her soul.

"No!" My voice echoed in the chambers of Hades as Beltrid's had. I threw myself in front of Kaylee as the sword fell, and it struck deep into my shoulder. Pain flooded my body. Though I yelled, it was drowned by the cry of the beast.

Where his black sword had entered my body, it ignited with a new fire, a light-radiating energy that could only be one thing—God's reality. It traveled up the weapon and into the creature. Divine glory engulfed the beast, and light burst from it, filling Hades with Paradise.

The screams fell silent, sand fell over me, the dry heat returned, and we all lay under the burning, desert sun again.

"Dad, are you all right?" Kaylee crawled to me and examined my shoulder. We both watched as the wound sealed and vanished. She plopped back onto the ground. "The ring?"

I nodded. "I believe so."

"Crystal!" Nathan's voice rolled over the now still air. He scurried to her body laying in the sand a stone's throw from us.

Kaylee and I also hurried to her. Her chest rose and fell with air, and her eyes cracked open as Nathan knelt beside her.

He grabbed her hand. "Are you hurt?"

"I...I don't know." She held his arm and a smile spread across her lips.

I gasped. What I felt now wasn't evil from her at all, but a warmth and true affection. But for only a couple seconds. Then her eyes grew blank, and the old feeling returned. This girl continued to mystify me.

She sat up. "I must have fallen and hit my head on something. Help me up, please."

Nathan lifted her up and supported her in his arms. I watched as he helped her to the horse, gathered with the others several feet away.

Kaylee retrieved her sword, then stepped before me. "Dad, I love you so much." She wrapped her arms around me. "Thank you for saving me."

I rubbed her back. "It's what any father would do for his daughter."

"You're not getting off that easy. It isn't every father who would willingly sacrifice himself for his daughter, and you know it."

"Maybe it's just I can't imagine a father not doing it." I held her in my arms. Even my heart felt I had done the right thing. I hadn't manipulated God as I did that morning. I whispered, "Thank you, Father."

The trail remained easy to follow and led us through two other oases. On the third day of desert travel, the climate changed drastically.

The sun dimmed behind clouds and cool air breezed across our faces, refreshing dry, hot skin. But the trail, which had turned into a defined roadway since the ground had firmed up a mile back, led straight into a fog bank. Once in, the fog thickened so much we could barely see a few feet in front of us.

The sound of lapping water greeted our ears and we arrived at a shore. Over the water stretched a wooden bridge, disappearing into the mist.

"Any idea where this is?" Kaylee ventured to ask.

I sniffed the air. "I smell food cooking. My guess is there's a city or village on the other side of this bridge. But we better walk the horses across."

We dismounted. Kaylee patted Rain's neck and mumbled something to her. Nathan moved his shoulders as if loosening up. I could feel the tension in the air. Not seeing far ahead cast shadows of the unknown over our fear. We readied ourselves to plunge into it.

I eased onto the bridge. It creaked with our weight as they followed, but it held. The wind had died, and the fog hung thick around us. The lapping of water and the creaking of the bridge blended with the sound of our own breathing, which caused eddies to swirl in the soupy, floating whiteness.

A few steps in and we could see neither end of the bridge. A swish in the water rang through the still air.

"What was that?" Nathan peered into the water.

Kaylee's scream pierced the quietness. "Help!"

We swung around to see big hands wrapped around her ankle. Kaylee clawed at the wet wood as she slid off the bridge and splashed into the river.

I gasped. "Kaylee!"

Nathan drew his sword and we both rushed to the bridge's edge. I heard water swishing below as they struggled. Kaylee grunted and the beast, whatever it was, let loose a guttural cry. "Ouch, stop that, meal!"

I wanted to jump in and save her, but what could I do but watch and get myself killed? I paused. But I couldn't get killed; the ring protected me. I placed my hand on Nathan's shoulder. "Stay here and watch your feet." I turned to Crystal. "Take the horses to the other side."

Nathan's eyes darted between me and the water churning below. "What are you going to do?"

"Arggg! Put that thing away," the gruff voice cried below.

I leaped from the bridge and sank waist high into the water before my feet landed onto a rocky bed. It felt like soaking in death itself.

"Father! What are you doing?" Nathan prepared to leap in.

I held my hand up. "No! Stay there."

He stopped, but confusion and concern twisted across his face.

I focused under the bridge. Among the dim shadows I could make out Kaylee's form slamming her sword onto a bulky hide with a thud, but the blade's edge failed to penetrate its skin. With her other arm, she held the beast's head back. It held her in one huge hand and attempted to fend off her blows with the other.

I pushed through the water until I stood by the creature's side. What could I do? Maybe if I distracted it long enough for Kaylee to get her point into its—

Kaylee's hand slipped off its head. The monster bit down upon her arm.

Her scream pierced the foggy, still air as she flung herself back. The sword fell from her palm.

Without thinking, I reached toward the blade and caught it as it hit the water. I grabbed the hilt firmly, and with all the strength I could muster, swung around to my left and plunged the sword into the creature's back. The point flashed upon hitting its hide, and the blade glowed a deep blue as it plunged into the monster. Satisfaction glowed within me as well.

The creature released Kaylee; she fell into the waters with a splash. I yanked the sword out. A wail and groan turned into a fell screech before its body crumpled in front of me. Its limp form drifted slowly downstream. I felt a burning sensation on my hand. I held it up, still gripping the sword, and noticed the ring glowed a deep, dark blue.

I had never seen it do that before and wondered what it meant. Kaylee rose from the waters, coughing and gasping for air. I swooshed through the murky liquid toward her. "Kaylee, are you all right?"

Her wet hair clung to her shoulders and her breaths came shallow and quick. "It bit me, is all." She grimaced.

I pulled her arm up. "That looks nasty. Let's hope there is a town at the end of this bridge, and they have a doctor."

Nathan's worried voice called from above, "Father, Kaylee, are you alive?"

I sheathed her sword and swung Kaylee's good arm over my shoulder. "We're alive. Help us up."

We returned to the edge of the bridge and Nathan reached out his hand.

I caught his eye. "Her left arm is injured, don't pull on it."

We laid her on the wooden slats and I rechecked her wound in better light. Blood oozed out of the bite-marks and the skin had turned a reddish-blue around it. Fog hung heavy around it; I brushed it away, yet it floated back thicker.

"Nathan, give me your knife."

He reached onto his left pants leg, retrieved a dagger, and handed it to me. I cut the skin on the bites; Kaylee allowed a brief groan to escape and she involuntarily pulled against my hand.

"Hold still!" I placed my mouth over the bite and sucked. I jerked my head back and spit out her blood. My whole mouth grew numb as soon as I had sucked it in, and her skin felt ice-cold around the wound.

I touched my mouth, and the skin felt rough and swollen. But quickly it disappeared and the numbness vanished. Kaylee's wound, however, had swollen and the bluish color had spread. I felt the skin around the wound. It was transforming her, and I would have been too, but the ring must have prevented it.

I checked the ring, the blue had given way to its natural golden color. Yet it felt different now. I couldn't place it, but something had changed. A knot formed in my gut. The flash of light when the sword hit the creature's hide, enabling me to penetrate its skin when Kaylee could not; the glow of the blade and the ring: I had killed with the ring! Beltrid had claimed I had used the ring to kill. I knew I hadn't then. Now—I had. But what else could I have done? Kaylee would be dead if I hadn't.

I wrapped cloth around the wound as best I could and glanced toward Nathan. "Help me. We need to get her to a doctor. Whatever is happening to her isn't a simple bite."

He pulled me up and we both helped Kaylee to her feet. She fixed her eyes on Nathan's face. "Dad saved me. He killed the creature."

"Father?" Nathan's eyes darted to me. "How?"

"With my sword." She groaned as another wave of pain hit her.

We continued over the bridge as my concern for Kaylee grew. The form of Crystal holding the reins of our horses materialized from the fog along with the shoreline. She watched us with no emotion as we passed before her, then she followed.

I sought out the city gate in the shadowy wall of the village ahead. We found it and the gatekeeper. After banging the metal plating with my hands three times, he opened a window in the gate. "You have no business here, I'll wager. Be off with you."

"We cannot leave, my daughter is injured and needs care. Do you have a doctor?"

"That we do. But he'll do you little good, I'm afraid. You're better off away from here." His eyes pleaded with us through the iron grate.

I had to get us in. "If we have to, we'll bang on this gate all night long. Now let us in!"

The man grumbled something about strangers and rolled his eyes. His face disappeared and only seconds passed before we heard the bolt of the gate shifting across wood and metal. We entered.

"I hope you're made of sterner stuff than most," he said as he latched the gate shut behind us.

Lights from various windows cast glowing beams through the fog-drenched streets. Bats dove into the lights for a brief moment to catch insects. Our own movement caused eddies to form in the stifling air as mist swirled around us, and, if I didn't know better, it appeared to be following us. Its gray-white appearance contrasted against the black and dull buildings, like silhouettes without the back-light.

Kaylee said, "Who would want to live here? Maybe we should leave."

"There's the inn up head. You need a doctor." I saw a sign reading, "Foggy Inn."

Nathan grunted. "How appropriate."

We opened the door and found the insides well lit. A man with an apron scampered out and greeted us.

"Hello, my name is Opus. How can I help you?"

"We would like a room. Also, we need a doctor. A strange creature under your bridge bit my daughter."

He gazed at her arm. "That troll's at it again. Yes, those troll bites can be nasty. My sister was bit by a troll once. Turned all blue and then…" His cheery smile faded. "Well, that's another story."

Nathan wrinkled his forehead. "Did you say, a troll?"

Opus nodded. "Oh yes. Been there for some time. He keeps people away." He stared to his left. "Or eats them."

I raised my chin. "He's a dead troll now. I just killed him."

Opus raised an eyebrow. "Oh dear. That might not be good. But I guess it's inevitable someone would." His eyes darted around, not wanting to focus on mine. "I'll need payment up front, then."

"Up front? Why? Afraid we might walk on you?"

"No, no." He tapped his fingertips together as he talked. "Just ensuring I get my money. There's some around who'll be quite peeved about the death of their pet."

I didn't like the way he said that. Sort of half sad, half happy, as if we were left out of his inside joke. Would other trolls hunt us down?

"But don't mind that. You're here now, and that's all that matters." He held out his hand.

"How many pounds?"

"Let's see. Four of you, five horses from what I can see outside, and a doctor to fetch—fifty pounds."

I allowed a low growl to escape. I didn't like being taken advantage of, but we didn't have much choice. So I counted out fifty pounds to him. He smiled as he stuffed it in his apron pocket. "This way."

We followed him down a creaking wooden hallway. He opened a door and pointed us in. The walls closed in upon bare furnishings: a couple beds, a table, and two chairs. Water roaches scatted into hiding as we lit the lamps.

"Make yourselves at home. Dinner will be ready about the time you get settled. So come right on in when you're ready." He stepped out of the room and shut the door.

Nathan wrinkled his nose. "Do we really have to stay here?"

"You have any better ideas? This is the only place in town I saw, and I doubt sleeping outside would be much better. Why don't you open the window to at least get some fresh air in?"

Nathan shook his head. "You call this 'fresh'?" But he opened the shutters and latched them back.

Kaylee rubbed her left arm, avoiding the wound. "I'm feeling cold."

I placed my hand against her cheek, but involuntarily jerked it back. The cold lifelessness of her skin shocked me. Not simply the skin's icy cold touch, but its texture had changed as well. The knot in my gut grew tighter.

A knock rattled the door. I opened it. A thin man with a bag bounded in. "I'm the doctor here. We have a troll bite, I'm told?"

"So it seems." I pointed to Kaylee.

He examined the bite and felt her skin. "Yep, it's started."

"What's started?"

"Troll poison. Before morning, she'll have turned into a troll."

Nathan jumped out of his chair.

I stared at the doctor, hardly knowing what to say. "Poison? Turn into a troll?"

He nodded.

"Can't you extract the poison?"

He wrinkled his brow as if I should have known. "It's not that kind of poison. She can't escape this poison anymore than you could escape..." He waved his hand. "...the air around you. I was told you did kill the troll, did you not?"

Desperation set in. "Yes, but what does that have to do with it? You have to do something. I can't sit here and watch my daughter turn into a troll!"

He sighed and nodded his head as if he'd seen this before. "I can give her something to make it less painful, but I can't stop it."

"Pills? It's just a bite! Bandage it up at least! It should heal." But the bluish color of Kaylee's skin contradicted my words.

"I'm sorry." He pulled some pills from his bag and placed them in my hand. "Those'll help. Five pounds please." He held out his hand.

I stared at the man in disbelief. The gatekeeper's words proved true; the doctor was useless. I gave up and waved for Nathan to give it to him. The doctor promptly took it and left. We placed Kaylee in a bed and covered her up. Her face had turned a pale blue, and her body shivered. Nathan scooted a chair over for me to sit in.

Why couldn't I still do miracles? Again, the pain of losing that ability had hit me where it hurts. But I had to try. Maybe God would grant my request anyway. "Father, please heal Kaylee from this troll bite."

I watched, but she didn't improve. Instead, she stared blankly at the ceiling. I hung my head.

"I thought you could do miracles," Crystal said to me as she stared at Kaylee. "Why can't you heal her?"

"I told you, I abused that power in the desert. Ever since then, I've not been able to do miracles like I did before."

"But the man who you knocked into the tree? Did you not do that?"

I locked onto her eyes. She stared at Kaylee with furrowed eyebrows. I shook my head. "No, God did that. One thing Beltrid had right—God won't allow anyone to take the ring."

She nodded slowly. "Still, you didn't ask God to do that, did you?"

I studied her face. It remained fixed on Kaylee. Did she think I could somehow use the ring's protection to save her? "You're right. I didn't ask. But I knew God would save me." Those words rang hollow in my ears. I had forced God's hand, without His permission. Crystal seemed to sense that.

"Then why not simply do it now? Don't ask, just use your own will."

Should I try? "I can't do that, I can only use the ring by God's power."

Kaylee groaned and her eyes widened.

"Quick, the pills." I grabbed one from Nathan and placed it in her mouth. She swallowed it with a drink. I sat on her bed and placed her head in my lap. I held her close, and rocked her like a baby.

I nodded to Nathan. "I'll keep the first watch. You two get some sleep."

Nathan sunk into a chair and slammed his fist on the table. Dust vibrated into the air from it. "I can't sleep! I can't do anything! Nothing!" He smashed his fist on the table again before wrapping his arms over his head.

Fog from the window hovered around the ceiling. And oddly enough, around Kaylee and me as I cradled her in my lap.

I rubbed her cold shoulders and she smiled through her pain. Her eyes gazed up at me. A rougher version of her voice came out. "Dad, whatever happens to me, I love you and will watch over you."

My eyes watered and I cracked. "Don't talk like that. We'll get you through this somehow."

She relaxed in my arms, trust beaming from her swollen face.

The ring, resting against her shoulder, gleamed in the lamp-light. Crystal may be right. I had used the ring to kill the troll without asking. But that happened without thinking about it. I hadn't done it intentionally. Perhaps I could use it without asking God. If ever a reason called me to do so, now would be it. Yet, every time I had failed to trust God, I had discovered the worst path I could have taken.

I wiped the tears back and hugged her close. No, I would not use the ring apart from God, not intentionally. I could do nothing, the doctor's help fell empty, and the ring wouldn't heal her. All that remained was trust in God, and that would have to be enough.

I waved the fog away from us, rubbed her icy back, and held her tight.

Kaylee groaned and a small growl left her lips at the end. My heavy eyes opened wider, and I hugged her tighter. Her frame had grown; her arms bulged to twice their original size. Her face had contorted with the expanding of her skin, as bones bulged against it.

I had to get out from under her. The weight had become too much. No sooner had I sat on a chair next to her bed when fluttering filled the air. I turned to the window and gasped.

Some type of bat flew around the room, but it appeared ghost-like, formed from the mist itself. Another flew in, and they both landed on Nathan's sleeping form at the table.

I leaped from my chair. "Nathan, Crystal, get up!" I swung at the bats, but my hands passed through them. Their mist-substance scattered for a moment and then they reformed, still attached to him.

Nathan and Crystal awoke. Nathan's eyes widened as he saw them. He fell to the floor and rolled, but they continued to reform on him as he did. Then I noticed: Crystal remained untouched. They had not gone for her. I checked myself and found three of them on me.

I've led us to our deaths!

12

More mist bats swarmed through the window, fluttering around Nathan and me. Crystal and Kaylee, however, they ignored.

Kaylee forced herself out of bed. "Must get us out," she said in a gruff voice, still hers but yet, not.

I had stopped trying to bat the creatures away from myself; it did no good. I watched as Kaylee, her now huge muscles bulging, leaped at the wall and kicked it. Creaking sounds echoed through the walls as dust floated to the floor. She kicked it again; the wall buckled. Again, and her foot crashed through. Once more, and the hole widened to a small doorway as dust and particles rained to the floor.

Reality turned surreal. Broken images flashed through my mind while foreign urges forced their way into my desires. Kaylee picked Nathan and me up as if we weighed nothing and carried us out of the inn. We lay on our horses. Crystal followed, her eyes empty of fear or concern.

I felt thin, as if I had slid into the fog with the bats. My tongue brushed across protruding fangs. My arms felt like flapping. The bats clung to me, flew around me. I could hear them now: squeaks that sounded like speech. They fluttered about me as if in a frenzy—addicted to whatever they drank from me.

More images flew through my mind with longer and longer periods between each. Riding through the street. Breaking through the city gate. Growling. The bridge and foggy water. Then, the desert and a night sky full of stars. I passed out.

When I came to, my head pounded like someone had been beating on it with a club. I groaned as I attempted to lift my head. A bright light from the door of the shelter didn't help matters any.

A face moved into view. As I focused, I realized Crystal hovered over me. She lifted me to a sitting position and gave me a cup.

"Drink this, it will help."

I took a swallow, and the bitter taste nearly caused me to spit it out, but I swallowed anyway. A warmth sank into my bones, and my head cleared. "What happened? How are Nathan and Kaylee?"

"Nathan is recovering as you are, but he hasn't gained consciousness yet. Kaylee…" She paused as if trying to find the right words. "She is sick."

"Is she a…troll?"

"Not totally. Getting out of the mist stopped the process."

"The mist?"

"That's what she said."

"The bats, did you see all the bats?"

She shook her head. "No. I think the mist gave you illusions. Nathan acted as if he fought some beast; you kept batting at him and yourself as if trying to brush something off. Then you both became incoherent and started to fade, as if the mist sought to claim you for its own. That's when Kaylee acted, while you were still physical enough to move."

I shuddered. "The bats were horrible. They swarmed all over me and Nathan. I felt like they sucked the life out of me." I met her eyes. "And for some reason, they avoided you."

Her eyes widened. "I'm not sure why. Maybe the mist's illusion projected what you feel inside. You said you felt evil from me."

I nodded. "Could be." I took another gulp of the liquid. I grimaced as it burned down my throat. "Is Kaylee awake? I want to speak to her."

"Yes, I believe so." She rose and helped me to my feet.

The light of the sun blinded me and caused my head to pound. But my eyes adjusted and we moved toward a shelter close by. I peered inside. "Kaylee?"

Her face, warped by the change, lit up. "Dad, you're all right!" She leaped toward me. Her thick arms wrapped around me.

"Careful now. That's a little tight."

"Oh, sorry." She sat back. "I thought I would lose you both."

"I thought I had lost you." I examined her closer. "Yet it seems you've gotten better."

She nodded. "I am. Getting out of the mist was the key. It's like the metamorphosis fed off of it." She pointed at her bandaged arm. "Crystal cleaned the wound and bandaged it."

"More than I can say for that stupid doctor." I placed my hand upon Crystal's arm. "Thank you."

She smiled, but pulled away and shifted her head around, avoiding our eyes. "I had better see how Nathan is doing and get some food going. You'll be hungry." She slipped out.

My stomach acknowledged her assessment with a growl. "She's right. I am hungry. How long have I been out?"

"All of last night since we left and half of today."

I shook my head. "But tell me, because I started to fade, what caused you to realize the mist fueled the changes? What did you see?"

Her eyes focused off in the distance. "The pain of my transformation made it difficult to think, but when you and Nathan screamed and rolled around, my mind sharpened. I could see two realities. One was you and Nathan acting like you tried to get something off of you, and Crystal sitting up in the bed, watching. That was very strange."

"Did you see anything attacking us? Did it attack Crystal?"

"I saw the mist swirling about you and Nathan. It grew thick as it entered through your noses. When I saw hints of the room behind you, I realized the mist was transforming you into itself. I knew if I didn't get you out of it, you would soon fade and be lost."

"But Crystal?"

Kaylee blinked. "No, it didn't attack her at all. But when I checked, I noticed the same mist entering me through the wound, but my transformation wasn't into the mist, it was to become a troll, to replace the one you killed. They wanted you and Nathan, because you had killed it. I heard the voices calling me and I felt their thoughts. I knew then that the only way to save us was to get us out of the mist."

I nodded. "Still, why did they avoid Crystal?"

Kaylee shrugged.

I breathed deep. "Ironic that I thought I had saved you, but it was you who saved us in the end. That's a nightmare I don't want to ever live through again."

"Me neither."

A growing swell of guilt burst through, as if on cue. Tears burst forth unbidden; I sank my head into my hands.

Kaylee wrapped me in her arms and rubbed my shoulder. "Dad, it's all right. We made it through just like you said."

I felt my limbs shaking. I couldn't control myself. "You don't understand. I led us in there, I killed the troll that started it all, I demanded the gatekeeper let us in despite his warnings. I nearly killed you and Nathan, and we would have left Gabrielle locked in her prison forever."

I felt her hand rubbing my back as I tried to gain control, but fresh sobs bubbled up again. "I nearly ruined everything!"

She didn't say anything, just held me. I could feel her tears dripping on my arm. We embraced each other for many minutes, before I felt enough control to face anything else.

But one thought intruded into my self-pity: had I forced the ring to heal her, assuming it would, we would not be alive now. It would have most likely taken both Kaylee and Nathan.

I sucked in a deep breath. "Nathan, how did he survive?"

"What do you mean?"

"You simply didn't get transformed all the way, and I believe the ring protected me from being totally taken over by the mist, but how did Nathan survive?"

Kaylee stared at the ground for a moment. "I don't know. You did regain your solid physical form faster, almost as soon as we left the mist. But Nathan remained very translucent. Crystal tended to him, and the next time I saw him he had returned to a solid form. She said he had made a recovery."

I noted her pinkish blue skin, her bulkier build, and a much more homely face than she used to have. "But what about you? Will you return to normal?"

"I don't know." She smirked. "Being half troll has its advantages."

"Especially when it comes to breaking through walls and gates." I winked.

I laughed, and it felt good after what we had been through. Tension flowed away on each breath I exhaled, causing the laughter to arise from more than humor—from the releasing of nightmares into the light of day.

Nathan regained consciousness later that day. After a few hours and a hearty meal, his strength returned. Though I rejoiced at this, it mystified me at the same time. He should have remained part mist like Kaylee retained her troll features. Did Crystal have some healing abilities she hadn't told us about?

We camped there four days, so that Kaylee could finish healing, and I felt I needed the time to process all that had happened. Though I had physically returned to normal, I had changed. I had killed an intelligent creature for the first time in my life. In the heat of the moment, I had used the ring to kill, and I could not undo it as much as I might wish it. I knew that would return to haunt me.

During the four days, Kaylee's scar mended and her temperature returned to normal. On the fourth day, she scurried about and helped with the chores. However, many of the troll features stayed with her. Her biceps bulged twice as big as Nathan's. Her legs rippled with muscles. Her voice retained a gruffer edge, but her sweet personality remained fully intact. Her face wasn't as tight as the first night's ordeal, but neither had it returned to her former beauty. Maybe it never would. She might have to live out her life as part troll. I pointed this out to her.

"It's probably for the better. Maybe now the boys will leave me alone and I can go to the convent and be a nun."

For sure, no boy would think twice about messing with her. Still, she seemed to be taking this too easily, even if it did make her feel safe from men with questionable intentions. I knew she tended to hide her hurts. She would deal with them in time.

We warned travelers away from the city. Nathan constructed a sign, which he drove into the ground by the side of the road. It read: "Avoid the mist at all cost. To enter will be your death. You have been warned." He seemed to find this cathartic, and regained an upbeat mood.

As I watched Nathan and Kaylee sparring, I knew the time had come to leave. I called them around me. "Let's get moving. We aren't getting any closer to my village sitting here."

They jumped at the mention of resuming the journey. The packing sped by. Kaylee loaded the horses faster than usual. In no time, we had mounted the horses and coaxed them into a trot. We skirted around the mist hovering to our left. As we left the desert, the forest trees gradually grew up around us, and we noticed a small path cutting through the woods. Apparently used by the few who knew not to go into the mist.

A small river flowing toward the mist soon crossed our path. No bridge crossed it, but we could see the path coming out the other side. It appeared shallow enough; we nudged our mounts to cross the river. The water flowed clear and cool. A fresh, brisk breeze caressed our faces.

In the distance, the river disappeared into the mist. I marveled that such a cheery atmosphere could exist beside utter despair and death. We crossed over, then dismounted to fill our bottles with the sweet water before continuing on.

The path led clearly through the forest. Sometimes it veered to the right, other times to the left. But based on the maps I had seen, it led toward the town close to where Gabrielle's family lived. The serenity of the forest soothed my troubled soul.

Troubled, because now that death no longer threatened us, my mind again turned to Nathan and Crystal. I had noticed her influence over him. He readily did whatever she wanted. He defended her no matter how silly her statement or request might seem. I had one question I knew would reveal much. But I didn't know how he would react.

Nathan and Crystal rode a horse-length ahead of us. I cupped my hand toward Kaylee riding next to me. "Tell Nathan I wish to talk with him, and see if you can engage Crystal in conversation."

She raised an eyebrow and nodded. She trotted up to him and he glanced back at me. After a few words, he dropped back to ride alongside of me.

"You have a question?"

"I do." I met his eyes. "Have you and Crystal…slept together?"

His eyes widened. "Well, no. No, we haven't. At least, not if you mean it like I think you're meaning it."

"Really?"

He sighed. "When I take a wife, I want to take a wife. Not a harlot, or a concubine. I would not disgrace her by uniting myself to her frivolously, without committing all of me to her."

I halted my horse, and he pulled up beside me. I waved to the girls. "Keep going, we'll catch up."

Crystal glared at me before Kaylee drew her attention back into the conversation and they continued on.

"Look into my eyes, Son."

His blue-green eyes stared at mine, steady and true.

I moved my horse close to his and reached out my hand. "I know you mean those words, and God will hold you to them. But I want you to promise me not to allow any seduction to pull you from your professed path."

His eyes remained fixed on mine, with barely a blink. "I promise that it shall be so." He reached out and grabbed my hand, and we squeezed each other tight. He smiled.

When he released, I felt something in my hand. I opened my palm to reveal an iron key; a crystal shaft hung from the iron end. I held it before his eyes and smiled.

His eyes widened and his mouth hung open.

I swung my pack up and pulled out the wrapped crystal ball. I held it in my hand and rotated it until I found the hole shaped in a round ring. Over it the letters, "pur" blazed in the sunlight. I couldn't help but let out a chuckle.

I caught Nathan's eyes and smiled. "Purity."

A wide grin creased his face and he sat taller in his saddle.

I inserted the key and twisted. The glow subsided, and I repacked Gabrielle into the blanket.

"Thank you, Son. Thank you so much. You've brought us one step closer to getting your mother back."

A tear rolled down his cheek.

"Come on, let's go tell the girls." I bumped the horse into a trot. Nathan followed.

A scream echoed through the woods ahead of us. It sounded like Crystal. Nathan shot ahead. I raced after him.

Father, let them be all right!

13

As I arrived at Kaylee and Crystal's location, I saw four creatures, swords in hands, attacking them. Their pitch-black exteriors, except for white eyes glaring from midnight-faces, blended with the shadows, rendering their ape-like shapes hard to track. Kaylee had cut into the sword-arm of one creature. Another had moved around the injured one and engaged her.

Meanwhile, one of the others had grabbed Crystal and pulled her toward a shimmering, door-like opening at one end of the clearing. Nathan scrambled off his horse and attacked.

I watched, quite helpless other than to pray. Kaylee dealt swiftly with her attacker. It attempted a stab at her chest. She pulled back, then flipped her sword to bump his hand to the side and thrust her blade through him. The creature let out a shriek, chilling my bones.

Nathan drove his sword in and slightly out to the right, pushing the creature off balance, and then brought the blade across its throat, severing the artery. It fell over with a cry.

The creature pulling Crystal, who kicked and yelled Nathan's name, stepped through the strange door. Nathan dashed after him, but the door shrunk toward its center. Nathan dove through the hole. His feet cleared the opening before it shrank to a point and popped out of existence behind him.

"Nathan!" I leaped off my horse and sped to the spot, but the door had disappeared, leaving Kaylee and I alone with the corpses of two shadow-creatures and the injured form of another.

I released a growl of frustration and turned to face the dark beast lying on the ground. Black blood flowed from the wound. No facial features could be discerned upon it, not even the outline of clothes. It moved as a shadow in the sunlight yet had substance and could hold a weapon.

"Where did they go? Take me there." I grabbed its neck and jerked it off the ground.

It sounded as if it spoke from a distant world, like a spirit. "You would go willingly?"

I glanced at Kaylee. The question didn't sound promising, but I had no choice. "Yes. I would go. Can you reopen the door?"

It shook its head. "No, I cannot. I will lead you to Shadow Mountain under which we live. They are kept there." It pointed with its good hand to a mountain barely visible through the trees.

"Enough." A voice behind me boomed.

I turned to see Beltrid standing half a stone's throw away. A chill raced through me. The demon picked the oddest times to appear.

"Are you behind this?" I focused on his eyes burning with hate.

He smiled. "I told you I could get to any of you any time I wanted. Well, I wanted."

"But why? What possible purpose could all this serve?"

"You will find out soon enough. By then, it will be too late."

Then Beltrid gazed at the shadow-creature lying on the ground. "And this one shall not lead you." He lifted his hand, but Kaylee jumped toward him with her sword.

"Kaylee, no!"

Beltrid held his hand out and she froze in her charge. He twisted his hand and the tip of her sword moved down. Her hand shook as she attempted to wrest control from him, but she couldn't stop it. Her face grimaced with the effort, but it continued to turn inward until the tip pointed at her gut.

"Beltrid, stop! What is it you want?"

"I told you. The ring. And I don't need this one to get it."

I tried to think. What could I use against him? I felt my pockets and the bones from the desert bulged in them. It sounded crazy, but I could think of nothing else to do as Kaylee gritted her teeth fighting to prevent the blade from plunging into her.

I pulled them out of my pocket and threw them with as much effort as I could muster toward Beltrid. The bones flared with a blue flame as they left my hand, and sped toward Beltrid as fiery darts. I saw the streak of blue follow my hand as it came down, and a burning sensation on my ring-finger.

With his attention locked on Kaylee, he didn't see them in time to react. The flaming bones plunged into his face, one landing on his eye. He jerked his hand to his face with a growling scream. Kaylee collapsed into a heap upon the ground, the sword falling harmlessly into the grass. Beltrid cried in anguish, then turned to me. He began to vanish, but as he did, I caught the glimpse of a smile.

The knot returned to my gut. I had done it again! He wanted me to use the ring without thinking.

Yet relief swept over me that Kaylee had survived. I scrambled to where she lay breathing hard. I scooped her into my arms. "How many times must I come so close to losing you?"

She said between breaths, "Dad, what did you throw at him?"

I smiled. "Bones."

"Bones?"

I nodded. "Bones of my old sin, now buried in his face."

She attempted to lift herself, but her shaking arms collapsed under her. "I'm afraid my struggle with Beltrid wiped me out. I need to eat."

"Just promise me you won't do that again? Please?"

"Don't worry, I won't be attacking him that way again." She smiled. "Besides, you're out of bones."

I stared past her. "Yes, I am." In more ways than one.

I turned my gaze to where the shadow-creature had lain, but he must have fled while we focused on Beltrid. "Looks like we lost our guide."

"At least he pointed the way."

I shook my head. "The sun is close to setting, and you're in no shape to travel. We'll have to bed here for the night. Rest against that rock, and I'll get something to eat."

Then I remembered. "Oh, some good news."

She perked up. "What's that?"

"I received another key."

"Oh, really? From who?"

"Your brother."

"Nathan? A key, from him?" She wrinkled her brow. "Which one?"

"Purity."

"Him? Purity!" She laughed. "I would have never thought it."

I stared in the direction of the mountain. "I hope he can remain that way. And alive." But Beltrid's words rang in my mind. He didn't need this one, meaning Kaylee, to get the ring. That meant he did need Nathan. But how would Nathan help him to get the ring?

Inheritance? Nathan would be expected to inherit the ring from me at some point. But he wouldn't willingly allow himself and the ring to be used by Beltrid. Something more had to be going on. But what?

The questions plagued me as I fixed a small dinner from the food in our pack, and cooked it upon a crackling fire.

I didn't sleep much that night. First half I sat on watch. I stared into the dancing flames of the fire and listened to the sounds of the night forest. Nothing else happened. No one attacked, except the thoughts in my head.

As the night creatures scurried in the forest, owls hooted, and wolves howled, I feared what would come next now that I had used the ring again. I hadn't killed Beltrid—after all, he is a demon. But I had certainly intended to, and it would have killed most people.

I glanced at Kaylee sleeping soundly in the shelter. Beltrid would continue to attack my family to force me to use the ring. He knew about my closeness to Kaylee and sought to use it. And I had made a habit of falling for it. But I didn't know what I could do differently.

A couple hours passed in these thoughts, when I heard the rushing of wind in the distance. A bright light raced through the dark forest toward me. I feared another attack brought on by my failure. I stood and walked to the edge, determined to face whatever came for me.

As the light raced over me like the edge of a rain storm, I shielded my eyes, for it hurt them. I felt my whole body ignited in flames and I fell to the ground, writhing in pain. I wanted to scream, but a bare breath escaped from my open mouth as if consumed by the fire itself.

Then, as if someone had punched me in the stomach, all air left my lungs, and I hung on the edge of suffocation for what seemed an eternity. When I thought I could take no more, air, sweet as honeysuckle on a summer's day, fled into my mouth, down my throat, and expanded my chest. A cool wind blew over me, and the burning sensation ceased. In its place, a bliss and joy flowed over me. I recognized it at once: Paradise.

But why here, and why did it burn so?

My first question received an immediate answer. A young girl around eight years of age strolled toward me. Her face shone with the brilliance of an inner light emanating all around me. It was Love, the girl I had met in my vision at the monastery.

"You burned because of the sin you held in your soul." Her young and pure voice floated like sunlight over me.

I hung my head, for I knew she came not to tell me I shouldn't feel guilty, but to confirm it.

"And why should I confirm what you already know, Sisko?"

I jerked my head to stare her in the face. She had read my thoughts; I could hide nothing from her. "I suppose you don't need to, but while I feel guilt over the ring's use, I don't see what other choices I had under the circumstances. She would be dead if I hadn't done what I did."

She stood before me now. Her face, so soft and welcoming, but harsh and full of judgment at the same time. "Why do you assume you had no other choice? Do you not trust God?"

I sat down and stared at the ground. "Yes, but it all happened so fast, I reacted. I didn't have time to think about it. It just happened. How can I stop that?"

"Sisko, you are making excuses. Trust must be a reaction, not just

71

something you do when you have time to think."

I felt tears rolling down my cheeks. She was right. When I traveled and did miracles, trust was easy. It was natural. Like breathing. I reacted with trust. But now? I no longer did so.

I sunk my head between my knees.

I felt Love's hand touch my head, and all sorrow fled in the presence of overwhelming joy. Then she spoke: "Father, as Your light has burned away the dross of guilt and sin upon this one, your child whose heart remains with You, show mercy upon your servant, Sisko, and grant unto him repentance, forgiveness of sins, and deliverance, pardoning his every transgression, whether voluntary or involuntary. Reconcile and unite him unto Your people gathered with you. Amen."

Sweet peace, joy, and contentment flooded over me as she prayed. All guilt fled away, and I knew beyond the shadow of a doubt that the curse would not take me into the abyss with it. I looked up, a sweet smile warmed my heart, and now I couldn't help but laugh.

She sat down with me. "You thought before that you had fallen under the curse of the ring. And to a degree, you were correct. But you had only touched it then. If you had continued to use it for yourself, however, you would have been pulled into it. For the curse isn't merely using the ring for yourself, but to use it apart from God's direction and will. To use it by your own power and from your own desires instead of listening to Him, like you used to do."

I nodded. "Of course, and that's what Beltrid wanted me to do. And what he got me to do."

"And that's why I'm here. Not only to heal you, but to warn you, and tell you that you now have a choice."

The last saint to give me a choice was St. Valentine, in Paradise. What would this one be?

"Take the ring off."

I jerked back in surprise. But I quickly understood. If it had come off in the desert twenty years ago upon only touching the curse, why wouldn't it come off now that I had been wallowing in it?

I grabbed the ring and pulled. It refused to stick to my skin, and slid off as if I had just greased my finger. I held it in my palm; it glowed a vibrant gold in the light of Paradise, as if its home were there.

I closed my hand around it. "What is my choice?"

"You must discover that for yourself. But if you think on it, and listen to your heart, it should be clear to you."

I sighed. Why did God have to be so cryptic and hidden?

She stood and giggled. "Because, my child—don't forget I'm much older than you—your healing comes through the journey of faith. We will meet again; you'll make it yet." A warm smile spread across her lips as the light of Paradise shrank until it collapsed upon Love into a pinpoint of light, then disappeared.

The darkness of a moonless night swooped back in upon me; the campfire crackled and popped, keeping the blackness at bay. Its light appeared so paltry in comparison to Love's.

I sat by the fire and rolled the ring around in my hand. Maybe I should bury it here in the forest? Beltrid would never find it. Yet I felt that couldn't be the answer. Or perhaps I should find some mountain to cast it into a fiery heat that would destroy it? No, that wasn't the answer either. Options continued to fly through my mind.

When Kaylee took over the watch, I lay in bed, staring at the shelter's ceiling, rolling over, back and forth as my mind worked on the question of how Beltrid intended to get the ring, and how my choice might stop him.

By the time I had risen with the first rays of the sun glowing in the eastern sky, I had come to a conclusion. Beltrid didn't need to possess the ring to have it. If he controlled whoever had it, then they would use it for his purposes, not God's.

I couldn't see Nathan being controlled willingly, but the demon might believe he could control him unwillingly. I figured Beltrid's confidence in his plan denoted his weakness. He hadn't taken into account a few things—like God. Nonetheless, in his vain attempts to gain the power of the ring, as he saw it, he would end up destroying me and my family.

A solution dawned on me, but I had been slow to accept it. Yet, the more I mulled it over in my mind through the night, the more certain I knew it to be the right decision. As I tightened the packs upon the horses, a certainty had settled in my heart. It was time.

I pulled the ring from my pocket and held it in my palm. The ring glinted sunlight off its surface. The Hebrew inscription, "It is more blessed to give, than to receive" blazed as bright as the day I had first saw it upon my finger, thirty-one years ago.

I wrapped my fingers around it. "Kaylee."

She stared up from filling a sack with dishes. "Yes?"

"Come here."

Her eyes focused intensely upon me, as if she sensed I had something important to tell her. She stood and drew near. One eyebrow raised as she peered into my eyes.

"Hold out your left hand."

She lifted it, and I cradled it in my palm.

I revealed the ring, between my finger and thumb.

She gasped. "The ring! It came off? What does this mean?" She stared at her fingers resting in my hand. "You don't mean to put the ring on me, do you?"

I nodded. "Kaylee, I figured when the time came, I would be passing

73

this ring onto Nathan, though I admit, I thought a few more years would pass before that happened, as he didn't desire it nor act mature enough to handle it."

She nodded. "I thought the same."

"But there are two reasons I've changed my mind. One, I've decided that Beltrid intends to use Nathan, in some way, to gain control of the ring. And I fear that he may have some way to do that. However, if I give you the ring, you will not only have the ability to help any of us, but God's protection will be upon you, as it has been upon me for all these years."

She nodded, but said nothing. Her eyes hardly blinked, her attention had so focused upon me.

"Two, I've come to realize though Nathan has many good qualities, patience and a humble heart he struggles with. They are two things needed to be able to handle the ring. Even then, it is a battle. One I fought and eventually lost.

"You've seen first-hand the results of falling into its curse." I knew the images of my vision at the monastery would bring the reality to life.

She nodded again.

"It's so easy to allow such failures to bury any other successes, like flowers covered in a killing frost. It has taken me many years to be healed myself, even as late as last night. If perchance you also fail at some point, don't do what I did. Find healing as soon as possible with His help."

"I will, I promise." She smiled.

"Good. But I should also warn you: by putting this on, it carries a burden to help whoever you can, to be a blessing. The ring acts as a vow to God, to allow Him to use you as He wills. He will guide you. You have but to ask, and He will grant it. But you must always ask for the benefit of others, never for your own."

"I know." She wet her lips. "But this is exactly what I want. I have no desire to marry a man. I really did seriously consider becoming a nun, because that's the kind of life I wanted to lead. But I see now that He's been preparing me for this." She set her jaw. "I accept the vow and burden of the ring."

I wrapped my arms around her, and tears welled up. I felt like a father giving away his daughter in marriage. And in fact, that's what I was doing. Who knows what difficult paths this decision would send her down. Yet, in my heart, I knew the ring should pass to her. I had no doubts.

I pushed her back and pulled her left hand up. "By the ring leaving my finger, God has said it is time to pass it on. May God grant you all the strength and help you need to fulfill His calling upon your life."

I took a deep breath and slid the ring onto her finger.

Part Two

Kaylee

14

I watched as Dad placed the ring on my finger. I felt a charge race through my body as if it had bonded with me. The gold glowed with an inner light.

"Wow, that was amazing!" I met Dad's eyes beaming at me. "Did you feel anything when you put it on?"

"Only once, and then barely due to my state of mind. The first time the steam house sneaked it on my finger and I wasn't aware when it happened."

"Not aware? How could you not be aware? It's magical!"

He laughed, and I realized I must be acting like an infatuated girl. My forehead grew hot, but I didn't care.

I held the ring before my face and rotated it in the gleaming sunlight, then grabbed it with my right hand and attempted to move it. The ring didn't budge, but held fast.

Dad smiled. "Yes, the ring agrees. You are its new servant."

In a mere couple of minutes, my whole life had changed course. I had planned to go to a convent when old enough. Instead, I would travel and help people as God directed. While not a nun, it still had a monastic feel to it. For a long time Nathan and I thought Dad's tales were just stories, but recent events had changed that.

I peered into Dad's peaceful eyes. "So I just ask—"

"And He grants. Yes."

I nodded. The impact of what had just happened still lingered, as if waiting to pounce on me once my attention turned to other matters. Could I really do miracles like in Dad's stories? Not that I doubted he told the truth, but hearing is one thing, seeing is another.

"What can I try it out on?"

His face fell, then grew stern. "No! Never, ever use it on your own volition. Always wait for God's direction, and always, always ask Him." He stared at me, his eyes filled with fear. "Promise me, you will always do that. I don't want you to go through what I have."

His forcefulness surprised me. He always approached everything with emotional stability, but I could see this arose from experiences he had gone through. Stories that he hadn't told us about the ring, perhaps. I slid my arm around his shoulder and could feel them shaking.

I rubbed his back. "Don't worry. I promise I'll use it right."

He sat up straighter, wiped his wet eyes, and pointed at my sword. "But you will have a temptation I didn't have. You have troll-like strength and skill with weapons. You'll tend to rely upon those, but I can tell you from experience that God has a way of providing what you need. Use your skills as God directs, but be aware at times He will have a different idea of how to deal with a situation."

He stared into the forest and sighed as if recalling one of them. "One of the reasons I decided to give this to you is because I've sensed a trust and love in you. Those qualities will go a long way to using the miracles as a blessing for others instead of a curse on yourself."

"Thanks for trusting me. I'll make you proud." I squeezed him with one arm, and he hugged back.

"I'm already proud of you, but it is God who entrusts it to you, not I. One other thing, no one, including Nathan and Crystal but especially Beltrid, should know about this yet. Once he finds out I've given this to you, he may kill Nathan, Crystal, and even me. So for now, I'll wear a similar ring upon the same finger. And if you have any gloves, you might want to use them, though I doubt Beltrid would notice a ring on you, and if he did, he probably wouldn't give it a second thought."

"You have another ring?"

He nodded. He pulled a necklace out from under his shirt. On the end of the chain dangled a ring. Gold like the ring I now wore, but a different design. It wouldn't stand out unless someone examined it close up.

"It's my wedding ring to Gabrielle. I didn't wear it on my hand, but have carried it with me, close to my heart on this chain." He removed the ring from the necklace and placed it on his finger. He spun it around and smiled. "Normal."

"I do have gloves designed for handling swords and bows. They won't completely cover up the ring, but it'll make it less noticeable." I pulled them out of my pack and wiggled my fingers into them.

"Perfect. Now, we had better get underway. We have a son and his girlfriend to find and save, if Nathan hasn't already done it for us." He swung himself onto the horse's back.

"One second, I have one more bag to tie on." I could help Nathan better now. But I would have to be careful not to reveal myself too soon. Yet another part of me felt a crazy excitement. Now I could do the things I had always wanted to devote myself to.

I tied on the last bag, then mounted the horse. "I'm ready."

We left, pulling three horses behind us. Two of which we hoped to fill with Nathan and Crystal once again.

The mountain the creature had called "Shadow Mountain" loomed over us, casting a darkness upon our path, even though the sun still shown in the sky. A sense of gloom had fallen over me as well.

It had taken us most of the day to travel here. We talked some on the way, but mostly I thought about all that had happened. The wound on my arm had healed, leaving a faint scar. Whether from the tough troll-hide that remained, or from putting the ring on, I couldn't tell. While many of the troll-features had receded, leaving a thicker and light-blue tinted skin, much of the muscle that had grown remained. I probably couldn't kick through a wall anymore, but I could do some heavy damage.

On top of that, I now had Dad's ring. Doing miracles, now that's a massive responsibility. But I still hadn't used the ring. My mind said the ring wasn't anything special. I had seen things on this trip that said otherwise; I knew now that Dad had performed miracles but had lost that ability before Nathan and I came along.

We arrived at the base of the mountain. I searched it, hoping for some sign of an opening. "So, now where do we go?"

"I don't know. Perhaps we should stop here and take a break. Besides, soon it will be dark." He dismounted.

I followed and helped him set up camp. We rested as we ate.

"Dad, do you feel depressed?"

"Yes." He gazed at the mountain. "I think this mountain is named 'Shadow' for more than just its looks."

"So how do we find Nathan?"

"That I'm not sure of. I think tomorrow morning, we'll start searching the mountain for an entrance."

I scanned the peak. "That's a lot of mountain. Could take us days to find one, if it's there." Nathan didn't have that kind of time.

"Then days it will take, unless you have a better idea."

I sighed. "No, I don't." Still, there must be a better way. "Unless we can do something to draw them out. That one shadow-creature acted excited to take us."

"But Beltrid didn't. I think he knows it would not turn out as the shadow-creatures think."

I scanned the area. "Then they will know we're at their mountain and come to get us, unless Beltrid has convinced them otherwise."

He nodded. "My thinking exactly. If they don't come, we will search until we find a way in."

"Or cut a door into the mountain ourselves." I didn't think we could do that, but it sounded good. I chuckled and Dad laughed with me.

We finished our meal and Dad took the first watch. I slept, but not solidly. Every forest noise jerked my eyes open, waiting for the expected attack.

A hand shoved my shoulder and woke me up.

"Kaylee, your turn."

I rubbed my eyes and saw Dad standing over me. "No problems?"

He sat down on his blankets. "Nope, nothing but owls, rabbits and who knows what other animals."

I stood and sheathed the sword lying next to my mat. "Get some sleep then." I yawned and stretched after exiting the shelter.

I pulled my pack next to me and dug out a bottle. It contained a concentrate that Jack had given us, a strong coffee. I poured some into a metal cup and added water, then set it on the coals to heat.

A snore rose from the shelter. Dad must have been really tired. I noticed he slept little the night before. While I hoped the shadow-creatures would show, for his wellbeing, I hoped they didn't.

While I waited for the coffee to heat up, I practiced a few sword-moves on a tree. Not as good as Nathan, cause trees can't parry or dodge, but I could imagine well enough. And the activity helped clear the sleep from my eyes.

I sat and took a sip. Too hot. It had sat in the fire too long. I placed it on a log to cool. A humming noise pierced the air; I turned toward the sound.

A doorway like before expanded behind me, and four shadow-creatures leaped from it. One of them dashed toward me; his sword-tip rushing to plunge into my chest. Another shot toward the shelter.

"Dad, wake up!"

I rolled from my sitting position onto my back, drawing my sword as I did. As he came over me, I kicked the tip of his blade into the air and pointed mine at him. He impaled himself onto it.

I pushed myself upon my feet. The other shadow-creature neared the shelter. Dad groggily rubbed his eyes. I grabbed the cup of coffee and flicked the contents toward the creature. The coffee splashed upon his face and the creature fell to his knees, writhing in pain.

I leaped to him and dropped my blade onto the back of his neck. A crack sounded and he fell limp. I moved between the shelter and the other two shadow-creatures. They halted just beyond my sword's range. Dad had risen and stood behind me.

"Move us toward the door," he whispered in my ear.

I moved to go around the creatures, but they moved back between us and the door. I whispered back to Dad, "I'll have to attack. When I take out one, make a dash for the door, I'll follow."

I stepped forward, and quickly pulled back, to get a sense of their attitude and balance. They acted tentative; I might have intimidated them. Still, I couldn't be overconfident. Even a lesser swordsman can strike a fatal blow if you make a mistake, and it just takes one.

Dad moved back, and I moved around so one stood behind the other. He kept me between them and himself.

I attacked again. I used Nathan's move, and my sword found its way into the creature's chest. He cried a shriek as he fell over. I immediately engaged the other. Out of the corner of my eye, I saw Dad heading toward the door.

The creature dodged my first blow. I pulled back in before he jabbed with his sword. I twisted to let it pass and drove my sword into his gut.

I didn't wait to watch him fall. I sped toward the door. Dad had fled through it, but the opening began contracting. I jumped and plunged into darkness.

I landed on a cold, stone floor. At first, I could see nothing, but then my eyes adjusted to the low level of light. I noticed Dad standing by an opening in the room we had fallen into. More and more details flowed into my eyes as he waved me over.

Apparently we had entered into a cave. Noises echoed from the opening, and I assumed the shadow-creatures talked in another room. Flickering flames ran along the tops of the cave walls, providing a dim glow.

I stepped lightly to the other side of the opening and peered out. Shadows moved in the room, chatting away in some unknown language. On one side of the cave, wooden cages held Nathan and Crystal. About five to seven shadow-creatures roamed about.

Dad motioned for me to drop back with him. We moved to the far side of the room and talked in whispers.

He pointed to the cave wall. "See those crystals over there?"

I followed his finger. In a hollowed out section of the wall, several crystals lay in a row. One lay by a pedestal designed to hold them. I nodded.

"Those crystals are set on the pedestal, and it opens a door to a location. Probably some form of magic Beltrid had given the shadow-creatures to do his bidding. When I saw you coming through, I removed the one standing there and the door closed."

So that's how they did that. Amazing!

He continued, "We need to distract the shadow-creatures in there, break Nathan and Crystal out, and come back here to escape. And we had better hurry. I'm sure they'll be wondering what's taking the raiding party so long and come to investigate soon."

"I assume you have a plan? Or should I fly in there with my sword swinging?"

He smiled. "You know, you would be one unusual nun. A warrior nun. Somehow those two don't go together."

I stifled a chuckle. I liked that about Dad. He had a way of finding the humor in a situation no matter how tense it became.

He pointed to the opening. "As a matter of fact, I do have a plan. On the other side of the cavern, you'll see an opening into another area. You have the strong arm. Find some good stones and throw one into that room. That should send most to investigate, and then you take out the other two with the rocks. Then we should be able to break out Nathan and Crystal."

I winked. "And if that doesn't work, then I'll use the sword."

The edges of his lips lost their smile. "If it comes down to it, yes."

He moved back to the opening while I gathered five good rocks. Once in position, I slung a rock toward the opening across the cavern. The speed and distance of the rock surprised me as I watched it sail across the room silently.

A second after the rock disappeared into the hole, a crash, as if I had hit dishes echoed from the room, and a piercing scream echoed across the ceilings. I had hit someone!

All the shadow-creatures guarding Nathan and Crystal froze and turned their heads toward the clamor. Shrieking sounds filled the cave, and all but two of them exited into the cavern on the other side.

I stepped out the opening while the other two still gazed where the others had gone. I threw a rock hard and quickly grabbed another and flung it before the other landed.

The first shadow-creature turned his head right before the rock arrived, and it zipped past him and clunked against the cave wall. The other found its mark on the second one's face and knocked him off his feet. He collapsed unconscious on the floor.

I quickly released a third one. The creature spotted me as the rock sailed its way. It let out a small screeching sound before my rock planted itself into its forehead and the creature fell backwards.

We raced to the cages. Nathan's eyes widened and a smile flashed on his face when he saw us, but then he glanced to where the other creatures had gone. Dad held his finger to his mouth and motioned for me to open the cages.

I examined the wooden bars and decided they should break without too much trouble. I reared my hand back and threw a punch at a beam. My hand stung. The wood buckled, but didn't break. I stepped back and jumped toward it, extending my leg for added impact. My foot cracked through and splinters fell to the floor. The sound echoed along the walls. That might draw them back sooner, but it couldn't be helped.

Dad pointed me to Crystal's cage. I attacked it the same way as he helped Nathan through the hole I had created. It took one blow to crack it, and I removed the wood enough to help Crystal through.

An odd feeling rushed over me as I helped her out. I had not noticed it before, but maybe the ring provided me with more of a sense of people, like Dad. Evil flowed from her like something tangible I could reach out and touch. If this is what Dad had felt, no wonder he reacted so strongly to her.

I realized I had been staring at her. I blinked and held her arm firmly as she climbed to the floor. She stared at me as well, as if sensing something in me she had not felt before. Something wasn't right, but we didn't have time to figure out what. We had to leave.

We bolted toward the opening. Shadow-creatures poured out of the cavern they had rushed into. Several cried out words in their language. Some took positions along the wall and fired arrows; the shafts snapped against the rocks around us.

Then Dad faltered. An arrow had pierced his back and wiggled as he attempted to move. I pointed Nathan and Crystal toward the cave-room we needed to reach, grabbed Dad, and pulled him along. His legs couldn't keep up with our pace, and I could tell by his eyes the arrow had hit a vital organ, maybe his heart. My own beat faster than it should have, and I had to shove the panic back. I had to focus on getting us out.

Nathan and Crystal flew into the room. I pulled Dad through the opening. Another arrow landed in his back, and he lurched in my arms. I saw the creatures galloping toward us. Horror filled me at the thought of losing him. A burning anger at the creatures who focused their shots on Dad swallowed it whole.

I pulled him to the wall, grabbed the crystal, and placed it on the pedestal. A doorway opened and I could see our campsite. "Take Dad!" I motioned for them to get moving. Then I drew my sword and moved back to the opening. I had to give them time to escape.

One creature flew into the room. I brought my blade down onto its neck before it saw me. Another followed behind it and I let my point penetrate its chest as I twisted to let its sword brush past my stomach.

I glanced back to see Dad's legs disappearing into the doorway. Another creature entered, but more cautiously than the rest. He saw me and drove his blade toward me. I couldn't get mine into position to parry, so I stepped back and to the side. His tip snagged my clothing, leaving him wide open. I plunged my sword into him and then pulled out the dark, blood-stained metal. The shadow-creature fell limp to the floor.

"That was for Dad!" I relished the moment, but knew more would be coming. I dashed to the shimmering door. As I passed by the pedestal, I reached out and grabbed the crystal off the stand and dove through the contracting doorway.

I fell upon the ground and rolled onto my back. A pain shot through my arm. I checked; blood soaked the tunic where the creature's sword had cut through. But it looked worse than it was. My trollish hide had prevented it from being more than a minor cut.

I rose to my feet and located Nathan holding Dad on his lap. Nathan worked to extract the arrows. Dad's pale face stared up at me and I gasped.

His eyes blinked back death, then a slight smile creased his lips. "Don't worry. I've been shot by arrows before. They're not fatal."

Nathan met my eyes. "We should leave. Those creatures could return at any second."

I shook my head. "They won't be here right away, though we shouldn't stay any longer than necessary." I held out my hand containing the crystal stone. "They can't get this door to open without its crystal."

A smile creased Nathan's lips. "Good work, little sister!" But it disappeared quickly when he focused on Dad. "But what are we doing to do about Father? He's dying."

One look at Dad's eyes, and I knew what he wanted me to do. And I knew I should. I felt it in my heart. But I couldn't attempt it while Nathan and Crystal stood by without revealing the truth to them.

Dad coughed and red drool trickled down his chin. Then again, if I had to, I would. Dad was more important than keeping a secret.

Crystal whispered in Nathan's ear. He shook his head. She whispered something else. He bowed his head and then stared at Dad.

"Father," Nathan said. "Maybe you should pass on the ring before it…" He swallowed and glanced at Crystal. "Before it is too late."

Dad's eyes narrowed. He said in a wheezing voice, "But you've never wanted the ring."

Nathan bowed his head. "I know. But you have to give it to someone, and I'm your son." He glanced at me before returning his gaze to Dad.

Dad coughed. "The ring will mean you and Crystal might never marry."

"But you did."

"Only after I broke its vow. He gave me a new vow, to marry your mother and raise a family."

Nathan rubbed his forehead. He pulled Crystal to the side. They talked, but barely audible. When Nathan raised his voice at one point, I heard, "…can't do that…" He glanced our way and then pulled Crystal off into the forest, out of sight and hearing range.

Dad nodded. "All right, they aren't watching."

I knew beyond a shadow of a doubt the path to follow. I marveled that such an assurance could be felt so strongly, as if a puzzle had come together into the perfect picture. It had to be the ring, or, as Dad would say, God using the ring. But in the moment, the "how" escaped me.

"What do I do?"

"Just ask God to heal me."

I hoped I did this right. Dad's life depended on it. Still, would it work? I had never seen him do anything like this. I breathed deep and laid a hand on him.

"Lord, heal my dad."

He jerked, and then color returned to his face. Blood stopped seeping from his body, and his wounds closed up. My jaw fell open. I couldn't believe it!

"It worked!" I cried, then quickly threw my hand over my mouth. I couldn't help but smile wide and hug him hard.

He sat up and rubbed his head. "Still left me with a little headache."

I reached out to touch his head.

"No, no, no!" He waved me off. "I didn't mean for you to heal my headache. Don't ever use the ring frivolously."

"I'm sorry. I just thought…" I didn't know what I thought. It was foolish.

"Always, always listen to your heart. God will guide you that way. You will know when to use it and when not to. And sometimes, it is best not to."

I nodded. This felt like my sword training class. "Yes, Sir."

Nathan and Crystal returned to the campsite. His eyes grew wide and he bounded to us. "Father, what happened? You were on the edge of death a few seconds ago."

Dad laughed. "I got better."

I covered my mouth to hide a snicker.

"Yeah, but how?" Nathan examined Dad's back.

"Let's just say, God decided it wasn't my time. He has a way of protecting me."

Nathan raised an eyebrow. "The ring?"

Dad smiled. "Yes, you could say the ring had something to do with it."

Nathan hugged him and laughed.

Crystal frowned, and again I felt evil flowing from her. She focused her attention on Dad as if frustrated. She had attempted to push Nathan to accept the ring. But why would she care? Was Beltrid using her somehow? Then I knew Dad had spoken the truth about Nathan and the ring. Dad didn't want to let on that he had already given it away, but it would have been playing into whatever Beltrid had planned to give it to Nathan.

One character trait Dad had failed to pass onto me was subtlety and tact. I stepped into Nathan's face. "What did you two talk about? Why is she using you?"

Crystal's eyes narrowed and her jaw set.

Just the reaction I had expected to get.

16

Nathan gritted his teeth. "Since when do you have the right to butt into my personal affairs?"

"If it has to do with the ring and Dad, then it isn't merely personal." I stared him down.

He didn't flinch. "It wouldn't involve you." His gaze focused into my eyes. "It's not like you'll get it."

My teeth pressed hard, in part to keep from blurting anything out. I turned to Dad, and he cocked an eyebrow my way as if to warn me against saying anything. I focused on Nathan again. "Maybe, maybe not. But the fact remains I'm still part of this family. What involves part of the family involves all of the family."

He huffed and then turned to get his things. "But what is between me and my wife-to-be is private, and I'll not share it with you."

Dad stood up. "Yes, we had better get a move on. There'll be plenty of time for talking on the road. The only thing we'll find here is more fighting."

I stomped off to pack. Nathan acted so unreasonable! The stress of the past days had ignited my frustration into a burning flame. The injustice of Dad and I putting our lives on the line to save their sorry butts and not so much as a thank you for it! Instead, Nathan acted more interested in getting his hands on the ring when before he despised the idea.

Of course, Nathan had been out of our sight the entire time. Who knows what words of enchantment Crystal had woven over him while they sat in those cells.

A weight settled on me. Not only did Amma lie frozen in a prison, but Nathan as well. I had to figure out a way to break both of them free.

Dad patted me on the back and winked as he passed by, hauling his stuff to the horse.

I winked back and smiled. No, it didn't all rest on me. But I did want to make sure when God said to act, I did so without hesitation.

I tightened the last pack onto Rain's back and lifted myself into the saddle. Dad led us down the trail that skirted Shadow Mountain. At least one special treat remained: to see Uncle Seth again. It had been a few years since he had visited us. He had given me my sword back then, and a desire had taken hold to learn how to use it. Maybe Nathan would have calmed down by then.

The crisis had died on the outside, but not on the inside. The thrill of healing Dad, getting to use the ring for the first time, all had settled a warm feeling over me. By a simple prayer, I had healed him from near death to his old self. Yet I couldn't tell anyone about it, or use it openly. Inside, I knew that should be standard practice and not just for this situation. Based on Dad's experience, people will find out soon enough and they'll seek me out, even if I do my best to hide it.

But the warmth from healing Dad clashed with another feeling: I had killed. Up until these events, I had trained with my teachers and practiced with Nathan, but had never taken a life. Even though I killed in self-defense and these creatures hardly seemed human, still it left me with a sick feeling in my heart. Dad's warning that my skills would produce temptations now reverberated with a fresh reality.

After all, would God consider the several shadow-creatures I had killed worth the saving of Nathan and Crystal? I knew I placed greater value on Nathan's life and stood ready to risk killing those who would kill him, but I had taken on the task of being my brother and sister's keeper, not their executioner.

Based on his stories, Dad had done quite well not being a fighter. God had protected him. I decided I would make every effort to not kill with my sword or hands. If using the ring for my own benefit would be a curse, how much more the sword?

I knew I might not be able to avoid it in every instance. But I vowed to think twice about drawing it to solve my problems.

But another question reared its head as we worked our way up the mountain to Uncle Seth's house. Beltrid had the ability to jump out at any time and take us. Why did he wait so long before appearing? Why did he not appear now?

If Dad had figured right, and Beltrid attempted to control Nathan, how? Only Crystal held sway over him to any degree. She had successfully prodded him to ask for the ring. Somehow she and Beltrid were linked. Maybe...

Did I dare consider it? After all, when Beltrid had appeared to Dad and I, Crystal hadn't been there. Could Crystal be Beltrid? I had no firm proof of it, and I didn't want to jump to any conclusions, but I couldn't discount the possibility either. And if so, we needed to be much more careful what we said and revealed around her.

I had to warn Nathan, though it would most likely prove fruitless. After the last conversation, I doubt he would be in a mood to listen, but I had to try, and I might discover more information in the attempt.

Nathan pulled his horse to a stop and dismounted. "I need to relieve myself."

This provided the perfect opportunity. "I think I'll do the same." I hopped to the ground and left in a slightly different direction from Nathan. Once safely out of his sight, I swung around until I spotted Nathan behind a tree surrounded by bushes. I sneaked up to the tree on the opposite side.

"Nathan."

The bushes rustled. "What? Are you trying to give me a heart attack?"

"Sorry, but I needed to talk with you. Alone."

"But now? I would prefer to have some privacy, even if you are my sister."

I had to chuckle under my breath at the scene. If an outsider saw us, rumors would fly. "Nathan, do you know why Amma was imprisoned in the crystal?"

He came out from behind the tree. "Beltrid hired that wizard to do it. He wants Father's ring is all I know."

"Yes, but those are related, somehow. I don't fully understand it yet, but apparently he has sent us on this quest in hopes that Dad will die and give you the ring."

Nathan wrinkled his brow. "Then he wouldn't get it if I had it."

"He wouldn't have to, as long as he controlled you."

"Control me? But I've never even seen the guy. How could he control me?"

I fixed my eyes on his. "Crystal."

His eyes widened. "Crystal! That's totally ridiculous."

"Nathan, it isn't just Dad who feels evil from her."

He paced in a circle. "You've never had a problem before? Why now all the sudden? Why do you pick this moment to sound like Father?"

I couldn't tell him the truth, yet. "Answer me this. When you followed Crystal into the disappearing doorway, were you with her the whole time until we found you?"

He stopped his pacing and stared at the ground. "No, but what of it?

She said they had their way with her." His face grew dark. He yanked his sword out and swung; it bit into a tree and stuck. "And some day I'll be back to take vengeance on them." He yanked it back out and sheathed it.

"While you two lay in those cells, Beltrid visited us in the forest. Nearly killed me. But Dad threw some bones at him and he left in pain."

"Bones? Where did they hit?"

"On his face, one in the eye."

Nathan moved dirt with his toe.

I stepped in front of him. "What? Did she have facial scars when she returned?"

He turned his back toward me. "No. Nothing, really. She said they roughed her up. Naturally she had bruises."

"On her face?"

Nathan remained silent; he kicked leaves into the breeze with his foot.

"Nathan, we have to consider that she is either working for Beltrid, or—"

He twirled around, pointing a finger at me. "Don't even say it! I can see the whole family is against me. Leave me alone and let me live my own life!" He stomped back to the trail.

"Nathan, I don't want to see you hurt. I'm saying this because I love you."

"Then let me worry about that and stay out of my life!" He disappeared into the brush.

I sighed and shook my head. Not only had he not cleared Crystal, the coincidences were too convenient. He also hadn't told me all he knew. Hopefully, though, I had planted enough doubt in his mind that he would stay on guard, if love had not blinded him to reality.

After taking care of my own business, I returned to the trail. Dad sat atop his horse, alone. His eyes settled on mine.

"What did you say to cause Nathan to leave in such a huff?"

I sighed. "I asked him about what happened to him and Crystal and told him of Beltrid's visit during their imprisonment."

"That hardly seems worth the reaction I saw."

I shook my head. "I basically accused Crystal of either working for Beltrid or they were one and the same person."

He nodded. "I see. That would explain it. Actually, I had thought of that possibility, that they are one and the same, but knew if I brought it up to him I would get the same reaction you did."

"I figured the same, but now at least I've planted that possibility in the back of his mind. In case it's true, maybe he won't be caught totally off guard by it. Unfortunately, what he said happened in the mountain confirmed that possibility, rather than dispel it."

"Let's get going. Nathan and Crystal headed on up to Seth's house ahead of us."

I pulled myself up into the saddle and we rode in silence for a couple of miles. My mind continued to go over the events surrounding Crystal, attempting to figure her out. Dad's sigh broke through my thoughts.

"What's the matter?" I studied his reaction.

He cast a half-hearted smile my way. "I've been having visions of late. Actually, a vision with Love is part of the reason I gave the ring to you. But this one happened when I nearly died. Very odd, actually, as it seemed the vision happened parallel to the reality."

He stopped talking. I waited a moment, but he didn't finish. "So... what was the vision about?"

He rubbed his forehead as if a pain attacked him. "I'm not sure I can talk about it right now. It was not an easy vision." He fixed his eyes on me. "But I would ask you to pray. Pray that I'll have the courage to do the right thing." Sweat beaded on his sun-reddened forehead.

"Dad, are you sick?"

He shook his head. "Just pray. Promise me you will."

I nodded. "Of course I will." I didn't care for the feeling his words gave me. A sense of dread hung upon them like sap on a tree. He didn't say another word as we rode to Seth's house, but slumped forward as if a great weight hung about his neck.

An old cabin came into view as we entered a clearing in the trees. A burly man exited the dwelling and trotted to meet us. We leaped to the ground and Seth wrapped us in a big hug.

He held me at arm's length. "Well, you've changed since I last saw you. Where did the blue-tinted skin come from? An ink well?"

I laughed. "It's sure good to see you again, Uncle."

"I'm so glad to see you, but I'm afraid I have some odd news to relay." Seth's eyes winced.

"Have Nathan and Crystal arrived yet?" Dad asked.

Seth nodded. "That's just it. They came, and promptly told me they were headed into the next town." Seth paused, as if afraid to say the words. "In order to get married."

I let my jaw drop.

"Marriage!" Dad ran fingers through his hair and stared at Seth. "We have to stop them."

17

Seth saddled his horse, and we all galloped toward Jerole, the closest town. Around each corner, I struggled to find a sign of Nathan and Crystal ahead of us, and each time the reality of an empty road trampled my hopes under its hooves. They must know we would follow them and be racing ahead of us. Or, they might have headed toward a city further away after convincing Seth that they rode to the closest one. In which case, we would arrive too late to stop their marriage. But if he couldn't find a minister who would marry without parental consent, we had a chance.

We arrived at Jerole's gates within an hour. We checked with the local priest and the town magistrate, but no one had seen them.

We dismounted in front of the *Last Leg Tavern* to discuss our next step. Upon entering, a constant buzz of conversation greeted us from an active crowd. That would allow us to chat without undue notice.

A barmaid brought steins of ale to place before us. I wondered, as I wiggled my rear trying to get comfortable on the rough, wooden bench, if all they served was ale since she never asked us what we wanted.

Dad took the time to fill in Seth on what had happened to Gabrielle and the reason for our trip. Seth's face fell upon hearing that his sister lay trapped in a small stone.

Seth took a gulp and wiped his mouth. "And now you have to deal with your son, too. If they aren't here, most likely they headed to Ramonth, a full day's journey. It's a bigger city, so more likely they'll find someone there to marry them."

Dad shook his head. "We'd get there too late to stop anything now." He chuckled. "What we need is the old dragon I rode."

Seth grinned. "As long as I'm not strung up again to bring 'em out of hiding!"

"What about the ring?" I asked. "Can we use it to get there?"

Seth raised an eyebrow toward Dad. "Ring? I thought you couldn't use it anymore? Much less for yourself."

Dad pointed at me.

I pulled my left glove off and held it out for Seth to see.

"Oh my, you gave it to her?"

"It came off and I knew the time had arrived to hand it on." Dad glanced around to make sure no one eavesdropped. "But Nathan and Crystal know nothing about it. I don't trust her, and she has undue influence on him. They both think I still have it." He showed Seth the other ring on his finger.

Dad fixed his eyes on me. "What does your heart say about transporting me?"

I tried to hear its song. "I don't know. I think my desire for what I want to happen gets in the way of hearing it."

He pointed at Seth. "Like, when Seth here had his hand cut off by his father, I thought about healing him right away, but my heart said not yet. So I didn't, even though it was hard."

Seth chuckled. "Hard for you? What about me!"

Dad smiled at him and then focused on me again. "Point being, you'll have to develop the ability to hear Him, learn to get past your own desire of what you want to happen, and hear what God wants. I had to learn it, and you will too.

"But as far as transporting me to Ramonth, no. You can only use the ring to heal someone of something, whether spiritual or physical. Not solely as a traveling device."

Seth hit the table. "Ah, but you transported me that one time."

Dad nodded. "Yes, because I thought it would help you spiritually. And it did. But I'm not the one that needs its help now, Nathan is."

I hung my head and took a swig of the ale. The harsh taste of the cheap ale didn't register as I mulled over options in my mind. There had to be some way to get to him.

"I'm sorry, Dad. This is my fault for coming on too strong with him."

He patted me on the back. "You didn't know. You'll learn."

I raised my head and focused on him. "There's a good chance the two of them won't be going fast all the way there. We might arrive in time if our stops are minimal. At least we have to try."

His eyes bore into mine. The pain in them struck my heart, as if I had said some word that triggered his reaction. Sweat returned to his forehead. I sensed then that he struggled inside. It wasn't sickness that ate away at him, but a difficult decision.

His jaw set and he sat straighter in his chair. "What else does your heart tell you?"

I glanced at Seth and tried to listen. I did feel there was a chance of arriving before Nathan, and who knows what God would do to help. But He wouldn't help someone who sat around waiting. Still, I could tell Dad wanted something more, but what?

"I don't know. That we should go is all I can get."

He leaned back in his chair and took another gulp of ale, then set it down with a snap upon the table. His face grew serene and his eyes shone with an inner light.

Seth slapped his forehead. "Oh no, I've seen that look before, and it usually precedes something bad."

That didn't sound promising. "Dad, what is your heart telling you?"

He smiled, but it faded as he spoke. "The vision I mentioned?"

I nodded.

He laid his hand on mine. "It told how I could defeat Beltrid and save your mother."

A flame of hope sprung up inside me. "But that's good."

"Yes, it is. But what I must do for it to happen will not be easy."

I sat up. "You don't mean that I go without you?"

He swallowed. "I must stay here."

I stared at the table, trying to understand. "But you have to come, I'm not ready." I met his eyes and saw a peace and confidence I hadn't seen of late.

He shook his head. "No, you're not ready. But I'll have to trust in God's guidance for you now. I have a different path."

"A different path?" He might as well have said tomorrow the world would end. "No, you can't have a different path. We need you...I need you. Amma needs you."

He sighed. I could tell this wasn't easy for him. He reached over and pulled me to him and cradled me in his arms. Despite my best efforts, I felt my eyes watering.

He rubbed my shoulders. "I'm doing this for your mother. And everyone else. I don't know the end of it, but God does. And I know I have to follow."

Seth shook his head. "And when he's at that spot, there's no arguing, my niece."

Dad pulled me back and stared me in the eyes. "God will use you. Your job is to keep Nathan from marrying Crystal."

"And what is your job?" I asked, wiping my eyes.

It appeared his face grew longer as he stared into the distance. "To do His will. Beyond that, I can say no more. We all have our crosses to bear."

I couldn't imagine anything more important than saving Nathan and Amma. What could Dad do against Beltrid anyway? "Certainly you would be of more use with me—"

His jaw set and he sat straighter on the bench. "You're wasting time, Kaylee. You need to leave. You have a brother to catch."

I opened my mouth, but his eyes grew narrow. I had no choice. But why would God send him on a different path? How could I continue without him? This made no sense.

Seth pointed behind himself. "Take the road headed east out of the city gate. That will take you directly to Ramonth."

I lifted myself from the bench as if I had been glued to it. "What about Seth? Can't he come?"

Dad shook his head. "No, I will need him. God will be with you. Just don't let Beltrid know you have the ring."

Seth met Dad's eyes. "Do I have a different path?"

"Than what? You'll still be here when she returns if that's what you mean." He turned toward me and swallowed. "Now go. I will see you again."

I nodded. At least that was something to hold onto. "Pray for me."

"I will, don't worry."

I could see the concern in his eyes, sending me out alone. Then I realized, not merely his concern for me, but my own concern for him reflected back at me. He no longer had the protection of the ring. The ring protected me now, but if something happened to him while I traveled, I would not be there to heal him as I had done earlier. Beltrid could appear at any time, discover the truth, and kill him.

I studied his thin face. Years of experience and wisdom had worn it down, yet through the guilt and spiritual battles he had fought, he still had a joy radiating from within. A confidence filled me that everything would turn out for the best. But oh, how I loved him, and hated to leave him now.

He must have sensed my concern. I'm sure he did, for he waved his hand for me to go on. I breathed deep and left the tavern.

Rain waited patiently for me. This would not be easy for her. I patted her neck and she nuzzled my cheek. "Girl, forgive me for riding you so hard now, but I have a brother in need." Her head bobbed as if she understood.

I remembered the ring. *I'm my brother's keeper*—this time in the most literal sense.

I hugged Rain and then mounted. She drank from a trough before I nudged her into a full-speed gallop. We flew out the gate and down the road, leaving a floating trail of dust behind us.

The wind whipped my hair around as Rain galloped down the road. I should have tied the strands back, but bigger concerns haunted me. Ramonth lay along the Furth Lake, down into a valley, so the winding trail kept sinking from the mountains. The trees blurred by; my interest in scenery not at the forefront of my thoughts.

While focusing on the road, my mind centered on Nathan. What would I do once I found him? Most likely, even if I could stop them from getting married this time, they would eventually do it. I had to do more than stop this wedding. Somehow I had to convince him that Crystal would mess up his life. If Crystal was this demon, their union held the worst possible life for him. I shuddered to think about the ramifications. Especially once the demon discovered I had the ring.

The smell of humidity filled the air. I gazed into the sky as we shot through the trees, and noticed storm clouds gathering. I slowed Rain down; I could tell she grew tired. I couldn't drive her this hard all the way. Light rain drizzled down, but within minutes a downpour cascaded waves of water over me, making it hard to see. But I didn't let up; I had to keep plowing ahead.

I rounded a corner, and a stream came into view. The road led through it to the other side. The rains had already swollen the stream into a small river, but I had to get across.

I nudged Rain into the water and allowed her to take a drink. Then we pushed our way through the rushing current. While the water moved fast, it only reached knee-high on Rain, and her legs remained steady. I rubbed her neck and kept her moving to the shore. It appeared we would make it.

A blinding light caused me to throw an arm over my eyes. Rain neighed and bucked but calmed down immediately. A sweet smell filled my nostrils: basil and roses. I tried peering at it over my elbow.

"Who's there? Who are you?" I feared it might be another trick of Beltrid's, to prevent me from reaching Nathan.

No answer came. Instead, a buzzing noise emanated from the light. Then I felt myself sliding off the saddle, and darkness swept over me.

The darkness flashed with glowing lights. Muffled sounds of thunder and bubbles surrounded me. I must have fallen into the river and sunk, yet my feet didn't touch the bottom. The river shouldn't be this deep. I paddled my way upwards, desperate for air.

I broke the surface to see dark clouds, pounding rain, and lightning. The latter didn't bode well for someone in a big body of water.

A big body of water? I scanned around in a circle and found a shoreline not too far behind me along with the lights of a city. I now floated in a lake, not a river! Where was I, and how did I get here?

And where did Rain go? Whatever brought me here didn't include my horse, or she had drowned in this water. My gut wrenched at the thought of it. I searched the waves for any sign of her. Only rough waves swallowing sheets of rain could be seen. In this weather, I couldn't stay to search for her either. Hopefully she had been left at the river and would find her way back.

I swam toward the lights. A wave burst over my head, and I gulped for air. After a few moments of struggling and gasping, I approached the shore, though it seemed like forever when the threat of immediate death by lightning could strike at any second.

I slogged upon the shore and lay down, letting my body catch up with my heart. Then I noticed a man staring at me. He squatted on a pier, working a knot holding a boat in the rough waters. He stood up and pushed his way through the downpour toward me.

I sighed. I didn't need a sailor, most likely with selfish intentions, to harass me. At least I might discover what town I had come to.

I stood as he drew near, placed my hand on the hilt of my sword, and wiped the excess water out of my eyes, as if that would do any good in this pouring rain.

He had on a soggy hat and a rain-jacket. His face radiated, underneath the brim, both a gentleness in his soft eyes, and a sternness in his square-set jaw, jagged and rough with the sun and sea's daily beating.

I decided to ask first and take the initiative. I didn't want to appear weak and have to fight if I didn't need to.

"Sir, where am I? What city is this?"

He cocked his head to the side. "You swam here. You should know."

How could I explain this? I didn't even know what had just happened. "I'm sorry, I have no idea how I ended up in the lake or where I am."

"Did you lose your memory?"

I shook my head. "No. I was riding on the road to Ramonth, but a bright light knocked me unconscious into a river, and I ended up here. Please, tell me where this is?"

He laughed though I didn't see the humor in any of this. "Why, you're in Ramonth."

"I am?" I still had a good half-a-day's journey from the river. "What time is it?"

"Hard to tell with the storm clouds, but the sun has just dived under the hills."

That made little sense. It would mean only a few minutes or seconds had passed. How could I have arrived so quickly?

I must have appeared pathetic, because he laughed hard.

He motioned for me to follow. "My place is up the street. I'll give you a place to dry off."

I didn't move. I had no desire to test this man's motives.

He stopped when I didn't follow, then turned back and approached me. He held out his hand. "I'm sorry for my bad manners. My name's Joel."

"Mine's Kaylee." I left his hand hanging in the air uncomfortably. He shrugged and continued staring at me. Then I noticed my clothing. Wet, it clung to my body, outlining my figure. No doubt this man had noticed.

"Look, I don't mean to be abrupt, Joel." I paused to gather my thoughts and words. "But I'm here on an important errand. I need to find the local priest."

His eyes roamed up and down my body. He laughed again. "You don't want to go to the priest soaked. You had better dry off first."

"Won't your family mind?"

He shook his head. "Oh no, not at all. They love company."

I relaxed. If he had a wife, I could dry off in relative safety. "All right. Lead the way."

He laughed again as he turned to head up the street. His attitude annoyed me. If he laughed at me one more time…well, I don't know. I just hoped he didn't. I didn't like being taken for a simpleton.

A visual flashed across my mind. I paused and blinked my eyes. The details remained fuzzy, but a feeling of pride—my pride, had hit me in the gut. His laugh had inflamed it, and I reacted. I glanced at the ring under my glove and wondered if it had warned me.

He turned. "You all right?"

I cracked a smile. "Yeah, I'll be all right. Let's go."

We trudged through the pouring rain, past rows of cottages barely visible through the falling water, until we reached the porch of a house. It sat upon a hill; the wide, long porch provided a vast view of the town. I could tell the area bore a healthy beauty, which would shine once the sun illuminated it.

He led me through the door and struck up a fire as I squished across the floor and huddled on a bench, shivering. I let my eyes wander around the room. Odds and ends lined the walls. If I had to guess what they represented, I would say traveling mementos. Some of the items, like a feather, appeared totally worthless.

Then I realized what I hadn't seen yet. "Joel, you said you had a family. Where are they?"

"Oh, you want to see them? I didn't want them to bother you."

I thought it an odd comment about one's family, until he stood and blew a piercing whistle. Cats flowed from a doorway and scurried around his ankles in anticipation. A few checked me out, sniffing at my feet.

"Your family is cats?" The nerve of him!

"Yeah. What did you think I meant?"

"What any right-thinking person would believe, that you had a family, a wife and kids." I scanned the area for available exits, in case I needed to make a quick one.

"Oh, I see what you mean. Silly me. I'm so used to thinking of them as family, I didn't give it a second thought."

Yeah, right. I have some property in a dangerous mist you can buy, too. I stepped toward the door.

"Whoa, where are you going?" He rushed over to me and stuffed dry clothing in my hands. "You'll get sick if you don't warm up. Go put this on and we can let your clothes dry out by the fire."

What did this guy take me for? A fish he could reel in on a thin line like that? I crammed the clothes back into his hands.

"I'll not be taking off my clothes in this house." I opened the door and stepped out. Somewhere deep inside, I felt I should stay. But I couldn't. Warning bells rang too loud in my head. I jumped off the porch and into the rain.

He stood at the open door. "Kaylee, I'm not like that. Honest. I just wanted to help."

Sure, help yourself. I know your kind. To his credit, he didn't chase after me. I stared at the city skyline until I found a cross atop a dome. I worked my way toward it while rain pushed against me as if I should go back.

I knocked at the rectory next to the temple. The door opened to reveal a man dressed in black. He frowned. "Come in before you die of sickness."

"Sorry to bother you at this hour, Father." I bowed and kissed his hand.

"No bother at all, my child. It's about time you arrived."

I raised my eyes to his face. "You expected me?"

He nodded. "Why yes. God said you would be here. Saw you on the road in my prayers today."

I sighed. "I sure wish God had let me in on these plans."

He chuckled, but then a knock at the door pulled him away. The door opened to reveal Joel standing in the rain.

Now he is chasing me!

The priest waved him in. "Come in. We have company."

He laughed. "We've already had the pleasure of meeting, Father. She thinks I have ulterior motives in wanting to help her."

"Oh, really?" The priest stared at me. "If you ask me, you probably do, Deacon."

"Deacon!" I blurted out.

Then they both laughed. I rolled my eyes and huffed. Let them have their fun at my expense. I had a job to do and I would do it, whether they helped or not. But these men laughed too much, way too much. I wondered what they drank here in Ramonth.

19

"Yes, he is a deacon." The priest motioned for me to sit. "And my name is Father Peter." He pulled up a chair. Deacon Joel poured cups of hot tea.

As he set the steaming liquid on the table, I caught Deacon Joel's eyes. "Forgive me, Deacon. I didn't know or I would have acted differently." He must think I'm an immature little girl.

He bowed. "Nothing to forgive. I don't fault you for being suspicious of a stranger's intentions."

I nodded and he smiled back. I still couldn't help but wonder if behind those eyes a desire for me swirled in his heart and mind. So much joy and excitement emanated from them. I no longer felt nervous. Instead, my cheeks flushed as I turned my stare into the steam rising from a cup of tea.

I breathed deep. "Father Peter, I believe my brother's on his way here to find a priest who will marry him and his girlfriend."

"Yes, and you want to prevent it. A wise decision considering the circumstances."

"What circumstances do you speak of?"

"Well, that he's about to unite himself to a demon. That's what."

I stared into his eyes. A great depth emanated from them, as if I gazed into eternity and found myself on the other side. "Father, how do you know that?"

He shrugged. "Like I said, God told me. How else would I know anything?"

His kind eyes pierced me like a bright light shining into the forgotten rooms of my soul so he could check for messes.

Deacon Joel sipped his tea. "Father Peter is known to be clairvoyant. He told me to check the boats at the pier, and I would see a girl come up out of the lake. Well, you know what happened."

Father Peter waved his hand. "It's nothing. He speaks. I listen and repeat. Pretty simple really. Much like your ring, Kaylee."

Apparently God had told him a lot. I took a sip of tea. A delicious warmth seeped into my bones and skin. I drank another gulp. "Wow, this is really good tea. What kind is it?"

"Thank you. It's a...family secret." Deacon Joel bowed his head.

"Father," I said. "Apparently, you know everything I'm going to say. So maybe we should cut to the chase, and tell me what we're going to do."

"What are we going to do? Why, have a wedding, of course!"

"Father, this is no time for jokes. You said yourself that my brother's about to wed a demon."

"Yes, and you will be the maid of honor." They both laughed.

"The maid of honor? You're making no sense, Father. What is your plan?" I leaned toward him in hopes of getting a real answer.

He leaned toward me as if ready to give one. "Do you trust God?"

"Of course."

"Then that is all you need."

I grunted and sunk back in my chair. "You're worse than my dad. What if I head out and meet him myself on the road before he arrives? That would make sense."

He shook his head. "And you would fail to save him."

Fail? Sure, but what chance did any of this have to work? Yet I knew he told the truth. All I had was trust in God.

"Have it your way, Father." I gulped the rest of Deacon Joel's tea now that it was cooler, and it warmed my heart with delicious comfort.

"Do I really have to wear this?" I pulled the tight dress over my head. "White's never been my color. Besides, this is getting too close to the wedding aisle for me."

The thirteen-year-old girl, Jamiel, helped me yank it down. "Oh, but you're so beautiful."

"Beautiful as a troll, perhaps."

"Besides, it's all we could find that's appropriate for a wedding on short notice." She pushed her long brown hair behind her shoulders.

She gawked at me as if she wished she could slip into the dress herself. And I wished she would. She tightened the girdle before tying the back closed; I gasped. "I can hardly breathe in this thing. Besides, I feel naked without my sword."

She put her hands on her hips. "You're funny." A giggle escaped her

103

lips. "And very strange."

"You would be, too, if you'd been through what I have."

After we finished putting all the frills and lace on, I wondered if I were the bride: ready to be delivered to some man. I shuddered. Not this time.

I hugged Jamiel. "Thank you for helping me, nonetheless."

She kissed my cheek. "You're welcome."

I shoved the veil and hat over my head. I couldn't believe I had entertained Father Peter's idea, much less agreed to do it. But he said I would know what to do when the time came. Very helpful, that one.

I stepped out of the room. Standing by the entry, my brother stood in wrinkled but colorful clothing. The puffy sleeves and flowing robe hanging to his knees accented his naturally handsome profile. Green tights covered his legs. A blue hat, the rim rolled on one side, and a blue-green feather added flourish to his stature.

I wanted to grab him and squeeze, but Father Peter had said to remain hidden from both of them until Nathan had changed his mind. I had a hard time imagining Nathan changing his mind about this, but decided to trust Father Peter. He must have something up his sleeve.

Next to Nathan, Deacon Joel stood clad in his white robes. They fostered an official air about him. The Deacon saw me and pointed as he talked to Nathan. "And she will be your bridesmaid. Well, not yours, but your bride's." His face reddened.

I lowered my head as Nathan examined me.

Nathan nodded and glanced out the window. "I'm sure she'll be fine. Now, can we get this underway? We're on a tight schedule."

I almost laughed. I wanted to blurt out, "How romantic." Leave it to my brother to hurry through what should be one of the most important days of his life.

Deacon Joel held his palm toward Nathan. "We're about to start. But keep in mind we don't normally do weddings this fast. Father Peter made an exception in your case."

Nathan bowed. "And it is very kind of him to do so. I am honored by his benevolence."

Crystal entered the narthex. Her long, flowing gown and queenly hairstyle spoke of an outward beauty. Yet something in her eyes gave me the impression she felt uncomfortable. I guess any demon would in a church. At least one would hope they would. I adjusted my dress as I sucked in my gut. Then again, it could be her dress.

Deacon Joel beamed. "Looks like we can start." He thrust his head into the nave. "Father, we're ready."

Soon, Father Peter entered the narthex for the betrothal. Nathan and Crystal gathered at the entrance and faced the altar. Deacon Joel and I stood behind them. Father Peter opened a book and read.

"Have you, Nathan, a good, free, and unconstrained will and a firm intention to take unto yourself to wife this demon, Beltrid, whom you see here before you?"

"I…" Nathan's eyes narrowed. "What did you say?"

"Sorry, I have to be accurate or the service is no good. You have to know who you are marrying. The proper response is, 'I have.'"

A realization blossomed into my mind. I knew exactly what I needed to do. Why it hadn't been clear to me before, I had no idea. Yet, now, at this moment, I felt my heart demanded action.

I reached over, touched Nathan's shoulder, and whispered, "Lord, heal Nathan's sight and allow him to see Crystal's reality."

"Are you crazy? This is a woman, not a demon." He swung his arm and head toward her. "Just look at—" He leaped back and nearly tripped over his shoes. He pointed at Crystal as he pushed himself against the wall. "What, what, what is that?" His eyes grew so large, I thought they might fall from their sockets.

Crystal frowned, but attempted to keep up the charade. "Dear, what's the matter? I've been waiting for this moment from the day we met. Can't we continue?"

Nathan didn't say anything. His mouth hung open as he pushed himself along the wall and into the corner. His eyes didn't blink, but remained frozen in shock, staring at Crystal.

I pulled the hat and veil off. "Nathan, don't be afraid. I'm with you." I stepped up to him and placed my arm around his shoulders.

He stared at me with unblinking eyes. "What are you doing here? I must be having a nightmare."

I squeezed him. "I only wish it were so."

His eyes stared at Crystal again. Horror danced across them with unbelief in its arms. He shook all over, and I feared he might have a mental breakdown.

Crystal growled. Her form wavered and it began to merge with another. For a split second, her eyes lost their sinister gaze and horror fled across them, then black robes overtook the white, arms thickened and legs lengthened until Beltrid stood before us.

"Years of planning and months of developing this relationship to be dashed in a single moment!" He roared, and the whole church shook with his thunder. A shelf rattled, then tipped over and crashed down on Father Peter.

Beltrid swung around toward me. "Troll girl, you had something to do with this! Now you will pay."

I braced for what would come. Would he try and control me again? And if he did, would he discover the ring?

Deacon Joel held out a hand. "Don't attack him, and he can't do anything!"

Nathan jumped in front of me. "You'll deal with me first, demon."

"No, Nathan!" I yelled and attempted to move from behind him.

Beltrid smiled. "Gladly, as I have no further need of you, either."

Nathan leaped toward him and plowed into Beltrid's belly. He cried out in pain as he crumpled onto the floor, holding his shoulder.

Beltrid raised a foot to stomp down on him. I had to act, or—

The demon gasped and flung himself forward, revealing Deacon Joel carrying a flaming sword. I stared in disbelief. Where did he get such a sword and why is a deacon wielding it?

Beltrid smiled. "I thought you looked familiar." Beltrid held out his hand and breathed into it, then ran his breath several feet above it. As he did, a sword of his own formed from the caustic blackness that flowed from him.

He held it ready while he circled Joel. "Appears now I'll get a chance to finish what I started last time we met."

Joel didn't appear phased. "That's the problem with demons. They don't finish what they start!"

Beltrid growled and thrust his black sword at Joel. Joel spun around and planted his across Beltrid's side. Fire swung against a black void and when they met, lightning shattered the air as if the two worlds would implode if held together too long.

I rushed to Nathan's side while Beltrid fought Joel, and pulled Nathan to the side. I laid my hand upon his shoulder. "Lord, heal Nathan's shoulder," I whispered.

Nathan's pained face relaxed and he rubbed his shoulder, then gazed up at me. "How did you do that?" His eyes flashed to my left hand.

"I'll explain later. But thanks for standing up for me."

He nodded.

I watched the fight again. Beltrid had burn marks on his sides and body, but Joel had been pushed back into a corner. He likewise appeared battered, and his dodges and parries failed to prevent Beltrid's blows from landing.

Something didn't make sense. Sword fights don't last this long. I couldn't have stood this long against Beltrid. There's something more about Joel than he let on.

Beltrid had backed him up against a wall. I had to do something quick, but what?

Nathan jumped up and grabbed an urn, but he couldn't lift it. "Kaylee, this is attached to the shelf."

I wondered at his plan. There were plenty of other loose objects around he could have thrown. Why this one?

As I drew closer I saw why. "Holy Water!" I grabbed both sides of the urn and pulled with all my strength. Cracks formed around its base.

Chunks popped into the air, then it pulled loose. I grunted as I tossed the whole urn, the water splashing out in a wave toward Beltrid.

He prepared to strike a final blow on Joel who now lay on the ground. As the water cascaded over the demon, fire like sparks of lightning crackled over him, releasing a putrid steam into the air. Beltrid cried in agony before fading into nothingness.

For a moment we stared at each other, and the shards of glass and chips of tile lying everywhere.

"Father Peter!" I rushed to the shelves and lifted them aside, allowing them to add to the rubble.

He smiled. "Well, did I miss anything?"

He appeared untouched. I extended my hand to help him up and shook my head. "Just the destruction of your narthex. Still feel this was the best plan?"

He scanned the room. "Appears we have met our objective, have we not?"

"Yes, we did."

"Then, it was a good plan."

Joel rose to his feet and dusted himself off.

I frowned. "Joel, who are you really? Deacons don't fight with swords."

"And do nuns fight with them as well?"

I gaped. "How did you know—"

He pointed at Father Peter, who shrugged his shoulders.

"But where did that strange sword come from, and how could you stand so long against Beltrid? He landed several hits on you, but you are not seriously hurt."

"The sword is under my robes. Wouldn't be proper for a deacon to display it openly.

"As for the wounds, you know nothing of fighting demons, do you? The outward physical manifestation is a window into the soul, which is what he's really after. He wants its death, not purely physical death. Death of the soul happens when it is joined to the darkness of evil. Thank you for putting an end to his attack."

While something bothered me about his explanation, it would do for now. I had other issues to deal with. "Actually, it was Nathan's idea." I turned toward Nathan. He sat on the floor, head buried in his hands.

"Nathan?"

He lifted his head. I expected to see tears, or sorrow. Instead, his eyes stared at me with purpose, and his jaw bit so tightly, his teeth barely opened when he spoke. "I will kill Beltrid. I don't know how, but I will kill him."

The conviction with which he spoke gave me pause. While I understood his rage at Beltrid's deception, I feared this would only pull him further in, not heal. But he needed to release the pent up feelings that boiled underneath.

A rage I shared to a degree, now that I thought about it.

"Dad!" His words flooded back into my mind, *I have a different path.*

"Deacon Joel." I turned back to him. "Is Beltrid gone for good?"

He hung his head. "Unfortunately, no."

I glanced at Father Peter, who nodded. "He's right. He couldn't handle holy water, but it will not send him into the abyss. That requires something more powerful."

I stared at the debris on the floor. Now that Beltrid's plan had ended, he would start a new one. That had to be what Dad knew was coming. "Nathan, we have to go. Now! Dad may need us."

We readied Nathan and Crystal's horses to travel back. I hoped Rain would find her way back to Uncle Seth's house. Or maybe I would find her along the road. But I couldn't spend time searching for the horse, not when Dad could be in danger.

Father Peter drew near and said, "Kaylee, you have a gift, but a gift that comes with a burden. Miracle workers are hard to hide, but work best in secret." He winked at me.

Nathan stared at me. "What did that mean?"

"I'll tell you later." I smiled as I focused on Father Peter. "Thank you, Father, for all you've done."

He shrugged. "All I did was try to marry them." He grinned.

I held out my hand for a blessing. He placed his in mine and I kissed it. He withdrew his hand and a key lay in my palm. A key with a crystal protrusion. My heart leaped and I gave Father my biggest grin. "Thank you!" I wondered which virtue it would unlock, but I wouldn't find out until we arrived back at Seth's where Amma's prison lay. I dropped the key in my pocket. Even Nathan cracked a weak smile.

Deacon Joel hugged me. "I've been wanting to do that."

I felt heat rising to my head. "Normally, I would slap a guy for doing that save my Dad or brother. But for you, I'll make an exception. Thanks for attempting to help me." I winked.

He laughed, and it didn't even annoy me.

We mounted the horses and galloped down the road, back to Uncle Seth's house. My thoughts now rested on Dad, hoping he would be all right. At least Beltrid thought he still had the ring. Maybe he wouldn't try anything for fear of being struck himself. But who knew what alternate plans he would instigate now that he couldn't use Nathan any longer?

The sun rose in the late morning sky as we exited Ramonth's gates and galloped into the open countryside by the lake.

20

The road to Seth's house stretched into forever. Beltrid's words rang in my ears as the horses' hoofs kept a rhythmic beat upon the dirt road. I had no idea what he might have planned for Dad. I knew it couldn't be good. While Dad had always taken care of himself before, he no longer wore the ring. Once Beltrid discovered that reality, anything could happen.

Another concern niggled at my thoughts. For one brief second, I had felt something different about Crystal right before Beltrid's form overtook hers. It happened so fast and the feeling touched me so subtly that I had trouble identifying it. Yet I couldn't stop thinking about it.

I shot a glance at Nathan. He appeared deep in his own thoughts. I could see the pain and guilt written on his face, seeping from his eyes. I wished we could talk, but at galloping speeds, the horses pounded too loud and the wind rushed past too strong. Opening a mouth meant dirt and an occasional bug flying into it. I glanced at the road from time to time, letting the horses follow it while I kept my head down.

After a while, we did slow the horses down to a trot. They couldn't keep up a gallop all the way without tiring them. We also stopped several times: to relieve ourselves, let the horses take a drink from a stream or river, and to dig out something to eat. But we didn't speak much even then. I thought it better to let Nathan speak first when he was ready. I knew it must be especially hard on him. But I hoped he wouldn't keep it all bottled up for too long.

Night fell, forcing us to find a place to camp. We would arrive at Uncle Seth's in the morning if we left at the first break of dawn. We unpacked. I started a fire, heated some water, and used dried meats and spices to create a make-do stew.

Nathan ate, staring into the fire. He finished and placed his cup on the ground before breaking his silence. "So how did you get to Ramonth before me?"

"I wish I knew. When we didn't find you two at Jerole, Uncle Seth figured you had headed to Ramonth, knowing we would check Jerole first."

Nathan nodded. "At least that worked."

"We talked about what to do, and I felt we should at least try to beat you to Ramonth. Dad agreed, but convinced me to go alone.

"When I crossed a river, I encountered a bright light and fell from Rain unconscious. When I awoke, water surrounded me; I ended up in the lake at Ramonth. I guess God transported me there."

He sipped soup from his cup. "God must have felt it important to do all that." He finally met my eyes and gazed deep into them. "Maybe He sees something in me worth saving?"

I smiled. "I know I do."

"Yeah, but you're my sister."

"All the more impressive, don't you think?" I winked at him.

He cracked an unsure smile. Then his head sank. "But I've sure made a mess of things."

I jabbed a stick into the fire. "In some ways it would have been better if we could have kept stringing Beltrid along. For some reason, he thinks getting control of the ring would give him some type of control over God.

"I guess he figured if you had it, and did things at his bidding, you wouldn't be doing it for yourself, but for him."

Nathan lifted his head higher. "So the longer we kept him thinking he would succeed, the longer we would have had to find the other keys to free Mother."

"Right. Now that he knows his original plan has failed, I fear what he'll do next. We could lose both Amma and Dad." I drank another gulp of soup. "But I am glad to have you safely out of his control."

He shook his head. "My anger at what you told me, the truth, drove me to push the matter of marriage. If I hadn't been so blind and hot-headed, Beltrid would still think his plan had a chance."

"And if I had the tact of Dad, I wouldn't have been so blunt with you, sending you down that path."

Nathan gazed into my eyes. "But you came after me, you didn't give up. You saved me from union with a demon, a union I would have regretted forever."

He reached over and wrapped me in his arms. I held him tight; my eyes watered. A conviction set in. Helping people, being my brother and sister's keeper, created a sense of peace and contentment within me. The inner joy it fostered provided all the motivation needed to use the ring for God. We sat there, in each other's arms for several moments.

A grunt sounded from the edge of the firelight. "Well, isn't this a pretty picture."

I swung around to see Beltrid standing by the edge of the trees. Nathan reached for his sword, but I placed my hand on his arm. Beltrid might very well kill us now but I knew not to provoke him.

"You know you can't have the ring or control God with it. Why don't you leave us alone?" I stood and faced him, unblinking.

He smiled, which caused me to brace for the worst. He held up his hand. "Never fear, I did not come here to attack. Only to pass on information as I agreed to do."

Nathan's eyes met mine. I would have felt better to do battle.

"Your father and I have come to, shall we say, an agreement. Your uncle can fill you in on the details. But as far as you're concerned, you will not see me again."

"What agreement did you make?"

"All I'll say is, if I can't have the ring, no one will." He laughed as he vanished.

A knot twisted in my stomach. "Oh, Dad." I sat on the log and wrapped my hands over my head.

Nathan sat beside me. "Kaylee, won't the ring protect him?"

I stared into his eyes. "That's just it, he doesn't have the ring. I do."

His eyes grew round. "You do?"

I pulled the glove off my left hand and showed him. "After the shadow-creatures captured you, Dad and I figured out Beltrid's plan to control the ring through you. But Dad felt the time had come to pass it on, and the ring agreed by coming off. He passed it on to me."

Nathan shook his head. "Wow. Better you than me. I've never wanted it, though I thought I would get stuck with it."

I smiled. "I think Dad knew that, Beltrid didn't. But he still thinks Dad has the ring. As soon as he realizes he doesn't, he'll probably kill Dad and come after me. Needless to say, we don't want him to find out I have it." I pulled the glove back on.

"Then we need to find out from Seth what this agreement is so we'll know what to do."

"Agreed. Let's get some sleep. And while Beltrid is a demon, I sensed he told the truth. I don't think we'll need to post watch tonight."

Nathan nodded. We cleaned up camp and bedded down for the night. Still, it took a while to fall asleep. The forest animals and crickets sang a hypnotic song as various nightmares concerning Dad swirled through my mind. I dreaded discovering the truth but couldn't wait to find out what deal Dad could have struck with Beltrid.

Nathan sank into sleep, but within minutes, he mumbled something unintelligible and squirmed upon his bed. I wondered what horrible dreams he might be fighting and hoped he would find peace.

Somewhere in the midst of it all, dreams invaded and interrupted my wandering thoughts with other nightmares I couldn't recall, and knew it was best I didn't.

Nathan shook me awake. "Daylight's burning. Let's go."

It didn't burn that strongly. The stars stared down at me, but a bare reddish glow emanated from the eastern hills. I yawned, arose, and began the process of packing. By the time we loaded the last of our supplies onto the horses, the first rays of sunlight shot over the hills and the sky radiated a dark blue, melting into a red haze on the western horizon.

Soon we trotted down the road again. The hooves of our horses beat out their song upon the dirt road. They splashed through creeks, sloshed through rivers, and beat like a drum upon the occasional bridge. The sun, like a conductor overseeing a production, had risen to mid-morning when the gates of Jerole broke into view over the crest of a hill. We didn't enter the city gates, but turned down the path leading to Uncle Seth's house, driving our horses as fast as we dared.

I patted my horse on the neck. "Sorry, girl, but we'll rest soon." They worked hard as we climbed the mountain path. By the time we reached Seth's clearing, they huffed in heavy bursts.

We dismounted next to the water-trough and dashed toward the cabin. Birds sang sweetly in the trees and sunlight splashed radiant colors over the world, as if it knew what we would soon discover and attempted to soften the blow.

Seth met us at the door. His face colorless, his eyes blank. "Your father…" He faltered, stared at the ground, and took a deep breath. "Your father, for lack of a better way to say this, sold himself into slavery to Beltrid."

I gasped. "He did what?"

21

"Your father struck a deal with Beltrid." Seth stared at the ground.

I glanced at Nathan and saw the same shock of disbelief frozen on his face that I knew must be on mine. "Beltrid told us that much, but what deal did he make?"

"Let's talk about it inside." Seth motioned for us to follow him. We sat at a table, and he provided us with hot tea before grabbing a chair himself.

"Beltrid appeared and told your father that if he couldn't have control of the ring, no one would. However, he couldn't force him to submit. So he threatened to harass his family and their descendants forever unless Sisko became his prisoner. After some discussion, he agreed to hand himself over in exchange for leaving you alone."

Nathan groaned. "So he literally sacrificed himself for us?"

Seth nodded. "Yep, but he did extract one clause from Beltrid for his release."

I raised an eyebrow. "Oh? What's that?"

"If both of you go into the steam house in his childhood village and come out better than when you entered, Beltrid will free him."

Nathan jumped out of his chair. "Oh no! If half the stuff Father said about that steam house is true, I'm not stepping one foot in there!"

I stood up. "But Nathan, if it's the only way to free Dad, we have to."

"Don't you understand? I know I wouldn't come out in good shape. I'm shot full of faults. I'll come out as a goat or something horrible."

"But you also have a lot of good qualities. Qualities the steam house would recognize and bless you with a miracle over. We have to try. Could you face yourself the rest of your life knowing that you might have saved

114

Dad, but you didn't give it a chance?"

Nathan seated himself and buried his head in his hands. "But why would Father want us to go in there, and why would Beltrid agree to it?"

I shook my head. "I don't know for sure, but in Dad's village, it was a rite of passage into adulthood. Perhaps he has the same idea for us?"

Seth leaned over the table. "And I'm sure Beltrid believes he can use the steam house for his advantage, to destroy you and gain the ring. As your father often said to me, prideful people didn't fear the steam house, when in reality, they had the most reason to stay far away from it. Beltrid is a demon because of pride. That will be your one advantage over him."

I nodded. "Come on, Nathan. We have to go in."

He sighed. "I'll give it some thought. We're going to Reol anyway and we still have to get Mother out of the crystal. Maybe by the time we arrive, I'll be ready."

I snapped my fingers. "Oh, I almost forgot!" I pulled the key out of my pocket. "I have a key for the crystal. Seth, where's Dad's pack?"

Seth jumped up and pulled a pack from behind a bed. I took it and found the ball wrapped in cloth. I searched till I found a hole in the shape of a sun. The three letters over it said, "HUM." A grin creased my face. "Nathan, it's humility. We found humility."

He smiled. "That's a major one. Put it in!"

I slid the crystal in and broke it off. A glow emanated from the rock and then died off. "Just three more keys to find. At least that's some good news. Maybe without Beltrid's interference, it will be easier to find the rest."

I wrapped the crystal and placed it back in the pack. Thoughts of Beltrid whipping Dad and locking him away in some forgotten chamber of the underworld sent shivers down my legs. I checked Nathan, and he sat deep in thought as well.

A deep breath escaped me. "Looks like it is just you and I, Nathan. Unless…" I met Seth's gaze over the tea's steam.

He smiled. "I've already arranged to go with you. I know the country from here to his hometown, Reol. I used to guide a gang of thieves along that road."

I let out a breath and placed a hand on Seth's shoulder. "Thanks so much, Uncle. Your presence will be very much appreciated."

"Once you save your father, I would've never heard the end of it if I hadn't come along. Besides, I'm interested in seeing, not going in mind you, but seeing this steam house of his. As much as he's told me about it over the years, I've never been there myself."

Nathan grunted. "So you'll know about any strange mist or places along the way to avoid, right?"

I cracked a smile. "What's the matter, brother? Don't you want to get troll strength too? Just one bite does the trick!"

He bopped me on the back of the head. "No thank you! I've had enough odd stuff to last me a lifetime."

The villagers at Jerole had found my horse, Rain, trotting down the road. They notified Seth and he claimed her. Unfortunately, the horse had become deathly sick. The villagers couldn't save her, but Seth recovered most of my stuff that hadn't fallen off. My heart sank at the news. Not only because I had lost a horse that I had raised from a young filly, but because her death cast a fear upon me that I would lose Amma and Dad as well.

While Crystal's horse rode well, it wasn't my horse. I wanted Rain back, but knew I wouldn't get her. One more reason I could add to the growing list why I should be depressed. But I knew depression wouldn't help bring Amma or Dad home. I had to focus on the hope that we could pull off the required task to free them. It was all I had, and I would hang onto it with a troll's grip.

After a noon meal, we set out toward the north. The forest thickened as we descended the mountain. A fairly wide path cut through the trees, running along a river that raced through the valley. The rushing waters over polished stones called out to hurry, and inside I felt we should.

But we wanted to find the three remaining keys too. We had to keep a watch for them even as we worked our way toward Reol.

Nathan cleared his throat as our horses trotted along the path. "So what three keys do we have left to get?"

"Generosity, contentment, and love."

"You know, I've already done my part to provide a key. When are you going to give us one?"

I cast a glance toward him. "It's not like I can command a key to come out."

"Can't you be generous? That should be easy. Do something generous and we'll have another key."

I shook my head. "It doesn't work that way."

"Well, it should."

I chuckled. "That would be nice."

As the sun dove toward the western horizon, our path led into a hall of trees interwoven with thorns. The tree-walls cast shadows, making the path appear dark and dreary.

"Uncle? What's this?" I asked.

He scratched his head. "Don't know. It's been a few years since I've come through here. Don't recall this being here before."

Nathan stretched. "Is there any way around this?"

Seth dismounted. "Don't know, but it's getting a bit late anyway. Maybe we should camp out here and give this some thought."

It sounded like a reasonable plan. My belly growled anyway. Food would do it some good.

As we set up camp, my thoughts returned to Dad. I wondered what he had to endure, and whether Beltrid had discovered he didn't have the ring. I also wondered why Dad wanted us to go through the steam house. I had everything I needed. I couldn't think of a miracle I would desire to have, so why risk what the steam house might do to me? But I didn't mind the risk if it would free Dad. I would go to hell and back for him if I had to.

Soon, we sat down and fixed a small meal: a light soup with flatbread. It tasted surprisingly good. Seth turned out to be a good cook and knew how to make even simple meals tasty. Mostly, we ate. But as our bellies filled, we discussed the situation.

"The road should go straight ahead," Seth said. "But it appears this hall of trees veers to the left and into the forest for who knows how far. It could take us way off course."

"Or be a trap," Nathan added.

I waved my hand into the growing darkness. "But I didn't see any alternate paths and the forest is thick with underbrush here. We couldn't pull our horses through that for who knows how many miles."

Seth chewed a piece of sopped bread and swallowed. "Problem is, the only other route I know is to go back to my place, take the road to Ramonth and follow that around to Siloest. But it would add another eight to ten days onto our trip."

I shook my head. "And we may not have that much time. Who knows what Beltrid will do once he discovers Dad doesn't have the ring? The longer it takes us to get to the steam house, the more likely that will happen before we can get Dad released."

I stared into the fire. "I don't get it. If God could transport me to Ramonth like He did, why doesn't He transport us all to Dad's village? Why allow these obstacles in our path?"

"That's one thing I learned from your father," Seth said. "He had a simple faith in God's guidance. Aside from his one slip on that account, he always trusted, even when it seemed as if everything would fall apart.

"The day your father stood down a dragon, I'll never forget that. He didn't run, he faced the dragon down. When the dragon blasted fire over him, I knew he would be roasted alive. I can't tell you the amazement that flooded over me to see him still standing there as if he had taken a shower. That's when I knew there was a God and He could be trusted."

Seth leaned back and stared at the stars. "Sisko is one of a kind. Never met anyone like him, ring or no ring."

I had heard Dad tell that story several times. But that's all it had been, a story. To hear Seth tell it, as an eyewitness, I realized these stories were real. I should have known that by now, but I had never thought of Dad as a great man who did amazing things. He was just Dad. Now, pride bubbled up inside me. At the same time, I realized I had some very big shoes to fill.

I watched Seth as he lay on the ground, lost in his thoughts. "So, Uncle Seth, you're saying God knows we need these experiences before we arrive in Reol?"

He nodded. "Yeah, I guess that's a good way to put it." He turned to face me and smiled. "Very good way to put it."

"Then, it's clear to me that we should go through the hallway, wherever it leads. Surely it can't take us further out of our way than taking another route, and most likely will be easier than cutting through the underbrush with our horses."

Nathan put his cup down. "I think you're right, little sister."

"Then it's settled." Seth rose to his feet. "Tomorrow we head into the hallway. But now, we sleep." He set up his bedroll under the shelter and settled in. Nathan followed, but I stayed up a while longer, watching the stars and thinking about the One who had created them all.

Guess He can manage a trollish girl like me.

The next morning, we packed up our gear and rode into the hallway. The trees and thorny vines grew thick, creating a formidable wall that towered over us. It would be very difficult, if not impossible, to hack through it. I thought about suggesting we try, but figured we should find out if an exit existed first.

The walls appeared closer in as we rode through them. I checked behind us and gasped. I tapped Seth on the shoulder and pointed. "Look, the path behind us closes as we go! I sense magic at work here."

Nathan groaned. "Great. This has to be a trap of some kind."

Seth said, "Probably is, but we've no choice unless we think we can hack through these walls with our swords."

"I thought of that, but we have no axes, and what use would a sword be on a tree? That would take forever. Nothing to do but see what trap lays ahead and deal with it when we get there."

Trap or no trap, our destination lay ahead. We rode on in silence while the trees groaned around us. A foreboding sense of doom cast its shadow into my mind; wild thoughts of what we would find at the end of this dark hall flashed through my head. Then it struck me: I would face my own dragon. Would I have Dad's faith to confront it?

I swallowed moisture down my dry throat and attempted to steady my hands by stroking the horse's neck. "Don't worry girl, everything will be all right."

Nathan glanced at me and sighed, but didn't say anything. We slogged on toward the doom awaiting us.

22

The hallway of trees led us around one curve and then another. Most of the day dripped by until late afternoon cast shadows along the path. The trees behind us continued to close up as we traveled; we could only go forward.

Life stayed outside the barriers. No singing birds or chirping crickets could be heard here. Even the wind remained aloof, so only our footsteps, the horses' hooves hitting the ground, and the creaking of moving trees behind us broke the stagnant air. I breathed hard.

As we rounded a curve, the tree-lined path opened into a larger area. Hope that we had finally come to the end of this dreary trail rose, but also dread at what we might discover there. As we left the one-way road, we entered into an open but solid circle about ten strides wide. We stepped into the center and the hallway closed behind us, leaving us encircled in wall of thorny trees.

Nathan ran his fingers through his hair. "Now what?"

No one answered, because no one had the slightest idea. Especially me. I dismounted to stretch while we planned our next action, and the others did the same.

I felt the ground give beneath me; I jerked my arms out to steady myself. I tried pulling a foot up, but it met resistance. I checked: my boot had sunk into the ground. "I think the 'now what' is quicksand."

Seth pulled his foot out, but the ground stretched up with it. "I don't think this is quicksand. More like a spell."

"Yeah, I'm being sucked in, not sinking in." Nathan struggled, but the ground had already pulled us down to our knees. The horses neighed as they struggled against the pull.

Nathan's voice betrayed panic. "Can't you get us out of this, Kaylee?"

"Maybe you all, but not myself."

"But we both have to go into the steam house to free Father. If you die, he's lost."

Yes! If I die, so does Dad, and possibly Amma as well. Nathan would be the last surviving member of our family. Saving myself would save others.

But Dad's story in the desert came back to me. No, I couldn't use the ring to save myself even for the promise of helping others in the future. I would have to trust God.

"I don't know what's going on, but I can't use the ring to save myself. I'll save you two so maybe you can save Amma at least."

Seth cleared his throat, the ground rising to his chest. "Whatever you do, you had better do it fast. We don't have much time left."

I nodded. "Lord…" My mouth froze. My heart didn't have the sense that I should do this. Dad had said to listen to it. It seemed the right thing to do, to save Seth and Nathan. I should be the only one dying here. And maybe the ring would protect me anyway.

"Sister! What's the matter?"

"I…I don't think I should try and save us."

The ground inched its way to my neck. The ground pressed in on my body, squeezing it.

"Why?"

"Well, I don't know. I can't explain it. But Dad said sometimes my heart would tell me not to, and it's doing that now."

Nathan sighed. "Are you really, really sure?"

I hoped I heard my heart correctly. I recalled what Dad had said: not acting when you could is hard. He was right. Watching the ground inching up Nathan and Seth's neck, knowing I could free them, and not doing it, wrenched my gut. But for good or bad, our destiny lay at God's feet.

Seth calmed down as he stared at me. "I've seen that look before."

I nodded. "Yes, I'm sure. I love you both."

Their eyes remained fixed on me as the ground passed their lips and we sank into blackness.

As consciousness flowed back, I blinked to clear the images before me. Vertical, iron bars slid into focus. I lifted myself to a sitting position and rubbed my temples. Nathan and Seth lay on the cold, stone floor with me. Crude, wooden benches lined the walls. A hole on one end buzzed with flies, obviously the toilet. We had been transported into a prison cell.

Nathan and Seth groaned as they awoke. Nathan shook his head and blinked his eyes. "Am I dead? Am I in hell?"

"Are you saying that hell for you is being locked up forever with your sister?"

He blushed. "No, that's not what I meant."

"Don't worry. We're not dead. What Dad described is nothing like this."

He grunted. "Don't worry, she says. Yeah, what do we have to be worried about? We just sunk into the ground, and now we're locked in a prison. We don't even know where we are. There's nothing to be worried about." Nathan sunk his head between his knees and wrapped his arms over himself.

Seth rose and strolled toward me. "Kaylee, you have any idea where we are?"

"Nope, came to a couple seconds before you two did." I arose and examined the surroundings, testing the bars. They didn't budge, but if I applied enough strength or leverage, they might bend. I grabbed them firmly and pulled outwards. My arms trembled with the strain, but I couldn't tell that the bars had moved in the least. When I could take no more, I expelled the breath I had been holding, and collapsed against the immovable iron.

I faced Seth. "But I do think this is a wizard's trap. The question is who and why."

"I have an answer for you, my captured troll," a squeaky voice said.

I turned to the bars to see who had spoken, but no one stood there.

"Down here." The high-pitched voice pierced the air.

I gazed upon the floor and saw a little mouse, waving at me. I squatted down. "Who are you?"

"Does the name Rodan mean anything to you?"

"You mean the wizard who imprisoned our mother?"

The beady-eyed head nodded. "Thought you had gotten rid of me, didn't you?"

This is Rodan! I swallowed a laugh and shrugged. "I don't know what you're talking about. And what's with this mouse thing? Did you change yourself into this on purpose?"

He stomped around, squealing in high pitches. His whiskers twitched rapidly. "As if you didn't know!"

I glanced at Nathan who shrugged while suppressing his own laughter.

"I'm sorry, we have no idea what you're talking about."

"Beltrid warned me about Sisko's ring. But I thought it was to help people, not punish them!"

Then I remembered. When we had left Rodan's house before starting this trip, Dad had said if his ring still worked he would say, "Father, send this wizard to the steam house." But he didn't think it actually happened. Yet the whole house had disappeared. Dad had said it in jest, but apparently God took it seriously.

"You mean, you really did go to the steam house?"

"Your stupid father did send me there, yes! And for that, I vowed revenge upon him."

"But don't you see, the steam house is attempting to correct the flaws in your soul. It left you a voice to repent with. Instead, you have used it to dig further toward hell."

"I don't need to be lectured by some weak girl." He bounced up and down on his hind legs.

"I wouldn't be talking if I were you."

"Ah, but my trap worked. Now you will stay here forever. Locked in my dungeon. I even have spells upon it so you can't break out. Your precious mother will stay locked away and your father will be dealt with by Beltrid." A high-pitched laugh chirped from his tiny mouth. "Now who has the last laugh?" He scurried away.

Nathan groaned. "Well, now we know who and why. Didn't get us very far. Trapped by a mouse!"

Seth patted Nathan on the back. "Don't worry. I have a feeling something will come of this."

They both stared at me. I gave them a weak smile. I certainly hoped it did.

23

Nathan put his mouth to my ear. "Just use your ring to get me on the other side of the bars, then I can get us free."

I shook my head and whispered back, "No, that would be helping myself."

He stomped his foot and said aloud, "Then what good is it?"

"Shut up!"

He stepped back.

I sighed and whispered to him, "Sorry, but I don't know if Rodan can hear us or not, and I don't want him to find out about the ring. He might tell Beltrid."

Nathan nodded. "Then how are we going to get out of here? We can't stay here."

"I know. I'm searching my heart. The ring should tell me something." But what? I couldn't use the ring, and even if I did, I didn't know if Rodan's spells would prevent it from working or not. My troll-strength didn't work either.

I plopped myself down on the bench and ran through various possibilities, hoping to find a solution.

Seth lifted himself from the bench and checked the bars and door. He peered into the lock. "You know, this doesn't appear that hard to pick. The poor wizard so depends upon his spells that he forgets the obvious."

I stared at Nathan, then turned back to Seth. "Really? You think you can pick the lock?"

"I used to do this kind of thing for a living." He grabbed a dagger from his boot and stabbed it into the keyhole. He wiggled up and down. I heard cylinders shift. Then a loud clank indicated the lock had turned. Seth pulled the door open.

I had to laugh. I had been too busy thinking of extravagant ways to get us out of this mess, and it took my uncle to see the obvious.

We filed out and worked our way down the hall. We came upon a locked door. Seth again picked at it with his dagger until it clicked open and we pushed the door out.

An endless hallway lay before us. A rock floor, bare walls dotted with torches stretched into infinity.

"How can such a long hallway be in this castle?" I wondered.

Seth stepped into the hall. "Don't forget, we have no idea where we are, but we do know we are in a wizard's abode. We need to be prepared for anything. Let's go."

We followed him and soon jogged at a brisk pace. After all, we had a long ways before reaching the end. But within fifty feet, Seth crashed into the air, and we plowed into his back. My hands felt something solid, yet they appeared to touch thin air.

"An illusion?" Nathan asked. He began feeling the walls around us. Seth and I followed his lead.

I jumped back unexpectedly when my hand sank into a wall. "I think I found it. I stepped through the wall and they followed.

We entered another hall, much like the last. Again we moved forward, more cautious this time. Seth held his hands out before him. Within an even shorter time, he found another invisible wall. We all patted down the walls around us. After a minute of searching, Nathan and Seth said together, "I found it."

They both turned their heads toward each other, their arms buried in opposite walls.

Seth pulled his arm out and his eyes widened. "Quick, back the way we came!"

I knew not to ask questions, just obey. We all three fled to the wall we had come through moments before. When Seth arrived, he tried to put his hand through it, but it thudded against hard rock.

Uncle stomped his foot. "I should have known! This is a wizard's maze. The exit route continually changes making it nearly impossible to find your way out."

Nathan kicked a wall and grunted in frustration.

I leaned against the rocks. "It's one prison after another with this wizard."

My support gave way and I fell backwards. I landed with a grunt on another stone floor, my torso embedded in the imaginary rock wall. My head pounded with a fresh knot, but my attention immediately focused on a ceiling full of bats. As if they smelled a meal, they released their grips on their perches and dropped toward me in a black cloud.

A scream bulged from my lungs, up my throat, and forced its way out, echoing through the hallway. I flung my arms over my eyes as they sank toward me.

Someone pulled on my feet and I slid back through the wall until I stared at Nathan holding my legs. My chest rose and fell in quick bursts and I could feel the sweat rolling down my face.

Seth rushed to me and knelt. "What did you see?"

I lifted myself to a sitting position. "Not all hallways are empty of danger," I said between breaths. "A horde of hungry bats nearly made a meal of me."

Nathan sighed. "A fine predicament we're in." He turned and paced the hall. No one dared to lean against a wall.

Nathan spun on his heals. "Kaylee, why don't you use…you know what?"

I wrinkled my brow. "What do you mean, you know I can't…you know."

He nodded. "Yes, but it does guide you, does it not? Tell you what to do sometimes, tell you *where to go?*" He raised an eyebrow.

His meaning hit me. "Oh, well, yes it does." Quite ingenious actually. I never asked for guidance, it simply came. I wouldn't be using the ring in any other way than I usually do. I only had to listen.

I rose to my feet and slowly stepped along the hallway, staring at the walls, attempting to hear the voice in my heart. Where on this wall could the right opening be? After a few minutes of staring, watching, and listening, no clear signal flashed in my mind where to go.

I stomped the floor and it echoed. "I can't do it!"

Nathan sighed. "You have to, Sis. You're the only one of us who even has a chance of finding the way out."

Seth rose and approached me as he undid a scarf he wore around his arm. "You're depending too much on your senses. They're getting in the way." He wrapped the scarf over my eyes and ears. "Nathan, don't make a sound. Kaylee, sink into your heart. Feel the direction it sends you."

I attempted to settle my mind: release the fears and frustrations, the tension and horror of our situation. The world closed in around me, and folded down until I discovered a wall within myself. Dad! A fear I wouldn't save him blocked the way. A fear I wouldn't prove worthy of the ring and his trust. Somewhere from the void of my mind his words returned to me. *God will use you.*

The wall of fear dissolved and a sweet, pure energy overflowed my soul. Then I knew. "This way." I placed a foot in the direction I sensed. Though I couldn't see, my feet stepped forth in confidence. "And this way, quickly, the door will close soon." I heard their footsteps behind me as if they echoed down a hall a few feet behind.

Turn after turn, wall after wall, but I could feel no end to the series of corridors. Still, my heart guided me from one hall into the next. I started to wonder if we would find the end. My face crashed into a wall. "Ouch!" I staggered back.

"You're doing fine, focus in your soul," I heard Seth's soothing voice whisper behind me.

I took a deep breath and dove back in until I found the trusting direction again calling to me. I stepped twice to my left and headed straight.

"We're out!" Nathan's voice exclaimed.

I pulled the blindfold off; a much different hallway, full of knight's armor in rows on the floor and coats of arms along the walls, greeted me. A rougher type of rock covered the floor, and windows high toward the vaulted ceiling allowed sunlight to cast its rays into the shadows.

A flood of excitement swooshed over me. God had used me! Relief settled and we proceeded forward.

As if we had tripped a wire, the suits of armor shifted on their pedestals and grabbed swords from the wall. Nearly a dozen empty shells of armor marched toward us with raises swords.

"Wizards!" Seth yelled. "Cowards who can't fight face to face."

We all drew our swords and met them head on. My heart jumped as I slashed through one's neck, and watched as the helmet rolled to the ground and the suit sank into a heap with a crash. Though I knew I hadn't killed anyone, I couldn't help but feel I had.

I discovered that using a slap with the flat of my blade against their chest or a well-planted shove with my shoulder, the empty suits lost their balance, setting them up for a final blow. Still, I grew overconfident at one point and allowed one to get its blade onto my chest. The mail I wore prevented it from penetrating, but the force knocked me back onto the floor. I rolled backwards and up onto my feet, avoiding a final stab of its sword, which smashed into the rock floor. Its head exposed, I dropped my sword and pushed through. The body collapsed and its helmet rolled away.

I scanned for the next target, but instead found Seth and Nathan leaning against a wall, panting as they watched me. Scattered pieces of armor lay like rubble over the floor.

Nathan winked. "About time you finished yours. Ready to go yet?"

I shook my head, too out of breath to respond to his jest. I wondered what the next wizardly trap would be. It probably wouldn't take long to find out.

We moved on to enter a room, much like the one we first met Rodan in when we discovered Amma's imprisonment in the crystal. The ceiling rose high above us, and sunlight lit the room.

"How did you escape?" Little pattering feet scurried across the floor toward us.

Seth grinned. "With some fine pickin'."

Rodan flung his paws toward Seth.

"Duck, Uncle!"

A flaming ball of fire erupted from Rodan's hands and fled toward Seth. It passed beside him as he leaped to his right, but Rodan had already released another. Seth couldn't respond in time.

"No!" I sped toward Seth; Nathan dashed toward Rodan. I watched as the fireball beat me to him and swallowed Uncle into its hungry mouth. When I reached him, the fire had encased him in ice.

I jumped backwards to avoid another fireball and spun around to keep ahead of them. I glanced toward Rodan, to see Nathan crashing into an invisible shield surrounding the wizard. But Rodan's eyes glared at me as he continued to fire his blasts my way.

He must be using the shield to focus on us one at a time. But maybe I could expend his energy.

I zigged and zagged through the room, his fireballs bursting close on my heels. Some I avoided by falling to the floor, rolling back onto my feet, and shifting directions. Others, by leaping over them.

I knew the ring would protect me if one hit, but he might suspect I had the ring if I survived one of his ice-traps.

Icy patches dotted his living room as I continued to dodge his volleys. He grunted in frustration. But I sensed where his next one would land as he threw it, and could dodge them. What I had hoped might happen, happened. His energy weakened in his attempt to get me, and Nathan broke through the shield. Distracted, Rodan stopped throwing fireballs my way and attempted to avoid Nathan's grasp. But Nathan trapped him between his hands and knocked him unconscious.

Huffing, I staggered over to Seth and laid my hands on him. "Lord, free Seth of this icy prison."

Cracks formed along the length of the encasement. I slammed my hand down upon it to speed the process. It shattered and fractured from head to toe, then fell from his body.

Seth cracked his eyes open, shivering. "Where am I?" His teeth chattered as he spoke.

I lifted him into my lap and rubbed his back vigorously in an attempt to warm him up. "We're still in Rodan's house, but we trapped Rodan. He hit you with one of his fireballs, which apparently ices you. Go figure."

Nathan approached holding a limp mouse by the tail. "Why don't you set Uncle by the fire over there while we figure out what to do with this wizard."

"Good idea. Is Rodan dead?"

"No, I don't think so. Just unconscious."

I sighed and realized I had hoped the answer would be yes. Thoughts of permanently getting him out of the way passed through my mind, but I couldn't do that.

I helped Seth into a chair by the fireplace so he could warm up. Nathan snapped his fingers. "I have an idea." He dashed back down the hallway. In a few minutes he returned without Rodan.

I watched his eyes. "What did you do with him?"

A sly grin creased his face. "I tossed him in one of his maze hallways. By the time he wakes up, that hallway will have moved to who knows where. I'll bet he doesn't know the solution to his own maze."

I laughed and shook my head. I couldn't imagine a better trap for a wizard than a wizard's maze.

Seth rose from the chair, rubbing his arms. "Come on, let's get out of here. We need to find out where we are and get back on the road."

We filed out of what appeared to be the front door. Once outside, we stood in a yard as it appeared on our first visit to his house. Our horses grazed on the grass. I glanced back and saw the same small cottage resting in the woods.

I groaned. "I hope we're not all the way back to our home! It would take most of another month to get to Dad's village."

We exited the yard. Nathan surveyed the area. "This doesn't look like the same road, though."

"I think you're right."

Seth shrugged. "If we are back, which direction would lead to your house?"

I pointed to the right, where the road descended. "I don't feel this is the same road, but if we have been transported all the way back home, that route will lead us back to the city and the road to our house."

We mounted the horses, which still had all our supplies on them, and we drove them at a light trot. Eagerness to discover our location pushed us onward. Yet the road felt different enough, I didn't seriously think we had gone back home.

However, I did find it harder to breathe here. We had to be high up. No doubt we would have to find a mountain trail to get down. The horses breathed hard as well. We slowed their trot so as not to push them too much.

After traveling for a few miles, we stopped to eat and relieve ourselves. I pushed through some brush to find a private place. As I did, I saw open sky ahead through the trees. I kept going, dodging a thorn bush, until I broke through.

I stood on the edge of a precipice. Wind whipped my hair around as I grabbed a tree to keep from falling off. I leaned over the edge to get a better view. Clouds floated far below us, and I couldn't make out any detail on the landscape below. Instead, patches of green and browns, with bodies of water dotting the land, lay serenely many miles below us. But the horizon appeared different than I had ever seen it from any height. It curved in an exaggerated arc, and layered over the blue I normally saw, a dusky black threatened to break through. And though the sun blazed in the sky, a few stars dimly sparkled above me.

A thought occurred to me. As improbable as it seemed, this land mass floated in the sky high above the ground. This is worse than being transported home. Here, we had no way to get off.

I leaned further out to verify my guess, and I gasped. I couldn't breathe! I pulled myself back and sucked in the air my lungs demanded. I flopped onto the ground and banged my fist into the dirt. "Rodan's prisons never end!"

I pushed my way back through the bushes after relieving myself and caught Nathan and Seth's attention.

"Uncle, Nathan, follow me. You'll have to see this to believe it."

They stared at each other and then followed. I leaned against a tree as they both scanned the horizon far below us.

Seth spoke first. "We're on a sky-island."

I asked, "You've heard of them before?"

He nodded as he stared downward. "Yes. From below, they appear to be a cloud. On top is flat land where various creatures live. But this is the first time I've been on one. A time or two, I thought I spotted one in the sky."

"But you said they look like clouds?"

"Yes, that's why they're hard to spot. But once in a prairie, a rock fell from the sky by my feet. I looked up and a big cloud floated overhead. Dust continued to fall from it as if someone above had kicked it off the cloud."

Nathan rammed his hand into a tree. "Now we're stuck up here! Rodan will eventually find us and then, zap!"

Seth frowned. "His prison is much bigger than we thought."

After a few seconds passed, we returned to our horses on the road. My horse neighed and stomped its hooves. I patted it on the neck to calm her down.

Seth pulled himself up in the saddle. "We might as well keep putting distance between us and Rodan. It might not do much good, but at least it's something."

I admit, depression had settled in. I tried to hold it off, but one problem led to another in a never-ending stream, and I grew tired of dealing with them. But I mounted the horse and nudged it onward.

As we progressed down the road, the horses acted strangely. My horse shook its head from side to side as if trying to shoo away flies. Nathan struggled to keep his trotting straight.

A small house came into view. A water trough sat in the front yard.

"Let's see if we can water our horses here." I pointed at the house.

We dismounted and Seth knocked on the door. A moment passed until the door cracked open.

Joel stuck his head out. "Well, hi there! Good to see you again. What can I do for you?"

I stumbled backwards, and Nathan grabbed me before I fell. I couldn't believe Joel's grinning face staring at me.

I steadied myself on the porch's post. "What are you doing here?"

"Would you believe, a deacon's retreat?" He smiled.

I shook my head. "No, I wouldn't."

"I didn't think so." He noticed our horses. "Oh yes, it's fine to water your horses here. As a matter of fact, it should be very beneficial for them. Meanwhile, you all come in and have some food."

Seth met my eyes. "I assume you know this guy?"

I frowned. "Yeah. He claims to be a deacon from Ramonth. Now I'm beginning to wonder."

"A necessary precaution," Joel said. "But please come in, we can talk more freely inside."

I felt I would soon get another unwelcome surprise. But he had helped me out the last time. Better to let him explain himself. This should be good.

He served us the same recipe of tea I drank in Ramonth, and the flavor still danced around my mouth. He placed crackers and dried meat before us. The smells and display drove my hunger into the open. Nathan and Seth ate well too.

After swallowing a tender morsel of beef, I glanced at Joel and noticed that he stared at me. "So who are you, really?"

"A friend."

"You mean a stalker. How did you know I would be up here?"

"Let's just say, God decided you needed more direct intervention."

"God decided? How would you know that?"

"I work for Him."

"Oh? And what is this job?"

He gazed at the ceiling. "Sort of like your father. He had his calling. I have mine."

I sat up. "Don't tell me, you have a ring."

He laughed. "Oh no. But I've been given a job and the means to do it." He stared at me with longing eyes.

A knot formed in my gut. "Does this job involve me?"

He nodded. "We'll be working…very closely together."

I sprang from my chair, knocking it backwards onto the floor. "We will not be together! I'm reserved for God, not for any man!" I stomped to the door.

I heard Joel rise from his chair and his voice called out, "Kaylee, why not? What are you afraid of?"

I flung the door open and swung around. Seth stared at me as if trying to understand my reaction; Nathan gazed uncomfortably at the table top. I met Joel's eyes. "I am not afraid of anything, least of all, you. Now, leave me alone!" I fled out the door, slamming it behind me.

I paused in the middle of the yard. I wanted to hop on my horse and gallop away. But if this man could follow me to a sky-island, where could I go to lose him?

I threw my head back and screamed in frustration. "God, what are you doing this for?"

"For you, that's what."

I twirled around to find Joel had sneaked up behind me. I whipped my sword out of its sheath and established my stance. Maybe I could scare him away. "For me? Come on, I'm not that gullible. Why don't you leave me be!"

He shook his head. "You don't need to do this."

My mind didn't agree. "Go away!"

"You saw me fight Beltrid, give it up."

"And I saw you nearly get killed. Who saved your rear?"

He smiled. "I fared much better than you did against Beltrid, so I've heard."

He heard? How could he have heard about that? Only Dad and Beltrid knew how he controlled me. "Did you learn that from Beltrid? Is he your real master?"

"I told you already."

I had heard enough; time to chase this man away. I raised my sword and swung toward him, intending to cut his tunic, maybe draw a little blood.

Out of nowhere, a fiery sword swung out to meet mine, and the flat of our blades clanked together, then slid downward until we locked hilts. A quiver fled down my arms as we locked eyes and held our pose.

He winked. "Sure you wouldn't rather have some more tea instead?"

I shoved him back and immediately jabbed to hit his shoulder. He pulled back and to the side as my blade passed by his arm. He pushed my blade into the air with his, and swung it down around my feet.

He pointed down. "Your shoe laces are untied."

"That's an old trick. You'll have to do better than that."

He pulled back and nodded downward. "I'm serious. I don't want you tripping and getting hurt."

I chanced a glance down. He had somehow cut my laces with his sword! Who is this man? I focused on him. "You're not scoring any points showing off."

"You mean, you're not impressed yet?" He winked.

"I'm not that kind of girl!"

I decided to try Nathan's move on him. I flipped my wrist, circled the blade, and plunged it toward him as Nathan had taught me. He circled the opposite way until his sword ran the length of mine, and his tip planted against my guard. Then he pushed me back and flipped his sword, ripping mine from my hand as I fell backwards onto the ground.

I landed with a thud. He raised his sword and drove it toward me. I flinched as he landed on his knee and stabbed the fiery blade into the grass beside me. He leaned over me and smiled. "And I'm not that kind of guy."

He arose and pulled the sword from the ground, then stepped back toward the house. I lay there, staring into the blackened sky dotted with hazy stars, panting heavily as I sought to regain my breath. Did God really send this man? Why? What sin had I committed that deserved this? I felt so helpless.

And yet, he didn't take advantage of it. Then again, he wouldn't try with Seth and Nathan around. Yes, they would be my protection from this crazy man, whoever he worked for. I rose to my feet and retrieved my sword.

Joel sat on the porch as if he waited for me. I felt fear, uncertainty, and curiosity battling for prominence within me at the same time. But I forced my eyes to remain confident. "Obviously I can't get rid of you. But know this. I don't want you with me, I'll do everything I can to get rid of you, and I'll make your life miserable."

He nodded. "Sounds like a deal. I'll take it."

I harrumphed in disgust and spit on the ground. "But stay out of my way. I don't need your help!"

I spun around and headed toward the horses. I froze. The horses, still slurping water from the trough, had grown wings. I stood there, my mouth hanging open.

Joel rose and stood behind me. "Like I said, the water would be very beneficial for them. I knew you would need a way down."

I didn't know what to say. We did need a way down, but I didn't want to accept Joel's gift. Not after what I had just said.

He moved around me. "This could work, if you give it a chance. I'm restricted in what I can do, what God allows me to do. We can be friends, can't we?"

I turned to face him. His eyes pleaded with me. Maybe I had overreacted. I sat down on the porch and placed my head between my legs, hands on my head. I breathed deep to calm my mind and clear racing emotions from my thoughts.

What did my heart say? I had forgotten about it in my reaction to all this. I didn't love him. But what of brotherly love, like I had for Nathan? Would Joel love me in such a way? Or was this an elaborate ruse to trick me into a relationship with him?

No, that couldn't be it. Father Peter knew God too well to be tricked in that way; he wouldn't have associated with someone deceptive. A sense that Joel told the truth settled in my heart. I still couldn't figure out why God would send someone like him to me. Even his smile annoyed me. I sighed. God forced me into this for some reason.

I lifted my head. "All right, here's how it is. Be my mentor, my guide, my prophet, whatever you want to call it. But understand our relationship can never go beyond friendship. No physical contact. No hugs or anything of that nature.

"But let this sink into your skull—I don't love you. Understand?"

He sighed. "I understand." He gazed into the distance. "We have a long road ahead of us."

Nathan and Seth rejoiced upon seeing the winged horses.

"This is great! Now we can get down. But how did you do this?" Nathan fixed his eyes on me.

"I didn't. Joel did it."

Nathan jumped onto his horse's back. "Hum. How do you get the horse to fly?"

Joel stood in front of Nathan. "Normally you would say, 'Upwards.'"

The horse spread its wings and flapped them as it leaped into the air. Nathan's eyes grew wide, but he held on. The horse fell onto the ground, jolting Nathan flat onto its back.

Joel pointed at the horse. "But it will be of no use to you up here. The air's too thin."

Seth cleared his throat. "Hate to disagree, but how are we breathing then?"

Joel waved his hands around. "It's the magic of the place. It enriches the air that is here to compensate, so even though it is thin, you get more benefit from what you do breathe in."

"So how do we get off this rock if we can't fly off?" Nathan asked.

"Head down this road. It leads to the edge of the floating island. Then you ride off it. You'll fall for a few thousand feet before the air is thick enough for the horses to gain control."

"You want us to fall off this rock?" Nathan's rounded eyes stared at Joel.

"That's the only way off. Short of getting Rodan to magically send you back. And I don't think that's going to happen."

"Why can't you do that? You have wizard-like powers."

Joel stared at the ground. "As I told Kaylee, I'm restricted. And I should add, the wings will only be available until you reach the ground. So you can't use the horses to fly to Reol, just straight down."

Nathan grunted. "Why does God make this so hard?"

Joel smiled. "I don't know all things. But I think it isn't so much that God is making this harder than it needs to be, but that you're not ready for the steam house yet."

Nathan's eyes drooped. "You mean I'm holding this up?"

"Like I said, I don't know everything. I'm not God. But I do know you're not ready yet."

Nathan met Joel's eyes. "No, I'm not."

"I think God's going to make it so you are ready by the time you arrive."

Nathan nodded. "I sure hope so. Guess I should put my mind to learning my lessons well."

Joel grinned. "Now, you all go jump off a cliff. Time's running out on those wings."

I stared at him. He did have a certain appeal. But I couldn't let on that I had any positive feelings toward him at all, beyond simple friendship. The last thing I wanted to do was encourage him. It would be bad enough putting up with his longing stares at me.

We mounted the horses, thanked Joel, and took off down the road. I nudged the horse into a strong gallop. The others followed, and we charged down the road as if running from Beltrid himself.

Seth yelled, barely audible over the horse's beating hooves, "Don't forget to breathe deep before we go over. It will be a while before we reach breathable air."

The end of the road came into view. My heart pounded in my chest as the edge approached. Everything in me said stop, but I kept the horse moving forward. Then it leaped into the air. I sucked in as much air as possible before sailing past the edge. Leagues of air lay below me. We dived toward the ground, leaving my heart several feet above me.

My hair whipped back as I plunged toward the earth. Biting cold numbed my fingers and nose. The horse knew what to do—she kept her wings flat against her body as we sped downward. I turned behind me to see the sky-island floating amidst the clouds. The trees disappeared from view as we sank; the cloud-looking bottom merged with other puffs of white until I had trouble discerning it from the rest.

Nathan and Seth held onto their horses, but Nathan's eyes flared wide in the wind. He didn't like the ride.

I, on the other hand, enjoyed it. The view from so high filled me with awe. Vast landscapes dotted the horizon. I felt free up here, like I should have been born a bird.

I glanced back at Nathan. One of his legs had slid out of the foot-strap. He rose out of his saddle and streamed behind the horse, holding only onto the reins. His mouth opened but I could hear nothing with the thin air rushing around me. He struggled to breathe.

I worried for him. Fear sang across his face. But the horses wouldn't be able to do anything until we reached thicker air.

My lungs demanded something to suck in. I expelled the stale air and attempted to breathe in fresh, but I gagged and struggled to find relief. My head grew light, and I feared I might fall unconscious.

The ground drew closer. I could make out individual trees below us, and the path cutting through the forest. The air grew warmer. My horse spread her wings, and angled out of the dive. The air grew thick enough to keep me barely conscious as I breathed in hard gasps.

I watched as Nathan settled back down upon his horse, but he landed off kilter and slid off the horse's back. He fell under the horse as she attempted to level out, and pulled the horse's head downward.

I banked my steed toward him. As I approached, his horse lost control and spun around. Nathan lost his grip and sailed away from his mount, his eyes and mouth wide open.

"Downward," I shouted and pushed on the back of the horses' neck. The horse folded her wings against her body and sank into a dive.

I guided the horse with the reins and pulled under Nathan. I grabbed his right hand and pulled him down behind me.

"Hold on!" I leveled the horse back out. Seth now flew a few feet above us and to the side. He shook his head. I smiled back.

The horses spiraled downward at a steady rate. The ground grew more detailed. Trees waved in the wind, birds fluttered from treetop to treetop, and the sun danced across bodies of water.

Now that we had slowed, I said to Nathan, "You really need to practice your horsemanship."

"Yeah. Remember to get more training on winged horses. Check."

I felt his heart beating rapidly against my back as he clung uncomfortably tight to me. I laughed inside, but smiled on the outside. I didn't want to embarrass him any further.

As we descended, I saw the tree-wall blocking the path. It had grown down the path for many yards. It would have been difficult to get around, maybe impossible if Rodan had designed it that way. At least now we could land on the opposite side.

The treetops rose above us as we descended. The horses leveled out and galloped upon the road before letting themselves settle onto it. Nathan's empty horse followed us. We pulled them to a stop.

I dismounted. "You all right, Uncle?"

He breathed hard, but grinned. "That was fun. But a little harrowing too." He dismounted with Nathan.

Nathan didn't say anything. With a pale face, he sat against a tree and rested.

Seth nodded. "Looks like a good idea. Let's take a breather before we get going again."

I noticed the horses had already lost their wings. "Do you think there are such things as winged horses?"

Seth gazed at the horses, grazing in a small patch of grass. "I've heard stories, though until today I had never seen one."

"If there's one to be had, I want one."

"If the stories I've heard are true, you can't own them. More like you befriend them."

I nodded. "That would be even better."

After Nathan recovered and vowed never to ride a winged horse again—not that he would likely get another opportunity—we rode on down the path. Seth said a city, Holoroth, lay not too many miles away. He promised the city held no big surprises. I feared he couldn't deliver on that promise.

As we drew near, more houses appeared along the road or up a path into the forest. As we passed one such road, I heard a wail echo from the path.

"Let's check it out," I said and nudged my horse toward the road.

Nathan frowned. "Kaylee, why? We don't have time to check out every little cry along the way."

"I have a hunch."

Seth laughed. "Just like her father. It's no use arguing, my nephew. Do what she says." He flipped his reins and the horse followed after her.

Nathan groaned and then did the same.

The closer we came to the house, the louder the wailing grew. When we broke into the clearing, a woman sat on the grass and a child, about eleven, lay in her lap. I jumped from my horse and ran to her.

"Ma'am, what happened?"

She raised her eyes to meet mine. "My son, he fell out of this tree and broke his leg. The bleeding inside has grown and now he dies. He's my only son."

My heart broke. I knelt beside him and felt his forehead. The cold sting of death radiated up my palm. I felt for a pulse, no throbbing of blood coursed through his veins. I hated to tell her, but he was dead. Yet what did my heart say?

I struggled to get past the sorrow I felt and see what God wanted me to do. It seemed the right thing to heal the child. Heal? More like bringing someone back from the dead. Yet that's what I heard the ring saying to do. The more I searched, the clearer I felt about it.

"Ma'am, I can try and heal him."

Her wailing turned to a whimper. She stared at me. "It's been twenty-five years since anyone could do such things—since Sisko roamed these lands."

I nodded. "I know." I placed my hand on the child. "Lord, heal this body and restore his life."

A couple seconds passed until the child jerked. Color rushed back into his face. His swollen leg shrank until it appeared normal again. His eyes flickered open. They darted between me and his mother.

"Momma?"

She fell upon him, hugging him in her arms and weeping tears of joy. "Oh my child, my child, my child…"

I glanced at Seth and Nathan. Seth smiled back. Nathan's jaw hung

139

loose. It dawned on me that Nathan had never seen the ring do anything until now. If I thought I could get away with it, I would have kidded him. But the mother had to remain my focus now.

She grabbed me and hugged tight. "Oh thank you, thank you, thank you!"

"You're more than welcome," I responded. "I only ask one thing of you."

"What? Anything! I'll give you everything I have."

"No, no. I don't need anything you have, but I do request that you tell no one about this."

Her face fell. "No one?"

I shook my head. "I'm Sisko's daughter and he's in trouble. If word of this gets out, it could mean his death."

"Oh!" She paused as if in thought. "I won't tell anyone, I promise."

"At least not until you hear others mentioning I can do these things."

She nodded. "But at least allow me to house you. Please stay the night here. I would be so honored." She bowed.

I glanced at Seth and Nathan. They both nodded it would be fine, even Nathan. "All right, ma'am. We'll stay."

She bounded up and pulled us toward the cottage. The wooden building stood among the trees, yet appeared small next to them. A six foot wide porch led to the front door; no curtains hung in the windows.

We entered, and the inside greeted us with warmth and simplicity: a couple of small beds in one corner, a half-full pot hung over a small fire under the mantle, and a round table stood in the middle surrounded by a couple of chairs.

She pulled a crate up to the table. "Sit, sit. I'll get you something to eat." We sat.

The boy stood by the table, watching me.

I caught his eye and leaned toward him. "You have a name, son?"

"Jacob."

"Hi Jacob, my name's Kaylee."

He smiled and a warm feeling flooded over me.

The lady placed three bowls of soup in front of us and a plate of bread in the middle. "I'm sorry. My name's Gabrielle."

We all froze. Nathan cleared his throat. "Gabrielle?"

She nodded. "Is there something wrong with that name?"

"No, no," I said. "Not at all. You see, it's just that…it's our mother's name."

"Oh." She smiled weakly. "I can see why that would give you pause." She sat down on the edge of her bed.

A rap sounded from the door. Gabrielle's face sagged. "One minute." She rose and answered it.

A man's voice could be heard, and he didn't make any pretense of caring if we overheard. "Who? I don't care who you have in there, it's my time to collect. Either I come in and get my due or you're out."

She mumbled some words I couldn't make out.

"Then tell them to leave, or I'll force you out with them! This place isn't free you know."

She mumbled more words.

"No, either I get it, or you're out of here tonight. I'll not wait."

Nathan gritted his teeth and stood up. He stepped resolutely to the door, his hand on the hilt of his sword, and flung the door wide open.

Nathan stood tall in the door-frame. "Sir, I'm sure it will not hurt you to wait one more day. We'll be gone and out of the way. But let the lady have her company."

"Boy, how dare you poke your nose into other people's business. I'll teach you a lesson."

Through the open door I saw the man draw his sword. Nathan swung his out and leaped onto the porch.

26

I flew to the door. Nathan stood in his stance while the man shifted back and forth. Blood dripped from Nathan's shoulder. Instinctively I reached for my sword, but I didn't draw it. I knew Nathan wouldn't appreciate me charging in to save him, but I would need to be ready if this man beat him. Still, I didn't want to kill anyone either. I wondered if the conflicting emotions would prevent me from acting when needed.

The man jabbed; Nathan dodged. He was testing Nathan, seeing what he might do before he committed. Nathan watched the man's sword, but I knew from training he took in much more than that.

The man twisted his wrist and pushed Nathan's sword to his right. Nathan flipped his tip under, around, and pulled the man's blade back up and out. Then he pulled his blade down and planted it into the man's upper shoulder.

The man yelled and dropped his sword. Based on the flow of blood, Nathan had hit an artery, and the man would soon die if not cared for. I sped toward them.

"Hold on, Nathan." I dropped by the side of the man and examined the wound. "You'll die soon if this isn't taken care of."

He stared at me as if not sure what to think.

"You're not going to heal the man, are you?" Nathan asked.

"I'm thinking, yes."

"He'll just try to kill me again."

The man's eyes stared off blankly into the air.

I shook my head. "I don't think so." I placed my hand upon him. "Lord, heal this sword wound and replace his life blood."

The man's eyes rolled up and then back down. He blinked. "What happened?"

"You almost died is what happened. My brother stabbed you in a sword fight, but I healed you."

He stared at me. "Why did you do that?" He blinked. "How did you do that?"

I smiled at him. "Maybe I figured you might take advantage of a second chance. Make your life better. Show others the kindness I've just shown you."

He stared at the ground. "And if I don't?"

"Well, let's say your fate in the next life might be even worse for having had the chance and ignored it." I stood up. "I wouldn't let it pass you by if I were you. But it's your life.

"However, I would ask that you return tomorrow if you want your rent. Let us stay the night, we'll be gone in the morning."

He nodded, apparently confused by my kindness. "Sure. But who are you?"

"A friend."

He stared at me for a moment, then rose and plodded down the path back to the road.

We reentered the house. Gabrielle, Jacob, and Seth had watched from a window. We sat at the table again.

Gabrielle stared at us for a moment and then said, "I don't know how I can ever thank you. But I feel so ashamed."

Seth placed a hand on her shoulder. "Don't be. Many have financial troubles."

She sighed. "You don't understand. He…" She glanced at Jacob. "He is paid with favors. Jacob is his son."

Nathan pounded a fist on the table. "You should have let him die, Kaylee!"

I shook my head. "He may be back tomorrow, but I have a feeling he won't be the same man."

Gabrielle approached Nathan and hugged him. "Thank you so much. I can't recall the last time someone has stood up for me like that."

Nathan blushed. "It was the only decent thing to do."

I remembered Nathan's wound. Dried blood had stained his tunic. "Nathan, let me take a look at your wound."

He waved his hand. "No, no, it's only a scratch. I don't need you to heal me."

I frowned at him. "Who said anything about healing you? I simply wanted to clean it up and bandage it."

Gabrielle jumped up. "I can do that." She grabbed a towel, dipped it in a bucket of water, pulled back his tunic to reveal his chest, and wiped carefully around the wound.

I had the distinct impression that he enjoyed the attention, the way he kept staring into her eyes. Hero syndrome, no doubt. I almost expected him to say he would stay there with her. A glance at Seth told me he had the same thoughts.

We finished our meal and bedded down on the floor for the night. I felt for this family—so destitute and desperate. I wished I could do more for them. Thoughts filled my dreams as the night wore on.

My dreams surfaced and I awoke with a start. The night had grown black. Crickets chirped loudly and a chill whipped into the room with each blast of wind. She didn't have oil. Only the very poor didn't have enough oil to keep a lamp lit at night. My thoughts swirled around in my head.

I felt I needed to walk them off, so I arose, and tip-toed toward the door. Nathan mumbled something in his sleep and tossed about, hitting a wall. I watched him for a moment, but he soon settled down, so I stepped outside.

A body sat on the small porch. "About time you came out."

"Joel? Did you wake me up?"

He gazed at me. "No, not at all. I knew it would happen is all. Have a seat." He patted the porch step next to him.

I hesitated, but figured it might be a good test of his intentions. I sat down and watched the stars blink in the sky. "I've often wondered what's up there among the stars. Perhaps I'll find out in the next life."

He laughed. "Your father found out, did he not?"

His mention of Dad reminded me. "You said you had a calling like my dad's. What is that calling?"

He paused while he bent down to pick up a stone and throw it at a tree. "In your father's stories, did he usually go around telling everyone what his calling was?"

"No, but his calling wasn't about a specific person either. You said your calling involved me. Shouldn't I know about it?"

His eyes met mine. "Unfortunately, I'm working under restrictions. To tell you that would destroy what I'm hoping to achieve." He gazed back at the stars. "However, I can say once we're in the next life, I would enjoy visiting those stars with you while they're burning."

I didn't know what to say. On one hand, his lofty opinion, even if I didn't share his assessment or have similar feelings toward him, sent a spark of joy through me. On the other, it sounded like another calculated statement to make me melt, and those tended to have the opposite effect. The feelings canceled each other out.

"If it were me, I would spend eternity visiting them."

He nodded. "I don't think you'll notice them."

"Why not?"

He stared at me like I should know. "Why, because God outshines everything else, and you can spend eternity exploring infinite love."

It sounded logical, but, "How would you know?"

He cleared his throat. "Haven't you ever read theology? St. Symeon the New Theologian?"

"Huh, no. Not really."

He smiled. "You really should. And I could tutor you, give you personal attention if you'd like."

Does he ever give up? "I'll give it some thought." I watched his face as he stared into the night sky. The glow of starlight outlined his profile; an inner strength and wisdom resided in him. I shook my head and rubbed my eyes. He was drawing me in, trying to get me to love him. "But I wouldn't count on it. I would really hate to break a prophet's heart."

"Oh, I'm a prophet now? No problem. Prophets' hearts get broken all the time. You wouldn't be the first."

I felt like I'd seen a glimpse of his real self for the first time. After working to help someone for years, then to have them ditch God and end up in hell—to preside over who knows how many untold horrors of sin and not fixing it as easily as I had fixed the man's shoulder earlier—I couldn't imagine the sorrow he'd lived through.

He was doing it again! I had to change the focus. "So, as my official mentor, how did I do today?"

"Beautiful. Your father would be proud."

"But this woman and her son, they live in such poverty. I feel like I should help, but I don't know how."

"You'll figure it out."

"You talk as if you know what I will do."

He nodded. "I do. That's why I can't say anything. Like I said, I operate under restrictions."

"I understand. Actually, I'm understanding a lot more now than I ever have before." I arose from the step and patted him on the back. "Thanks."

He remained silent for a couple of seconds as I reached the door. "You're welcome?"

As I opened the door, I realized why he had ended his sentence with a question. I had touched him, without thinking about it, and it surprised him after all my talk about no physical contact. I had to be more careful. It was innocent enough, but he would interpret it as more than that. I shut the door behind me.

As I snuggled under my blanket, my thoughts centered on Joel. Such a mystery, yet his whole demeanor provoked a negative reaction in me. He appeared for all the world like a love-sick puppy begging for attention. Starved was more like it. But for all that, something about him appealed to me. No, I couldn't let thoughts like that cloud my judgment. I had to keep my guard up with him.

I drifted off to sleep.

The movement of creaking boards and shuffling feet woke me. Nathan and Seth already sat at the table, eating more soup and bread. I hated that we ate all their food. But before I could protest, Gabrielle had placed a bowl of soup on the table and urged me to eat.

I sat and ate. I kept thinking about something I could do for this lady and her son. My mind recalled a prophet many years ago who had come to a widow and her son. He had provided oil so they could make bread. Is that what I needed to do?

We finished our breakfast and packed up to leave. Still I had no clear idea of what I should do, and I knew enough not to invent something myself. Either God would make it clear, or He knew it would be best for me not to get involved, as much as I wanted to. The former would be easier to handle.

I prepared to put my foot in the stirrup when Gabrielle tapped me on the shoulder. I turned to face her.

"You have done so much for me and my son, I could never repay you."

"You don't have to. Your joy is payment enough. Trust me."

She reached out and took my hand. "Still, we want to give you something, even though it could never be enough." She pushed two coins in my hand. Not even enough to buy a pound of grain.

I put my palm back in her hand. "No, I couldn't take this. I have plenty, really."

"No, you must take it. I am giving it to you." She pushed my hand back.

I felt something more in my hand now. I opened it up and saw beside the coins a key with a crystal protrusion. I picked it up and showed it to her. "Gabrielle, you have already richly paid me."

She wrinkled her brow. "Where did that come from?"

"Too long a story and you likely wouldn't believe it. But know that this means all the world to me, and it came from you." I already knew what virtue this represented: generosity. I also knew I couldn't give her the coins back. She wouldn't hear of it.

I wrapped my arms around her. "Thank you so much for your generosity." I glanced up to see Nathan and Seth beaming.

146

I pulled myself upon the horse and waved as we headed down the path. I felt great, except I never felt any idea click as to how to help her. She had given to me instead.

No sooner had we entered the main roadway when we saw Gabrielle's landlord traveling up the road. I figured we would pass on by him. I knew he probably came for Gabrielle, and it didn't appear he had changed. But as he approached, he waved us down much to my delight.

"I wanted to say thank you. I've done a lot of thinking, and visited the priest this morning." He stared at the ground. "I've done this lady wrong. She doesn't have much, barely two pennies to rub together."

I felt like I had been hit in the gut. She had given me everything she had.

He continued, not noticing my reaction. "So we agreed to pay for the rent by sexual means."

"We discovered as much, Sir," Nathan said with a hint of disgust on his lips.

The man shuffled his feet nervously. "Well, I decided to set things as right as I can make them. I'm going to propose to her. If she'll have me, we'll get married and I'll take care of her and Jacob. If she doesn't want to, then I'll help her somehow to earn a living so she can pay me rent with money."

I smiled. "That's very good of you." Then a thought landed. "Hold on, Sir. I have something you can use."

I dug in my pocket and pulled out the two coins Gabrielle had given me. I handed them to him. "If you will plant these between the two biggest roots of the old tree in her yard, I think you'll find the money multiplies for you. That will give her something to invest in getting a business going."

He took the coins from me. His eyes narrowed. "Are you pulling my leg?"

"Would I do that after I had brought you back from the edge of death?"

"What's your name?"

"I would rather it wasn't spread around right now. Just do what I said and all will be fine. And, Sir?"

"Yes?"

I patted him on the back. "I hope she says yes."

He grinned. "Me too."

We trotted on down the road. Nathan rode up alongside of me. "Are those coins really going to grow money?"

I laughed. "No. God told me an old treasure chest lay buried between those roots by thieves long ago. When they dig down to plant those coins, they'll find it."

Seth snapped his fingers. "I knew that place looked familiar! That's where my gang and I buried our loot many years ago. I never could remember where we had put it."

Nathan and I couldn't help but laugh. Seth joined in with us, though I wondered if he wished he could go back and get some of it. If so, he didn't show it. So far, this miracle worker job had turned out great. Though I would feel better when we had freed Amma and Dad.

We hadn't ridden too many hours before the city gates of Holoroth loomed before us. While not big, a lot of people still lived within its walls. Once through the gates, people strolled while others stepped about briskly as if on important business.

Along one road, a market lined the street. Reds, yellows, blues, and deep purples contrasted against the gold and silver sparkling in the sunlight among the many tables. A cacophony of voices haggled and chatted among the various vendor stands. The smell of fresh-cooked meats lingered in the air, stoking feelings of hunger. I could picture Gabrielle and Jacob selling here at some point.

An inn stood on the corner from which songs and cheer could be heard over the street noise. Seth halted; I stopped alongside of him. "Uncle, we don't have a reason to stay here. We should ride on through. There's still plenty of daylight to travel by."

He nodded. "Yes, but we should stock up at the market. There's not another chance before reaching your father's village."

We found a place to leave the horses. Nathan dropped down. "Why don't you two go do the shopping. I'll stay here and watch the horses."

"Sure, brother. Don't get in any trouble while we're gone." I laughed as he drew his sword.

I quickly drew mine and parried his attempt. "Now, now, brother. People might get the wrong idea and you'll have a whole town rushing to aid the damsel in distress."

He glanced around. A few did indeed watch us. He sheathed his sword and grinned. "You don't get into any trouble either. I would hate to get off my lazy rear to rescue you."

I sheathed my sword and smirked at him. Seth and I strolled down the market street. Seth searched mostly for dried meats and cheeses. While he bartered for those, I grazed among the jewelry. All sorts of rings and necklaces filled the stands. Bracelets beat from gold glittered in the sunlight.

As I browsed, one bracelet stood out. The metal circled around into an oval at the top. A picture had been engraved upon the oval—a winged horse. I stared at it, entranced. Memories of flying through the air returned. The freedom and thrill found its way back into my mind.

The merchant ducked behind his counter and popped back up. I didn't notice, until he spoke, that Joel had replaced him.

"Would you like to try this bracelet on? It appears to have been created just for you."

I jerked my head up. "Joel? What are you doing here? You can't take over someone's booth!"

"As long as I make him a good profit, why would he care?"

"Where is he?"

"Taking a nap on the floor." Joel stared at the ground. "And he needed one too. Works too many hours. It'll do him some good."

Joel pulled the bracelet out and placed it on my arm. "Beautiful! Matches the person it's on."

I stared at him. "I don't get it. Why do you call me beautiful? I was before the troll bite, but now I'm pretty homely."

"Maybe because I see what's inside, not what's on the outside."

Did he have a list of perfect things to say to swoon any girl into his arms? I held the bracelet up. A warm glow emanated from it. The lines of the winged horse flared with an inner fire. Ripples of subtle reds and blues spread across the golden surface. It held my eyes in its trance.

He smiled. "You must have it. It's yours."

I glanced up. "But I shouldn't spend money on this. We may need it for food and supplies. We have a long trip back home once we have finished at Reol."

Joel pulled a purse out and slipped several coins into the merchant's money box.

"No, you can't do that!"

"Sure I can. I'm doing it now."

I grabbed the bracelet to take it off. It wouldn't release me; it held securely around my arm. "Let me take this off. I don't want it!"

"I meant it when I said it was created for you. It's yours now."

"No, I'm serious. Get this off me."

"I can't. Once it's on, it's on."

I groaned. "Is all jewelry from God like the ring? Put it on and you can never take it off again!"

"Shush, not so loud."

I stomped the ground. I did like this bracelet. Why then did I fight having it? The answer settled in me: because Joel gave it to me. I didn't want to feel like I owed him, like he had bought me anything. What would he expect in return? But it appeared I had no choice.

"Fine. So now I have a bracelet that won't come off. What does this thing do anyway?"

He grinned. "I can't tell you."

I held the bracelet up into the sunlight. "Great. Another puzzle to decipher. Do I ever get any answers?"

"Eh? What do you mean?"

I dropped my gaze back to the counter. Joel had left and the merchant now stood rubbing his eyes. He focused on my arm and pointed.

"Did you pay for that?"

I nodded. "Yes, Sir."

He checked the cash box and his eyes lit up. "Oh, all right. Guess my mind blanked out for a moment. I should do that more often."

I strolled back to Seth as he gathered various supplies into his shirt, converted into a carrying bag.

The bracelet sparkled sunlight into his eyes, and he squinted. "Where did you get that? You didn't waste our money on it, did you?"

"No, Uncle. I wouldn't do that. Joel, well, he bought it for me."

He raised an eyebrow. "Bought it for you, eh? So, you two discussed marriage plans yet?"

"Uncle!"

"You're not getting any younger."

"I'm sixteen! And I wouldn't marry him even if he were an angel."

"Then who? A demon?" He grinned.

"Uncle! I'm marrying no one save God."

He rubbed his head. "I don't know. Accepting a bracelet like that sort of commits you to him, I think."

I swung at him, and he ducked laughing. But I did want to hit him. I wanted to release the frustration I felt.

"You're as bad as Nathan. I didn't accept anything!" I stomped back to the horses. My face felt flushed. I stared at the bracelet. What did this mean? What did it do? I felt like I had just been swindled into something I would regret.

27

As soon as we left the city, and the solitude of the open road surrounded us once again, I recalled the key we had received. I pulled the pack open and unwrapped the crystal ball. Amma stood frozen in the faceted rock, hands raised and face turning away. "We're close to freeing you, Amma. Don't worry." I pulled the key out and examined the protrusion. It had the shape of two overlapping coins. I found the hole and, as expected, it read "GEN" over the top of it.

I inserted it and broke it off. "Two more, and we'll have freed Amma." I packed it away.

Nathan sighed. "Two more, but they both will be difficult to find. Someone who exhibits true contentment and love will be rare." He flipped his reins and we continued our journey.

Seth pointed to a distant set of hills. "Your father's village is on the other side of those hills. About another three day's journey."

As we rode along at a good trot, my thoughts returned to the bracelet. Maybe it would lead me to a winged horse. But who knew what it could do, or how to use it? Could there be some words that would activate the thing? Why did God want me to have this, or did Joel try to win me over as Seth suggested? Though I knew he was kidding me, and if he thought I had taken him seriously, he would say I had overreacted, still...

I sighed. When God knew I could handle it, He would reveal it. Until then, it belonged to me. Though I did hope in some way it allowed me to befriend such a winged horse. The thought struck me with awe, and my mind wandered through the clouds as we rode along the ground.

The rest of the day drifted by without incident. A nice change of pace. I hoped maybe the rest of the trip would be like this and no more surprises would pop up. Not likely, based on all we had experienced so far. I examined my bulging, trollish arms. These last weeks had been the craziest in my life. Surely I would wake up and find out this was all a dream.

The ache of sitting in the saddle all day reinforced it wasn't a dream. Before the sun sank behind the horizon, we set up camp. The hills now loomed closer. The stars unfurled behind the retreating sun to watch over us. We ate a meal from the dried meats and cheese Uncle Seth had bought, along with bread.

We chatted about various items of interest. Uncle Seth even told us stories of Dad when they wandered together. I had heard them from Dad, but Seth tended to put a funny spin on the events, and he took note of things Dad didn't.

The story of his own transformation held me in its grip the most. He related how Dad had broken through the rage that had haunted himself and his father, and what it felt like to suddenly go from uncontrolled anger to being stabbed by Dad across the belly, and thinking all had been lost. Then Dad had healed him, and Seth had experienced his wounds sealing up, his cut-off hand restored, and life flowing back into him.

"Uncle, couldn't you control the rage?" I asked.

"Yes and no. I had some control, but it was very difficult. Much easier to just let it fly. Everything in me wanted to let it happen even though I knew it wasn't right." He stared into the starry sky.

"That's what was so amazing about your father. He took my rage on himself and ended up defeating it. I'm sure with God's help, but he did it when the rest of us couldn't."

Nathan stared deep into the fire, as if struggling to keep his own animal in its cage. I knew he hadn't finished with his grief and guilt over Beltrid. Seth's story appeared to have struck a chord with him.

Nathan arose. "I think I'll say hi to dreamland." He entered his shelter.

Seth and I chatted for a little while longer, and then I decided to turn in as well. As I passed by Nathan's shelter, he mumbled and tossed around. I pulled back the flap. A pained expression lay on his face as he squirmed and flailed his arms in the air. Apparently a nightmare stalked his dreams of late.

My heart nudged me. I stretched out my hand and laid it on his head. "Lord, heal my brother of his nightmares."

He calmed down, yet I could tell he still fought within himself. Some battle raged inside him. Maybe the ring took longer to deal with mental sickness.

I left and entered my own shelter. I lay awake for a while, thinking, praying, hoping that our trip wouldn't end up as a nightmare. I had a feeling it wouldn't, but I had no idea what God would take me through to get there. If I knew, I would probably run home as fast as my legs could carry me. Gradually, my eyes closed and dreams formed in my mind.

A landscape materialized into view. A deeper blue than normal filled the sky and richer green colored the grass. I scanned around to see a vivid forest, while a peaceful meadow and still pond lay before me. I checked my body, but it wasn't mine—it was Nathan's.

Kaylee?

Yes?

Am I dreaming you here, or are you in my dream?

I don't know. I could probably ask you the same question.

But I've had this dream many times, and you've never been here. Never been inside my head.

I know I've never been here. Where are we?

No specific place I know of, but I've had this dream ever since the foiled attempt at marrying Crystal.

So this involves her?

Yes, and she should appear by the forest's edge…now.

Indeed, Crystal stepped from the forest and smiled. I could feel Nathan's hatred rise as if I were him. He drew his sword and moved toward her.

Nathan, what are you doing?

I have to get rid of her, kill her. Atone for my sins by wiping out however many of her there are in my memory.

But something's not right. Not if you have killed her over and over.

He didn't pay attention but lunged toward her. Her smile disappeared into fear, and horror filled her eyes.

Her eyes—something in them gave me pause. Recognition bubbled just underneath the surface of my thoughts.

She attempted to dodge the sword, but Nathan's blade wouldn't be denied. The tip swung around and plunged into her chest, cutting right into her gut. Blood poured across her stomach. Her eyes grew wide, frozen in the surety of death's grip, then she collapsed upon the grass.

She reached out a hand. "But Nathan, I love you."

He snarled. "You don't love me, you used me! You tricked me. I was nothing more than a pawn in your hands. You couldn't possibly love me."

We stood there, watching her bleed to death; revulsion filled me. I wanted to do something, but I couldn't control him—only watch the events unfold.

She cried and screamed as pains tore through her body. She lay upon the earth, calling between cries of agony, "No, I did love you. Whether you believe it or not," until her voice could no longer form the words.

His teeth ground together, and through his eyes I could see them narrowed into hate. "Die, demon of my soul, and never return."

Connections formed in my mind, and I realized what had bothered me about her eyes: she displayed the same expression right before she changed into Beltrid at the wedding. Crystal wasn't an illusion!

Nathan, listen to me. You must heal her.

Heal? Her? No way, I have to destroy her…destroy him.

Trust me. Heal her and I believe this will end.

He didn't say anything. His eyes didn't blink as he stared at her dying form. *How could I do that? I don't have a ring.*

You don't need a ring, this is your dream. Just do it.

But I hate her, how can I heal her?

Because you hate Beltrid, not Crystal. I believe Crystal is real, Beltrid possessed her. Your hate for him is conflicting with your love for her. Heal her, and you'll break the circle of hate.

He stomped around her like a wolf circling its prey. I could feel the turmoil churning in his mind. Hate and love, fighting against each other, struggling for dominion. Then I recalled the story Seth had told us; I knew what he needed.

Nathan, please use hope. You need to know there is healing. You can stop hating her. Dad did it, you can too.

He stopped circling and stared at Crystal; her blank eyes bored into the sky. Shock had taken over. He knelt beside her, reached out a shaky hand, and placed it on her body. I could feel tears rolling down his cheeks, and the force of will breaking through the hate.

"God, heal…" He sobbed, shook his head, and steeled himself. "God, heal…heal Crystal, because…" He broke down again but gathered his strength of will and forced the words out. "Because I love her!"

Since we shared the same body in this dream, I felt as if I cried along with him.

He fell upon her, holding her bloody body in his arms and pressed it to his chest. He sobbed like a little baby, rocking her back and forth upon the ground.

Then I felt her arms encircle him and a kiss upon his cheek.

Her eyes locked onto his. "Thank you, Nathan. I will always love you. You've freed me."

She vanished leaving Nathan alone upon the ground, crying.

Nathan, don't you see? That was the real Crystal, the body Beltrid used and took over. He had trapped her in his prison, and she could only be released by you, if you loved her.

He slammed both his fists upon the ground. *And all this time I've been keeping her trapped in his prison. Why can't I see these things?* He wept.

Nathan, you can. But you've allowed your hate to blind you is all. Crystal isn't the only one who needs healing.

He fell back upon the ground, staring into the vivid blue sky. He reached out his hands. "God, heal me!"

A flash filled my vision, and I jerked up from my bed. My breaths flowed shallow and quick. In a matter of seconds, Nathan's head burst through the opening. I met his eyes in the dim, moonlit darkness, staring at me.

"Were you really in my dream?" he asked.

I nodded. He leaped into the shelter and rushed to me. He hugged me tight and kissed me tenderly. If it had been any other man, I would have slapped him. Instead, I wrapped him in my arms as joy flooded over me. God had used me to heal him; I could think of no higher praise.

The next morning, I watched Nathan sipping coffee as he sat on a log. His face radiated peace and joy. I found it hard to say exactly what had changed, but I could tell a heavy weight had lifted from him.

Seth stared at him as well. "Why are you so chipper today?"

He gulped down another swallow. "Because Uncle, everything is so much more wonderful today. Life is…well, it's absolutely great!"

It had been a long time since I'd seen him this happy. "I take it your dream didn't return last night?"

He shook his head. "Nope, and I don't expect it will. But what did you do to get in there?"

Seth cast a raised eyebrow our direction.

"All I did was pray for you. Maybe God felt you needed some encouragement." I glanced at Seth. "Long story, Uncle."

He shook his head, waved his hand at us, and returned to his packing. "We should be able to make it to the hills today. Barring any tree hallways and such getting in the way."

Nathan's expression grew somber. "Kaylee, I know we need to free Mother and Father first. But after that, I'm going to find the real Crystal. Maybe I freed her from Beltrid's hate last night, but I need to know how she feels about me, and if she's truly safe."

I nodded. "And circumstances permitting, I'll go with you to help." I watched for an affirmation. "If you'll have me, of course."

A smile creased his lips. "That would be great. Thanks, Sis."

After packing, we followed the road toward the hills. As the morning wore on, the weather changed. Sunny skies grew dark. Black clouds rolled in, churning above us. A heavy shadow fell across the land and the air felt thick with moisture. The wind whipped across our faces in growing blasts.

"Looks like rain," Seth said, stating the obvious.

The road led across an open field, leaving little protection from the growing storm. Rain pelted down into sheets, soaking everything.

Seth motioned for us to hurry. "Quick," he yelled over the growing wind. "Let's cross this field before the storm gets any worse. We can take shelter in the trees."

The road crossed a stream that had swollen; water threatened to race over its banks. We pushed the horses onto the bridge and worked our way across. Then I heard a roar. I swung my head to face a churning, blackened funnel cloud bearing down upon us.

I nudged the horse into a gallop, but its hooves slid on the slick wood and its feet flew from under it, throwing me onto the bridge. I jumped to my feet—Seth and Nathan had neared the bank, but Nathan had stopped and began to race back toward me.

Then I heard the bridge ripping apart, and the world crumbled before me as shattered glass. The boards of the bridge lifted me into the air and I fell flat against them. Debris pelted me, stinging my skin. For a moment, as I sailed through the air, the board protected me from the pounding branches flying at me. Then it flipped and flew away, leaving me exposed to whipping dirt and limbs, eating away at my clothes and skin until raw pain flooded my body.

After thinking it would never end, the ground raced up to meet me. My body crashed onto the bank of the raging stream. Most of it sank into the waves, but rested against some rocks leaving my head above water. I couldn't feel anything, nor move.

As I stared half unconscious into the sky, I noticed a horse tossed among the winds, its legs flailing about. It didn't make sense; the horse had no wings. I should know why it had none, but reality grew fuzzier as the world flew above me. Consciousness slipped from my grasp, and I sank into darkness.

28

As I attempted to open my eyes, colors swam. I couldn't focus, but someone in black stood over me.

"Don't move," echoed in my mind. I tried to get up, but pain screamed through my body, and my mind spun back into darkness.

When I came to again, my eyes focused more clearly on the surroundings. I lay inside a cabin. A sound of someone moving echoed in the room. I turned my head, which resulted in the world swirling in and out of view. I grimaced at the pain, but held on. I didn't want to black out again. The world settled back into focus.

A man dressed in a black robe stood over me. His long, black beard, traced with gray, dangled from a thin face. He wore a black skull-cap and his long, wiry hair had been tied behind his head into a ponytail.

I tried to ask a question, but my throat didn't respond. It felt like dry chalk. The man seemed to sense this because he placed a cup of water to my lips.

"Gently now. Small sips."

My head pounded from the movement, but I sipped the water and it tasted like nectar. He kept feeding me the water, and I drank until I couldn't take the pain in my head any longer.

"Are you a monk?" The words had to fight against crud in my throat to get out.

He nodded. "By God's mercy."

"How long have I been out?"

"Almost a day."

I instinctively jerked my head around in surprise and wished I hadn't. Sounds entered my ears but they reverberated into indistinguishable noise, and I fell into a dark sleep again.

I opened my eyes. Crickets sang through the windows. I moved my head a bit, and though I felt a pain, my focus remained firm. I turned my head around to find the monk.

He moved into my sight. "Feeling better?"

"Yes. But I was going to ask, before I blacked out again, if you had seen two other men. They were with me."

He shook his head. "No, I'm afraid not."

I groaned. "One was my brother, Nathan. The other my uncle, Seth. I hope they're all right."

"I'm sure God will take care of them."

"This messes everything up. We had a couple more days before reaching Reol. Now who knows when we'll get there."

"Certainly not tonight."

I stared up at the ceiling. "I think a certain prophet fell asleep on the job!"

"I'll have you know I watched the whole thing. On pins and needles I was." Joel came into view next to the monk. "Like I told you, I work—"

"Under restrictions. I know."

"But I did get you to Ambrose."

Ambrose turned and bowed. "I'm at your service, Joel."

I stared at them. "You two know each other?"

Joel stood tall. "I know lots of people. You aren't the only person God's given me to guide."

Ambrose glanced at Joel. "Is she the one you told me about?"

"Yep, isn't she a beauty?"

"That she is."

I shifted my eyes to examine my body, but a blanket covered it. They couldn't be talking about my face. It sounded more like they discussed a horse.

"Pardon me, but you two do know I'm listening, don't you?"

Ambrose smiled. "Sorry, but I didn't think you would mind us talking about your soul before you."

"My soul?"

"Why, yes. What did you think we talked about?"

I didn't know whether to feel insulted or relieved. I decided I had better go with the latter. "What most human girls would think you were talking about."

Joel turned to Ambrose. "She does, however, have some maturing to do."

"Yes, but it is all there, she will grow into the role."

The role? What did he mean? Being a miracle worker? Yeah, I knew that. Yet I couldn't help but feel they meant more.

Ambrose stared into my eyes. "She still needs rest. And we do need to speed this healing. Time is short."

"I know, I need to—"

"Sleep." He laid a hand on me. "You need to sleep."

My eyes closed and dreams rolled in to take the place of reality.

I awoke and felt much better. Daylight shone through the windows. I couldn't see Ambrose in the room. I sat up. My head hurt, but I managed without too much trouble.

I felt a gnawing at my stomach. I hadn't eaten since yesterday morning. Bread and cheese lay on the table, along with some water. I sat on a chair and devoured the morsels, washing them down with plenty of the liquid. As I ate, warmth and strength flowed through me.

I felt well enough—I should go search for Nathan and Seth. Not to mention I had to find the pack containing Amma. I hoped the crystal hadn't broken or been lost. I shuddered.

I heard laughing outside; not voices I recognized.

"Hey, old man, did you get what we asked?"

"You must learn contentment, my friends."

I moved to the window and peeked out. I saw Ambrose sandwiched between two muscular men.

"I'll teach you contentment, old man." One of them swung his fist into Ambrose's gut.

He doubled over, but no cry arose from him. The other kicked him. They continued beating upon him, but he simply stood there and took the blows. He didn't even try to block or dodge them.

I couldn't take anymore. I grabbed my sword leaning against the wall by my bed and flung the door open.

"If you two need someone to beat up on, why don't you try me?" I stepped into the yard and held my stance.

One of them smiled and drew his blade. "And if I win, I get you for myself."

I shook my head. "I would fight till the death before that would ever happen. But if you know what's good for you, you'll leave." I knew he wouldn't. Not without convincing.

He stepped toward me, his sword held in front of him. "I'll have you know, I'm the best sword fighter in these hills. You've bitten off more than you can chew."

I jabbed at him, to see what he would do. He jerked back, but didn't move his feet properly. He wavered unsteadily, and I took advantage of it.

I pushed in with my sword toward his right foot, which sat too far under him. He swung his arms into the air to steady himself as he dropped his foot back. I swung across his belly, ripping his shirt and leaving a thin, red line over his navel.

He dropped his sword and covered his stomach with his hands as he fell to the ground upon his rear.

I smiled. "By the way, I'm not from around here. Where I'm from, you wouldn't make it past the first round of our contests."

He glared at me from the ground.

I jabbed my sword at him. He jumped back, grabbed his sword, and scurried backwards. Then he arose and they both fled down the hill.

Ambrose came up beside me. "You didn't have to do that. I don't mind having the body buffeted. They help me in my discipline."

"But they might have killed you."

He shrugged. "If it is my time, that is fine with me. I only desire one thing, and it can't be had in this world. Here, there is nothing for me. The more I'm reminded of that by such people, the more my focus is upon God. He uses all things to move me to Him."

"I wasn't going to kill them. Just wanted to scare them away."

"That you did very well." He chuckled. "Though you didn't have to, I thank you nonetheless."

"I do need to find my brother and uncle, though."

"I believe you do not."

I wrinkled my brow. "What?"

"You don't need to find them, your brother has found you."

I heard rustling in some bushes to my right. I turned to see Nathan emerge from them. His hair hung clumped about his head, moss and leaves clung to his clothing, and he appeared as if he had been up all night.

He staggered toward me. "Here you are, doing fine. And to think all this time I was worried about you."

I raced to him and wrapped my arms around him. "Have you seen Seth?"

"Yes. I left him by a tree at the stream. His leg is broken so he can't move."

A relief flooded over me, knowing they were both alive, even as concern for Seth's condition nagged at me.

Then I remembered. "Oh!" I turned to Ambrose. "This is the Monk Ambrose. He took care of me this past day and night. The storm knocked me unconscious, and I awoke in his cabin."

Nathan bowed to Ambrose. "Thank you." He examined me. "It appears you've healed fast."

"Thanks to Ambrose. He has a touch." I smiled.

Ambrose bowed to us.

"I would rest," Nathan said. "But I need to get you back to Seth so you can heal him, and we can get going again."

I nodded. "Let me get my gear, what little I have left."

Ambrose raised a hand. "Go, but please return. I wish to send you off properly."

I raised an eyebrow and nodded. "I'll make sure we return."

29

Nathan led me to Seth and I healed him. Nathan had found much of our traveling gear washed up alongside the bank. Only one horse had survived. We would have to go on foot, which would add another couple days to our trip. Nathan handed me Dad's pack. I checked inside—Amma stared from inside the crystal. A welcome sigh escaped my lips. I pulled my arms through the pack's straps, and it settled onto my back.

After we had packed what we could on the horse and ourselves, we prepared to leave.

Nathan pointed down the riverbank. "We should get moving. We've lost enough time as it is."

"But I promised him. We have to return."

"Promised who?" Seth stared at me.

"Monk Ambrose. He took me in and cared for me. I might have died by the time Nathan found me if he hadn't."

Seth nodded. "Then we must return. It would be wrong not to."

Nathan grunted and stared at the sky. "All right."

We worked our way back to Ambrose's cabin. When we entered the clearing, a table had been set in the center of the yard. Bowls of a hearty soup surrounded a serving plate of fish and cheese. A loaf of steaming bread sat on one end.

Ambrose exited the cabin. "Welcome! Thank you for returning."

I bowed. "You're welcome. It's our honor. But where did you get all this?" I scanned the area for a storage house I might have missed. "I know this wasn't in your house."

"God provides, does He not?" He spread his arms out. "Let us pray and eat."

He offered a simple prayer for the food before we dug in. The food tasted so delicious, I felt I could sit and eat all day long. It filled, without weighing me down. The more I ate, the more strength I felt return to my bones. Even Nathan appeared glad we had returned, based on how much he put away.

As we finished the last on our plates, Ambrose arose. "Now I would have you join me for ninth hour."

Nathan frowned. "But we need to get moving."

Ambrose bowed. "Your time is short, indeed. All the more reason to stay and pray."

I eyed Nathan. His shoulders sank.

I stood up. "We would be delighted to pray with you."

The service didn't take long. He did it simply, but with full sincerity. I could feel his words pulsing through me as he read and felt as if the whole world swayed to the rhythm of his voice. For precious moments, eternity penetrated our world. The same paradise I experienced in Dad's soul flooded over me.

When he said the dismissal, I wanted much more and almost asked him to do another service. Then I realized how silly that would sound; he would use a set schedule.

He held up a hand. "One minute. Let me get something before you leave." He glided into his hut and returned with three bags. He handed one to each of us.

"These contain food I've cooked for you. Nothing fancy, but it will keep you full of energy for the rest of your trip."

Then he pulled out a locket and placed it in my hands. "This is a relic from another brave girl: Love."

I froze in awe, then smiled. I kissed the locket and put it around my neck. "I actually met her."

A corner of his mouth turned up and he nodded. "I know. May her prayers aid you in your journey, and I will pray as well."

I wondered if he talked with Love as freely as he did with Joel. I bowed and extended my hands for a blessing. He laid his in mine and I kissed them. "Thank you." I hugged him.

His eyes widened, and then he hugged back. "May you and your family go in peace."

I bowed once more and we left down the road.

Nathan stepped up beside me. "Did you get a key?"

I shook my head. "No." I had wondered. He embodied contentment. But apparently God had other ideas. Still, if he didn't exhibit it enough, then who would?

The hills drew near. I felt a tingle in my step. Soon I would see my grandparents for the first time, assuming they still lived. But I wished Dad could be here. I hated to break such news upon first meeting them. Would we get there? Beltrid's shadow loomed over us.

While Beltrid had not appeared to us or directly opposed us, he still attempted to keep us from our goal, perhaps through Rodan. It had to be more than a coincidence that a tornado happened by, on top of everything else that had befallen us.

I shouldn't have been surprised. Only a fool would trust a demon to keep his word. Beltrid would take advantage of any loopholes he could find. Why did Dad make a deal with him?

I stepped quickly to travel along side my uncle. "Uncle Seth?"

"Yes?"

"I'm pretty sure Beltrid is behind some of these recent events."

"I wouldn't be surprised."

"I think he doesn't want us to get to the steam house. I'll bet we encounter more obstacles before we arrive."

He nodded.

"I'm wondering, maybe we should leave the main road. He might not expect that."

He shook his head. "It would be too difficult to find a way over the hills where there is no path. It could add several more days to the trip."

"But I feel like we're sitting ducks, waiting until he throws the next punch, and we'll be too late to dodge it."

Seth cracked a smile. "Do you seriously think going off the road will fool him?"

I shrugged. "I don't know. But we need to take some action, go on the offensive. Try to anticipate and defend against his next move."

"Spoken like a true warrior."

I wasn't sure I liked that title anymore. "Do you have any ideas then?"

"Sure. Follow this road over the hill to Reol and get you two into that steam house."

"No, Uncle! I'm talking about preventing Beltrid's next move."

He glanced at me. "You have an inside scoop on what his next move will be? Based on what you all told me of your trip to my house, and what we have experienced since then, it has been one unbelievable event after another. I would have no way to predict what he will do next. I'm sure I would never see it coming, and neither will you."

I sighed. "You're probably right. Still, I hate waiting, hate not having some control over the situation."

He winked at me. "I think you have more control than you know, but risk losing that by worrying about it."

I thought about his words for a while. I stared at him. "Those are wiser words than mine."

He laughed. "Your father taught me a lot." His eyes focused into the sky. "I owe him my life, in more ways than one."

We set up camp at the foot of the hills. After a meal, some discussion about the next day, and what we would do once we arrived at Reol, we settled into our bedrolls for the night. Distant wolves howled into the night. Others farther away answered back. I fell into my dreams.

I stood on the porch of a house. The dark wood and aged overhang gave it a cold and distant feel. As I opened the door, my attention focused on a sense of dread emanating from the entryway. Despite nagging feelings that I shouldn't, I entered the house.

The door opened into a hallway lined with mirrors. I stepped in front of the first one. The reflection of a girl dressed in a beautiful white gown sparkled like a beautiful star on the other side of the glass. I peered closer. The girl was me! I couldn't believe it. The beauty shone so bright, I had to squint to look upon her. I had never looked so good before. Then again, I had never been one for lacy dresses. Hard to fight in those and too attractive to the boys.

I stepped further down the hall, and the next mirror revealed a troll, holding a sword, and slashing at unseen enemies. That wasn't really me either. True, I did have some troll blood in me now, and I used a sword, but I didn't have such an appearance. What did this mean?

I moved to the next mirror. I smiled, for the mirror showed me riding a pure white winged horse. A grin beamed from my face as if having the time of my life. My hair whipped back as we flew, and even watching I felt a wonderful joy.

I stood there for a while, enjoying the sight, before I moved to the next mirror. I stepped to the side, but jumped back and screamed. Before my eyes, Beltrid's face stared back at me from the mirror. A menacing smile creased his lips, as if he would reach out and grab me right then.

I felt hands shaking me. I awoke to Nathan holding me by the shoulders. "Kaylee, wake up. It's just a dream."

I forced myself to breathe deep as I sat up. "Oh Nathan, it was horrible."

He rubbed my back. "It's all right now."

"I looked in a mirror, and I saw Beltrid's face."

"That would be enough to make anyone scream." He smiled. Then he pulled a piece of polished metal from his pack. "But see, you're all right now."

Beltrid's face grinned back from the metal. I screamed.

"Kaylee, wake up!" Nathan's face stared over mine as I opened my eyes, trying to catch my breath and my heart. I sat up; my eyes darted around, expecting Beltrid to leap out at any moment.

"You're having a bad dream."

"Nathan, I don't know what happened, but when you showed me a mirror, I saw Beltrid's face in it." Tears formed in my eyes.

He reached into his pack and pulled out a piece of polished metal. "But this isn't a dream, look."

I crawled backwards and turned my eyes away. "No, no, don't bring that close to me. I don't want to see!"

30

Nathan thrust the metal before my face. Beltrid laughed in the shine.

I cried out, "No! Take him away!" I crawled out of the shelter and sped toward the forest. A root caught my foot and threw me crashing onto the ground; the taste of blood flooded my tongue.

"Kaylee, stop screaming, wake up!" Seth called out. He stood over me.

I squished my eyes shut. "No, Uncle, I don't want to wake up. Please leave me alone!"

"Have some coffee, that will help."

I cracked an eye open to see him holding a cup out. My shaking hands received it from him. As I put it to my lips, the moonlight shining in the cup revealed Beltrid's grinning face and beady eyes.

I flung the cup away and cried, "No, please go away, leave me alone!" I writhed on the ground, my hands upon my head.

"Kaylee, get up! The shadow-creatures are upon us!"

I jerked my eyes open and craned my neck toward the voice. "Dad?"

"Hurry, Kaylee. They're coming, Save me!"

Shaking, I grabbed my sword and raced to him. "Dad, I'm coming!"

But I arrived too late. I watched helplessly as three of them ran their swords through him. Dad's eyes locked on mine, and he reached out toward me before falling limp.

"Dad—no!"

The shadow-creatures turned my direction. They morphed and joined together until Beltrid himself grinned before me, a long sword in his hand.

My legs shook and I stepped back. "Dad! Help me!" His death still fresh on my mind, my anger grew. I squared my feet and prepared to defeat this monster and wipe that grin from his face.

He swung from above; I glanced his blade against mine as I stepped to the side and it swished through the air. A confidence settled in my mind and I attacked with a greater force. He stepped back against my blows, but blocked each one. Each swing and jab I parried and dodged, and likewise, I couldn't bring my blade to meet his flesh.

I tired as the battle raged abnormally long. My blade warped from the clashes with his, and chipped in spots along the edge. All the while, he appeared to grow stronger, faster. Desperation set in.

I blocked another blow from his sword, but I couldn't hold the grip. Pain shot through my hand as my sword twisted out of my fingers and through the air to land with a thud several feet away.

I stood there, holding my hand, slowly backing away as he grinned and approached. This is what it felt like to see death coming, to know there's nothing you can do. All control lost, all self-assurance gone. He lifted his sword over his head.

I held my hand up. "No!"

He plunged it toward me—blackness swam over the world and I lay on the ground, curled up into a ball, crying. I hated him!

A small, soft hand touched my shoulder.

"Kaylee."

My eyes blinked open. I turned to see a small girl. "Love?"

"Yes."

"What's happening to me?"

"Beltrid is playing upon your weaknesses. He's trying to trap you in your own mind."

Tears flowed down my face. Adrenaline pumped through me and my heart beat rapidly within my chest. "How do I get out of this?"

"You know, if you think about it."

"I'm too scared to think."

"Let me help." She poured water into a bowl sitting next to us and held it toward me. "What do you see?"

I shook my head. "I don't want to look."

"What do you see?"

I stared into her gentle eyes. The soft skin and slight smile disarmed me. I felt my heart slowing down. I thought about looking in the bowl, but I couldn't. I didn't want to see his evil grin again. But she held it out, as if knowing I had to eventually.

I raised my head. Shivers rolled across my arms. I brought my eyes over the bowl and gazed in. My mouth dropped open.

"I see Joel." My eyes met hers. "Why?"

"What does he represent to you?"

"Well, he's a guide of some sort, sent by God."

"I didn't ask you about him, but what he represents to you."

I thought for a second. "A man who is out to make me his next catch."

"Do you love him?"

"Why, no. I mean, not if you're saying husband and wife."

"God calls us to love everyone."

"Well, I don't hate him, but he is annoying."

"Indifference and hate, neither is love. Do you love Joel?"

"I...I don't know." I knew what I should say, but couldn't bring myself to say it. She would know if I lied, I could sense it.

"Kaylee, Beltrid discovered a key weakness of yours. You can't love when you can't control the relationship comfortably. You can't control Joel, nor most men."

"I don't see what control has to do with love."

"You're afraid of committing to another unless you can control the outcome. Your desire to be a nun is a way to avoid those relationships."

"No, I wanted to be married to God. That's all."

"A noble and honorable reason to be a nun. But in your case, you're running from commitment, running from love. That's not an honorable reason."

I thought back. Yes, I've avoided men. I didn't date, didn't hang around men other than my dad and brother, turned down all advances. The encounter with...with...

Love placed a hand on my shoulder. "Yes, let it out, focus on it."

I locked onto her eyes; she could hear my thoughts. I swallowed. "You know, don't you, what I'm running from. I've tried to forget, to not think about it."

She nodded. "Yes. It prevents you from loving everyone, allowing Beltrid to trap you with hate."

I breathed deep, and decided it best to speak it, as if confessing to her what I had kept buried deep inside like an embarrassing sin.

"He was drunk." I stared at the ground. "He...wanted me." Images flooded through my mind as I continued. "He reached out his hand and touched me. I wanted to run, but fear had frozen me in place. I didn't know what he was doing, and too scared to ask or stop him. I felt..."

The word caught in my throat, but I choked it out. "Helpless." I noticed my hand had locked onto the grip of my sword lying next to me. "If it hadn't been for the people who happened by...he would...would have..."

My muscles tensed; I raised my sword and slammed it into the ground. The forest shook, a crack formed in the earth, and a black stench spewed into the air. I choked on the filth, but then a sweet breeze swept over me. The black stench broke apart and dissipated into the sky above.

I raised my eyes to meet hers. She waited for me to say it. I sucked in another breath. "He would have used me for his own...pleasure." I shook

169

my head as if to convince her. "I vowed I would never be controlled that way again, by anyone."

"And what does Joel represent to you?"

I dropped my head. The answer paraded before me. "Someone I can't control or run from."

"And yet, he's not taken advantage of you, has he? Kaylee, love means trusting someone, being open to be hurt. If you can't trust, you can't really love."

I sank my head between my knees and wrapped my arms over my head. "How can I change years of fear? Years of hiding and running?"

"Kaylee! Wake up please!"

My eyes fluttered open. Joel hovered over me. He stared into my eyes, as if waiting for something. I felt revulsion rising like bile. It rose into my mouth, and I tasted hate. I swallowed hard, pushed it back down, surprised by its force. My eyes watered. My hands shook. My body quivered. A flood built up behind a dam in my soul, and cracks rolled down it. Chunks exploded off and I felt the gates open, the wall crashing down.

I blinked back tears. "Joel, hold me please."

He wrapped his arms around me as if he had waited for eternity to hear those words. Warmth spread through my limbs, into my toes, across my arms, and into the very thoughts flowing through my mind. A burning heat blasted through for a brief moment, and then a bright light swelled until I could take no more.

"I think she's coming to." It sounded like Seth's voice.

I cracked my eyes open. Nathan, Seth, and Joel sat around me by the campfire. I lay on a bedroll, the stars twinkling above me.

I opened them wider. "Am I really awake?"

"Kaylee!" Nathan placed his arm on mine.

Seth sighed as if releasing tension he had held back; he smiled.

I sat up and reached out for Joel. "I'm so sorry, Joel."

He grinned from ear to ear. He slipped into my arms and eternity flowed through him, joy from some distant world I could only dream about.

I saw Nathan's wide eyes glancing at Seth. Seth shrugged.

I paused. "No one answered me. Am I really awake?"

Joel grabbed a piece of polished metal. He held it, but didn't give it to me. "You truly want to know?"

I tightened my lips and nodded. He passed it to me. I eased it into my line of sight. My own face stared back. I relaxed and handed the metal back.

"Kaylee," Nathan said. "You've been out for nearly a day. What happened?"

I dropped my mouth open. "A day?"

"We figured you had fallen into some sickness or spell. At one point we thought we had lost you. You kept jerking around and bashing into things so we had to bring you out here."

"Somehow Beltrid discovered a weakness of mine and used it against me. He tried to trap me in my mind."

Seth shook his head. "What did I tell you about predicting his next move?"

"Yes, Uncle. You were right." I grabbed Joel's hand. "And you helped me get out."

He squeezed it. "You broke through with God's help. I embodied your fears that Beltrid used to trap you with."

I felt free, which surprised me. It felt wonderfully open and free to hold his hand. To admit I loved without feeling threatened by it. He knew more about me than my own father did, than anyone save God Himself. We shared a unique bond.

Acknowledging and expressing that, my own love for God flowed stronger as well through Joel. I pulled out the locket containing Love's bone fragment and kissed it. "Thank you," I whispered to her.

The next morning arrived with the red sun breaking over the hills. I awoke from a sound and refreshing sleep—such a change from the previous night. I ate well and then we packed our bags, loaded the horse and ourselves, and started the climb up the hill.

As we ascended, the wind whipped into a brisker pace. A familiar scent passed my nose. "Smoke." I kept sniffing the air and scanned the area. Then I saw the source of the smell.

"Look behind us!" I pointed down the hill.

A wide fire raged below us and worked its way up the sides of the hill. It roared toward us, as if it had eyes and chased us.

Seth picked up the pace. "Run!"

31

Nathan pointed up the hill. "Hold on. I see a cave."

We rushed toward it as the fire chased us. I released the horse, hoping it would find its own way out of the fire. We dashed into the tight cave entrance and sank in as far as we dared, not wanting to lose the light shining in, but wanting to get as far away from the fire as possible.

The air at the entrance heated up. Flames leaped around it, reached in, and attempted to ignite us into its glory. Sweat poured down my face as the temperature rose.

I had no idea how long the fire would last, but I figured it would eventually die. However, after several minutes, it raged as hotly as when it had started.

The light from the fire reflected off the back end of the cave. The room sunk a few feet into the mountain with no way out. Nathan and Seth had settled onto the floor. Their red skin glistened with sweat.

Nathan stared at me. "Kaylee, can't you do something? It's like an oven in here. I don't know how much longer I can last."

I checked Uncle Seth; he breathed hard as if getting little air and stared back at me with a scarlet face. I wondered for a couple of seconds why I didn't feel the heat as they did, then I realized the ring protected me. I stepped closer to the fire flaring around the entrance. Its tongues licked out toward me. While I felt some heat, it didn't increase as I came closer. Indeed, it actually felt cooler.

I stepped up to the fire and thrust my hand in.

"Kaylee!" Nathan leaped toward me, grabbed me by the shoulders, and pulled me back. We both fell backwards, landing with a grunt. His eyes squinted at me as sweat dripped from his eyebrows. "What magic caused you to do that?"

I smiled and held up the hand I had thrust in. "Look, nothing happened. Not even a red mark." Indeed, the skin felt cool to the touch.

Nathan felt my hand. His mouth dropped open, and then he gazed at me. "Just like Dad's story about the dragon."

A loud crack erupted from outside. A burning tree fell across the cave entrance. The flaming limbs began to grow into the cave. Rivers of fire flowed in. Seth and Nathan scurried as close to the back wall as possible.

The fire flowed around my legs, but I couldn't feel any heat. I turned back to them, flames wrapping around my body, and held out my hands to them. "Come, I can take us through this."

Nathan and Seth glanced at each other. Their eyes cowered as they pushed themselves up against the back wall. Nathan shook his head. "I'm not sure I can. I don't have a ring like yours."

"Trust me, I can do this." An inner check clicked in me. "That is, God can do this. Trust Him."

Seth's face relaxed. "She's right. I've seen this before. I'll not run this time." He stepped out and held a hand out for Nathan.

Nathan swallowed hard. The fire inched its way toward them. "All right, I'm coming." He closed his eyes. One would think his blood boiled underneath his skin, as red as it was. He held out a shaky hand to Seth. Seth locked onto it and pulled him up.

I stepped toward them and placed my hands on theirs. "Lord, protect them from the fire and get them through it."

With their hands in mine, we stepped into the inferno. Nathan followed with his eyes closed firmly shut. Flames licked around us, blues and reds glowed and flickered. Yet none of us had caught on fire. Nathan's face had turned back to its normal color, as well as Seth's.

I jiggled Nathan's hand. "Check it out, Brother."

One eye cracked open, then both followed all the way. He stared all around himself. "Wow! This is absolutely amazing!"

Seth chuckled. "I'll say. It was amazing watching from the outside, but inside is indescribable."

Indeed, what appeared dangerous and menacing just moments before, now shown with a unique beauty. A beauty I had seen before. "The fire in Dad's soul, with Love. That's what this fire looks like." It had that same surreal light pouring from it, what Dad said felt like Paradise.

Nathan released my hand and swung in circles. The flames rippled as his hands passed through them. The fire sizzled around his hair, as if moisture vaporized inches above him. A pure joy flowed from him, a happiness I hadn't seen from him in a long time.

I couldn't stand it any longer. "Nathan, may I have this dance?"

He stopped twirling, straightened his back and held out his upturned hand. "Dear maiden, I would be honored."

I couldn't help but laugh, like a little girl who knew nothing but fun and joy. I placed my hand in his.

Seth bowed to us. "And allow me to offer the song." A glow radiated from him as he broke into a melody and lyrics I had never heard before. He must have created it on the spot.

Upon the rising of the Sun,
Flows the life within its light.
Upon its penetrating gaze,
Flows the death within its flames.
Upon the rays of distant fires,
Beats the rhythm within two songs.

But one note leads to life,
And one note leads to death.
The song you chose to sing,
Defines the dance that you must dance.
The music of death and of life.

Upon the anger of one man,
Rose a furnace filled with fire.
Upon the bonds of three young men,
Flowed a faith unquenchable.
Upon the coals of burning wood,
Danced the joy of three plus One.

But one note leads to life,
And one note leads to death.
The song you chose to sing,
Defines the dance that you must dance.
The music of death and of life.

Upon the stocks of sacrifice,
Rose the courage of one man.
Upon the breath from one fell beast,
Flushed the sulfur straight from Hell.
Upon the dragon's scaly back,
Rode the faith untouched by fire.

But one note leads to life,
And one note leads to death.
The song you chose to sing,
Defines the dance that you must dance.
The music of death and of life.

I couldn't recall a time of greater joy as Seth's voice floated through the flames while Nathan and I danced among the fire. He twirled me around and I fell into the arms of—Joel?

He smiled and glanced at Nathan. "Mind if I cut in?"

Nathan stepped back and bowed. Joel took my hands in his, and we swung back and forth. The fire kept beat around us as Seth continued his song. Joel's warm eyes glistened with excitement. Joy coursed through my body, a joy I had never imagined I could experience with any man.

He said as he twirled me into his left arm, "When we get to Paradise, we can do this eternally."

Before I thought about my words, I said, "I would like that." And I felt as if I could go through eternity dancing. It would never get old.

He held me and stared into my eyes. His upturned lips sank for a moment, but then returned to a smile though weaker than before. "You need to be on your way. Beltrid's given up here."

A flash of light blinded me. A wave of pressure knocked me from my feet as Seth's voice screeched to a halt. My rear banged onto the rock floor. As my sight returned, I sat in the cave with Nathan and Seth, but the fire had vanished along with Joel. Little flames caressed the tree at the cave entrance, and smoke rose in streams over the burned foliage outside.

I stared at the cave ceiling. "You could have done that a little less abruptly." As if answering what I imagined Joel would say, "Yeah, restrictions, I know."

Nathan stood and held out a hand to me. He wore a wide grin. "You're amazing, Sis." He pulled me to my feet.

"Me?" I grabbed Seth's arm and helped him up. "I just asked, is all."

We exited the cave and surveyed the charred ground. Smoldering piles dotted the landscape and blackened trees entertaining flames continued to burn.

Nathan headed up the hill. "I'll go find the horse. You two get some rest."

I lay flat on my back. "Will this never end?"

Seth sat up. "I can say resolutely that this will end at some point. When and how might be the more unknown question."

I pulled my pack off and dug out the food Monk Ambrose had given us. "Want some, Uncle?"

He nodded and held out his hand. I placed some of the cheese into his palm, then reached in to get myself a handful. Something felt cold and hard. I fished it out and held it before my eyes. An iron key held a sparkling crystal on its end, shaped like a cross.

A chill raced down my body. "Uncle, Ambrose did have

contentment." I showed him the key. "He was too humble to give it to us directly."

He drew near and checked it out. "What do you know."

Nathan returned with the horse in tow. "The horse was just over the ridge and not harmed at all." He stared at the key. "One more to go: love."

I smiled and pulled out the crystal prison. I found the hole, inserted and broke it off, and watched as the glow dimmed. I held it in my palm. Amma still lay frozen inside, distorted by the facets of the stone.

I sighed. "Yes, one more. Still, her release seems so far away. I'll not relax until she's freed from this prison." I continued studying the rock, deep in thought.

A shriek rang out above me, and I jerked my head upward. An eagle dove toward my hand, snatched the crystal from it, and flew to a burnt tree limb up high. I could barely make out a rider on the bird: a small mouse sat in a saddle.

A high pitched laugh rose from the eagle's back. "Now what do you say? Thought you could get rid of me easily, did you? No, not me."

Anger at myself beat back my fear for Amma. "Rodan, bring it back!"

"You mean, this crystal with your mother in it? Why would I want to do that?"

"Because you have nothing to gain by keeping her."

"Revenge, that's as good of a reason as any to make you all suffer."

"But I really—"

He launched the eagle into the air, and they flew upwards.

I stomped my foot and dashed to the horse. I hopped upon the horse's back and jerked the chord holding the packs on. They crashed to the ground.

"I'm going to see if I can follow him." Then I sent the horse galloping through the burnt trees. Thankfully, the underbrush had all burned away. But I had to be extra careful that I didn't lead the horse into a place littered with holes.

I watched the ground and the air. The eagle soared higher and farther out. Soon, I came to the end of the burnt forest, and underbrush thickened, slowing me down. As I struggled to push through the undergrowth, the eagle shrank into a small dot on the horizon.

I buried my head in the horse's mane. I had failed! Failed Amma, and the feeling grew that I would likely fail Dad as well. I turned the horse around and trotted back to camp. I didn't want to face Seth and Nathan. What would Nathan think? I hadn't protected Amma as I should have. That's what he would think. That's what I thought.

After returning to camp, I sat down and ate without saying a word.

Nathan patted me on the back. "Should we go after Rodan and get Mother back?"

I shook my head. "Dad's time is limited. Once we're finished with the steam house, I'll make it my personal quest to find Rodan and rescue Amma."

Seth said, "Not to mention, better to make sure you two can get through the steam house first. If you come out better, your father will be freed and all three of you can rescue your mother. If you come out for the worse, then perhaps it would be best not to free her to face those facts."

Nathan nodded. "Yeah, you're right. Beltrid is probably betting that we will chase after her, delaying our trip to the steam house."

Beltrid. His shadow still hung over us even though Dad had arranged otherwise. Inside I wanted to scream and cry. I should have been more careful; I should have known she might be a target of Beltrid or Rodan's tricks. Inside, I knew if ever the chance arose, they would be an exception to my decision not to kill.

We returned to the road and climbed until we reached the crest of the hill. Over a couple smaller peaks, we saw Reol in the distance. Smoke rose lazily from several homes.

"Should be there in two more days," Seth said.

I nodded. The faster, the better at this point. I felt guilty for not rushing to Amma's rescue. But Dad needed rescuing too, and unless Rodan broke the crystal, Amma could wait. He probably wouldn't break it, at least until he could do it in front of us, if revenge was his motivation.

Seth patted me on the back. "Kaylee, it wasn't your fault. There's no way you could have foreseen Rodan flying in to take her."

"I know, but it hurts."

He hugged me.

We began the descent. While inside I felt dreary and sad, the sun blazed brightly in the sky. A cool wind breezed across my face, refreshing my spirit. Like God Himself caressed and hugged me with His warmth. I decided to focus on getting to Reol and freeing Dad. I would need all my attention to prepare for the steam house.

Nathan slipped in beside me and squeezed my shoulders with his thick arms. "Don't worry, we'll get her back. Rodan doesn't have a chance with us on his trail."

I nodded and smiled at him. "Thanks." I hugged him back.

We reached the bottom and decided to set up camp a stone's throw from the road in a clearing. We had lost the shelter, so we would have to sleep under the stars. Luckily, no threatening clouds lingered in the sky.

Soon we had set up camp, and a crackling fire fought back the night.

We sat around it and ate our soup and cheese. Between bites, we chatted.

Nathan set his bowl down. "It's a good thing we're almost to Reol. Camping under the stars is fine when the weather's good, but one rain storm would have us wishing for a roof."

I swallowed. "Just think, by this time tomorrow, we could be in Reol. Hard to believe we're almost there after all we've been through."

Seth waved a piece of flatbread at me. "Keep in mind all the delays we've experienced so far. I'm sure Beltrid and Rodan haven't given up yet."

As if answer to Seth, a pair of wolves howled in the distance. Seth paused and gazed into the forest covered in black.

I listened intently. A couple more howls broke the still, night air. I heard some leaves rustle behind me. I swung my head around and peered into the trees, but could discern no movement. But for a brief second I thought I saw the firelight reflect off two beady eyes.

No one said a thing and I heard no further noises. "Must have been the wind."

Heat flared across my body; Nathan and Seth both gasped as they fell backwards. I spun back around to see the fire rising into a pillar, spinning in blues and oranges as it rose higher and higher.

The heat grew unbearable, and I jumped back onto my feet. Nathan and Seth had also backed away on the opposite sides of the clearing. Still the heat bore down, but I didn't want to enter the forest if I didn't have to.

A growling noise erupted from within the flames. The pillar split down its center until several strands of fire cascaded to the ground like a willow tree. Then they each spun around upon the ground, taking shape, until they formed into an orange-haired set of wolves. Their eyes burned with a white light. Bright and dark patches moved in patterns as if molten lava churned within their bodies.

"Rodan's behind this, I'll bet," I yelled out.

With a loud growl, they all attacked us at once. Four rushed toward me while several others raced after Nathan and Seth. I started to draw my sword, but if I allowed them to attack as a group, I didn't stand a chance. I had to find some way to string them out.

Nathan and Seth must have realized the same thing, for they dashed into the forest. I wanted to scream in frustration, but I had no choice. I sped into the night woods hoping to find a solution before they overtook me.

32

I raced through the forest, moving as fast as my troll-legs would carry me. Even so, I expected the wolves to gain on me at any second. Yet they held back, as if wanting to push me toward something. But what would that be?

I didn't want to find out. I scanned the area with the little moonlight I had, searching for something I could use. I soon spotted the perfect formation. A stand of trees created a doorway framed by stout trunks. To avoid it, my pursuers would have to go around a big cluster of bushes and trees. They would follow me through that narrow doorway.

I leaped through it and skidded to a stop as I whipped around, unsheathing my sword in one motion. The first wolf sped toward me, then upon seeing the sword, tried to skid to a stop. It couldn't dodge the point of my blade, which pierced the fire-wolf at its neck and into its upper torso. Lava-blood spewed from it, burning my skin. I tumbled back as the next wolf leaped over its fallen comrade. I landed on my back, but kept the sword trained on the wolf flying toward me, skewering it. I screamed as more hot lava erupted from the beast and flowed over my arm. But the pain quickly subsided as the ring reacted to it and healed me.

I jumped to my feat as the other two wolves raced toward me. I turned to run again, but as I did I gasped, for behind me a cliff-face dropped many yards to a river I could hear far below. I barely had time to grab a tree before my feet fell off the precipice. Only my grip on the tree trunk kept me from careening down the side of the cliff.

The two wolves approached at a slow walk, rumbling a low growl, and attempted to bite my hand. They wanted me to fall—they had chased me toward this canyon drop. I sheathed my sword and moved my hands beyond their reach. I could feel my fingers growing tired; it would be a matter of time before I fell unless I did something. Though the ring might protect me, I didn't want to tempt God with assumptions of what He should do.

As one wolf reached its neck out to snap at my hand, I swung my legs up and locked it between them. I let my weight pull the beast over the side of the cliff, and I let go. It squirmed as it dropped, yelped as it hit rocks, and then it was quiet.

The lone wolf pulled back, growling. I shifted to a limb above me and swung my feet until I had gained some height. At the apex of my forward swing, I released the branch, sailed through the air and rolled onto my feet while drawing my sword, crouched and ready should the remaining one attack.

Instead, it backed up further. I growled back and shot toward it. The beast attempted to gain traction in the dirt before it fled yelping into the forest night.

I leaned against a tree, attempting to gain my breath. I glanced down the cliff-face. Ring or no ring, that would not have been fun. Seth and Nathan—did the wolves chase them over a cliff? I knew I couldn't rest any longer.

I jogged back to camp, no further wolves appeared. How had Nathan and Seth fared? I shivered.

When I arrived at the campsite, no wolf or person waited. I stomped my foot. I would have to track Nathan and Seth down to find out what happened to them. I grabbed a long stick from the fire for light and checked the area where I recalled Nathan had disappeared into the forest. I found his footsteps among a series of paw-prints and followed them.

The route led through brush and between trees. After several yards, the trail circled around a few trees covered with bushy undergrowth. Like me, Nathan must have realized that they drove him to some destination, and had attempted to thwart their plans. I studied the tracks all the way around and found where the wolves left, but didn't see any sign of Nathan other than within the endless circle.

"Nathan?" I listened, hoping he could respond. I circled the trees two times before my makeshift torch revealed some broken branches on a bush. I shoved them aside and peered in. Nathan's body lay on the ground with a dead wolf next to him. Blackened rock streamed from the dead animal, like hardened lava.

I gasped. I lay the torch on a nearby rock and pushed my way into the bushes until I knelt by his body. I felt his wrist; a bare pulse beat in him.

I placed my hand on his chest. "Lord, heal Nathan of these wounds." He convulsed for a moment, and I feared God might not do it. But then he settled down and opened his eyes.

They blinked and then focused on me. "Kaylee?"

"Yes, I'm here."

"Where are the wolves?" He sat up.

"Looks like you killed one. They must have figured you were dead."

He gazed at the dead wolf. "This one followed me in here, and we fought. I killed him, but not before he had seriously hurt me. I knew I would die."

He smiled at me. "Good thing you found me."

I helped him to his feet and we worked our way back out of the bushes. "Now to find Uncle Seth."

I traced our path back to the camp. When we entered the clearing, Uncle Seth sat by the fire.

He turned and grinned. "About time you two came back. What took you so long?"

Nathan laughed. "How did you get away? I didn't think you could run or fight as well as us."

"I've been using a sword long before you. But sometimes a little wisdom can take you a lot further than a sword."

"And what wisdom might that be?" I asked.

"Wolves are guided more by smell than sight, especially at night. As I fled from them, I took my vest off. When I came to a good set of thorn bushes, I tossed it in, then ran around it and out the opposite side. You should have heard the yelping and crying of those wolves as they plunged into those thorns!" He laughed and slapped his leg.

We both laughed with him; that would have been an interesting sight to see.

Nathan sat down. "But Uncle, do you have any idea what they were driving us toward?"

"Maybe not driving us toward something as much as away from each other."

I glanced at Nathan and could tell he hadn't thought of that possibility. "My wolves nearly ran me off a cliff, but maybe they wanted to separate us, delay our entry into the steam house?"

Seth nodded. "Seems likely. Beltrid can't kill us because of his promise to your father, but he's doing what he can to prevent you from getting there."

Nathan huffed. "If Kaylee hadn't found me, I'd be dead by now."

I frowned and faced Uncle Seth. "So…I guess your solution is to keep plowing ahead and hope he can't throw something at us we can't handle?"

He locked onto my eyes. "Sometimes, perseverance is one's greatest asset."

I nodded. What was important? My comfort and ease in completing this task, or that we finish it no matter what Beltrid threw at us? Uncle Seth's words had struck a chord in my soul; I had to push ahead no matter what. My will strengthened, and I determined, no matter what distractions Beltrid threw our way, I would stop feeling sorry for myself and focus on reaching the steam house.

The next morning, the sun shone and the birds sang as if nothing had happened the night before. We set out on the road again. We would arrive tomorrow if nothing stopped us, and I feared something might.

When mid-afternoon rolled around, we came upon a girl, about ten years old, crying by the side of the road.

I knelt beside her. "What's wrong?"

She pointed down a path leading into the forest a few feet away. "My mommy is sick and dying. I tried to find someone to help, but no one will." She bawled louder.

Nathan frowned. "What about Father? He needs saving too."

"How can I leave her? If her mother can be saved, I would feel guilty the rest of my life for not healing her."

"Will you feel guilty if we're too late to save Father?"

I gritted my teeth. "Of course I would." I turned to study the little girl. "But this one's in my face. We don't know that stopping to help her will be too late for Dad. For all we know, this might help us save Dad."

Seth put his hand on Nathan's shoulder. "If you could heal, would you pass her by and let her die?"

Nathan stared at the ground and sighed. "No. But we're so close to Reol." He stared down the road. "But Father would say to help her."

Seth slapped him on the back. "That he would."

I said to the girl, "Show us where your mother is. Maybe we can help."

She stopped crying and smiled. "My name is Angel."

"Angel? Nice." I smiled back. "Now, let's get going, we can't waste time."

I pulled her onto my shoulders, and she directed us down the path and into the forest. Angel? Somehow the name didn't fit her. I couldn't place it, but something bothered me about this girl. Maybe she was so distraught that I had picked up on those feelings. But I had to help.

I figured the mother must have been a little ways from the road, but that proved untrue. We traveled until the sun sank to the western horizon and shadows stretched through the forest. She occasionally directed us what path to take when it split, or to avoid dangerous areas.

"Angel," I said. "How much farther is your mother?"

"Not too much farther. Just over that hill."

I shielded my eyes from the sun as I gazed at its crest. She had said that about four times now. A knot of worry grew; Nathan may have been right. This could be a ruse by Beltrid to delay us, but how to find out without seeming improper? She wouldn't tell me outright if that was her purpose. An idea popped into my mind.

I grabbed Angel under her arms and lifted her off my shoulders. "I think I'm getting a little tired. Let's rest here for a while, maybe eat something."

Her eyes watered up and tears fell down her cheeks. I breathed a sigh of relief. If she had been happy to stop, I would have suspected she didn't tell us the truth.

I rubbed her arm. "I know you're eager to save your mother. Maybe Nathan can carry you a while, and I can eat a little as we walk?"

She calmed down. "All right."

Nathan grabbed her and lifted her onto his shoulders. Then we resumed our trek through the woods.

This time she had told the truth. Over the small hill, a house rested on the opposite side. The sun had sunk behind the peaks, and darkness grew in the eastern sky.

As we entered the clearing where the house sat, I scanned for signs of a sick woman. "Is she inside the house?"

Angel nodded.

We approached the house, but before we could step onto the porch, a wolf rounded the corner of the house. Atop the wolf sat a mouse in a saddle with a cloth bundle behind him.

He patted it. "Looking for this?"

My jaw tightened. "Rodan, give that back, now!"

He laughed. "Only if you can catch me!" He flipped the reins and the wolf shot toward the forest.

I raced after them.

"Kaylee, don't! He's trying to distract you!" Nathan's voice sounded distant.

I couldn't let this pass. Amma was so close, I had to save her and rectify my mistake. I followed the wolf into the trees. I wouldn't let them get away this time.

33

My troll-muscles pumped to the limit. Rodan kept ahead of me, always in view, but I couldn't gain on him. At last my body revolted, and I couldn't maintain his pace no matter how much I wanted to capture him.

I collapsed onto the ground, gasping for breath. Why did I keep failing to rescue her?

I lay there for a few moments until my breathing returned to normal. I stood up and searched the area. Wolf tracks trailed deeper into the forest. Stars peered out from the night sky one by one. I rested against a tree and tried to think.

Obviously Rodan wanted to lead me away from the steam house. He dangled the possibility of getting Amma back before my nose, and like a horse wanting a carrot, I followed. But why did I do that? Too big an ego? Did I think I could trick him? Out maneuver him?

No, I knew my heart said to follow him, even though logic said otherwise.

I heard footsteps approaching. I remained very still. They grew louder until Nathan passed me. He stopped at the spot where I had fallen. He examined the ground and then his head turned my direction. He jumped back at first when he saw me. I chuckled.

He put his hands on his hips. "Some help you are, hiding from your own brother."

"I wanted to see how well you tracked me. You would have never heard the end of it if you had gone on by without turning around."

He reached out a hand and pulled me up. "So what happened?"

"He was too fast and I couldn't keep up. But his tracks are pretty clear."

"You did much better than I would have. Your strides were pretty

184

long."

"So I guess we should go back, if logic dictated our next move."

He stared back toward the house. "Yes, if logic dictated it. Point is, why did you go after him if you knew what he was up to?"

"I felt in my heart I should."

Nathan nodded. "Uncle said that might be the reason, and if so, to tell you this: Angel's mother was in danger, but by Rodan. If we had not returned with her, he would have killed her. The girl was honest about that part. Uncle said he would head back to the road and go to Reol. We can continue to track Rodan and meet him there later."

I smiled. "Great. But it's getting late. Better camp here tonight and pick up the trail tomorrow. It's too dark to keep following."

Nathan slid the pack off and broke out the dried meats and cheeses the monk had given us. After eating, we prepared for sleeping on the bare ground. We built a fire to keep the darkness at bay. We each took a turn staying on watch. No telling when the wolves might attack again, or what Beltrid might try next.

While on watch, I gazed at my bracelet. The winged horse shimmered in the firelight. I wished I had such an animal to carry Nathan and I. We would be in Reol in no time or be able to track and follow Rodan easily.

"But that would take all the fun out of it."

I jumped and swung around, drawing my sword. Joel emerged from the trees.

"Don't scare me like that!"

He grinned. "There's no good way to approach someone when they think they are miles from anyone." He sat down across the fire from me.

I sheathed my sword and sat down. "I assume you were talking about my desire to use a winged horse. What 'fun' would I be missing out on?"

"I wish I could tell you. But that would ruin it all."

I sighed. "Then why mention it."

"I'm sorry. I shouldn't have."

"Where have you been? I began to think once you helped me over this love and control problem I had, you had sunk back into obscurity."

He nodded. "It's true. My task with you is finished. Only one other loose end to tie up."

"And I suppose you can't tell me what that is either."

"Nope."

For the first time, I realized he might not be around much longer—a lump rose in my throat and I tried to swallow it down.

I met his eyes. "And will I see you after you finish?"

He stared into the night sky and bit his lip. "That's up to God. Sort of goes with the calling."

His words didn't sound promising. "I guess I'm lucky that God sent someone specifically to help me."

"To be honest, it wasn't just you."

I raised an eyebrow. "What do you mean?"

"We knew you had a problem dealing with men. A problem we had to correct if you were to continue with the ring, because you couldn't be biased in its use."

I hadn't thought I might not keep it. Where would it go if I didn't wear it? I sat up straighter. "You talk as if you had consulted with God one-on-one."

He smiled half-heartedly. "I guess you could say we're pretty close." He cleared his throat and changed the subject. "The cure involved forcing you to deal with your past and realize that not every man is out to rape you. Ironically, Beltrid's attempt to trap you in your mind, to mind-rape you, ended up being what we needed to reach you."

A chill ran down my legs thinking about the dream I couldn't end. "You mind if I sit next to you?" I couldn't believe I had said that.

He patted the flat space next to him. "Sit."

I scooted next to him and laid my head on his chest. He wrapped his heavenly arms around me. I admit, I liked it. Not just for the physical sensation, but because I felt as long as he held me, I didn't have anything to fear. No wolves would appear, no evil events attempting to peel us away and drive us to our deaths. As long as he sat next to me and hugged me, the world would stop for a while and I could rest without a worry.

I snuggled deeper into his arms. "So why did you show up this time? Any special abilities we need or warnings you have for us?"

"No, I came because you needed encouragement."

Warmth spread through me knowing one of God's best stood guard. I could sleep in peace. My thoughts drifted to love and wondering if Joel loved me, or whether my inexperience caused me to imagine he did. Did I love him? I suspected the later could be true. And if so, I didn't know whether to be glad or sad, for I might not see him again.

"Get up, lazy bones." Nathan shook me awake.

"What time is it?"

"First daylight. But you fell asleep on watch."

"No, no. Joel stood watch."

"Yeah, sure. But never mind, no harm done."

I frowned at him. I could tell he didn't believe me. So what? It didn't matter.

We ate cheese for breakfast and then set out to follow the tracks.

They wound through valleys and over hills. We walked at a quick pace, but didn't run. We didn't want to tire ourselves out or miss a key clue due to haste. When the sun sat high in the sky, the trail ended at the top of a hill in a meadow. Knee-high grass waved in the wind's gusts. We searched the area for the continuation of his trail, but no tracks could be found—as if he flew away on this spot. And knowing him, he very well could have.

"It's no use," Nathan said. "This is a dead end."

A fireball erupted from the grass on the far side and sped toward us. The unexpectedness of it caused me to freeze at first, but we both jumped to the side as it flew past us.

"I'll bet it's Rodan. If we're low, he can't see us."

A small bolt of lightning shot past me, causing the hairs on my arm to rise. It left a trail of smoldering, blackened grass to my right.

Nathan rose and dived forward. I followed. He rose again. About then, a bolt shot from the grass and a giant bubble enveloped Nathan and floated him into the air. It hovered a few feet, but didn't go any farther.

"Rodan, what are you doing?"

I stood. A bolt shot my way, but I spun around and it flew by. I zigzagged randomly as balls of fire and bolts zinged their way in front and behind me. I tacked my way closer toward him. As I dove to fall close to his location, I heard him scurry away in the grass, creating a wake as he pushed through the knee-high weeds. I jumped to my feet to chase after him. A ball of fire flew out and before I could react, hit me in the arm. Its force knocked me backwards onto the ground; a searing pain blasted through my body. The pain quickly left due to the ring's power.

A wolf rose from the grass. Rodan hopped into the saddle, and sped down the hill.

I jumped up and stabbed my sword through the bubble encasing Nathan. It popped, and he dropped to the ground with a thud.

"Hurry, maybe we can catch him!" I raced after Rodan.

I pushed myself again. If the wolf tripped over something, I would have them. Nathan had trouble keeping up, but I knew he could track us down, so I pumped my legs as fast as they would go. Still, I couldn't gain on the quick beast. The bag with the crystal dangled and bobbed on the wolf's hind legs. I hoped it wouldn't break.

As we flew down the hill, I saw a cut lawn nestled in the valley below, but no house sat on it. Rodan headed straight for it. I had no idea if he led me into a trap or if he raced ahead blindly. It didn't matter. If I could catch up to him, the race would end, and I could get Amma back. I breathed long and deep as I pumped my legs, attempting to keep myself full of fresh air. However, soon my breaths grew rapid.

The distance between us grew, and I watched as they disappeared into the forest. But I kept up a pace as well as I could manage. Then I broke into the open clearing. I searched for Rodan but could see no sign of him.

A fire ball shot toward me and I ducked. I raced to the spot, hoping to get there before another fireball could go off. But a bubble enveloped me, and I rose off the ground. I didn't even see him shoot anything at me.

Rodan's head rose above the grass and he hopped onto the back of the wolf and laughed. "Now I've got you!"

Nathan burst into the clearing. He glanced at me, then focused on Rodan. He narrowed his eyes, drew his sword, and sped toward him. But before he had taken five steps, another bubble formed around him. He slammed into the side of it and slid to the bottom.

I hadn't seen Rodan so much as mumble a spell or wave a hand. Had he become so good he only had to think a spell? I attempted to penetrate the bubble with my sword, but from the inside, it wouldn't break. Instead, it stretched with the point of the blade.

Rodan's eyes darted between us, and his mouse-mouth hung open, but then he clapped his paws in glee. "Excellent! I should get paid well for this."

A new voice commanded from the other side of the clearing. "I doubt you'll get a thank you, much less pay after I'm done with you."

I turned to see who had spoken. An older man who looked to be in his fifties stood a few feet away. He wore a white robe and sported a short, gray beard.

Rodan twitched his whiskers. "Who are you?"

"If you need a name, it's Josh."

The named sounded familiar. Could it be my dad's childhood friend? I could only hope.

"Josh? Not the apprentice of Milore, are you?"

"One and the same."

"He was an old fool."

Josh laughed. "A wise old fool, if you ask me. You, on the other hand, appear to be the true fool—unless you prefer existing as a mouse."

Rodan jumped up and down on the wolf's back. He stretched out his paws and muttered a spell I couldn't hear. A blue, streaming flame erupted

189

from his hands and shot toward Josh.

Josh lifted his left hand casually and the flames spread around him as if a shield protected him. Then he flicked his fingertips out; the flames shrank back toward Rodan. The fire collapsed into his body. He flew off the back of the wolf and tumbled into the short grass. Josh strolled toward him.

Rodan rose and muttered another spell. Arrows materialized before him and then sped toward Josh. Josh spun his fingers into a circle and held out his palm. The arrows pointed skyward and gathered into his hand before he closed his fingers around them. Then they dissolved into nothingness.

Rodan stomped his little feet. "How did you get so powerful?"

Josh smiled. "Clean living, I guess. Now, do you wish to repent before I decide your fate?"

"Repent? Me! You're the one getting in my way, you should repent."

Josh shook his head. "Even after getting a second chance in the steam house, you still can only think of yourself." He sighed. "Oh well, have it your way."

Josh thrust his hand forward and spread his fingers.

Rodan didn't budge. He scanned around himself. "Seems you missed."

"Nope, I didn't miss."

Rodan tried to move, but his feet appeared stuck to the grass. He muttered a spell, but even though a glow spread around his feet, still he could not budge them.

Rodan stared at Josh. "What do you mean to do? Keep me in this spot forever?"

Josh shook his head. "Let's just say, I've constructed a mouse trap." Josh mumbled a spell as he traced a circle with his hands.

A light emanated from Rodan like a small star in the grass. It grew brighter and whiter until Rodan's form disappeared. I shielded my eyes. A squeaky scream pierced the air. When I thought I'd burn in the light's heat, it collapsed within a second. Once my eyes could focus, a smooth ball set upon a plain, black base lay in the grass. Inside, I could see the tiny figure of Rodan jumping around.

The wolf headed for the woods. I pointed toward it. "Get the bag on the wolf's saddle. My mother's in there!"

Josh waved his hand. The wolf froze in its tracks, and the bag floated into his outstretched hand. Then he approached my bubble and studied me. "You wouldn't happen to be Sisko's daughter, would you? You bear a striking resemblance to him, despite your odd look."

"I am, and that's my brother Nathan. My name's Kaylee."

His eyes traveled up and down my body, as if he judged me at a horse show. Of course, I felt like that anytime someone looked at me with anything more than a cursory glance—a reflex I couldn't control. Yet I knew my perception bore little resemblance to reality.

I sheathed my sword when I realized I still had it out. "I don't suppose you could let us out, could you?"

"Oh, I'm sorry. This is an automatic trap I had set up. The mouse and wolf didn't register since they weren't human." His talk turned to mumbling, but I caught enough of it to hear, "I'll have to adjust the spell for intelligent life of all types, I guess."

He waved his hand and the bubbles popped. We both collapsed onto the ground.

"Come on in, we have much to discuss." He stepped toward the center of the clearing. A black house trimmed in white materialized before us.

I glanced at Nathan as I dusted myself off. He appeared as interested as I did. Dad had mentioned Josh, and told us a few stories. But we didn't realize how much of a wizard he had become. Apparently a very powerful one, and hopefully on our side.

I cleared my throat. "Uh, excuse me, Josh. But what about Rodan?"

He stopped and turned. "Oh yes, practically forgot about the fool. Guess I should at least give him a spot on my mantle." He lifted the ball from the grass and held it to our eyes.

Inside, a little world of forests and mountains existed. Rodan dashed around a meadow, stopping occasionally to say something and thrust his tiny paws out, but nothing happened.

I pointed at the ball. "Is this the 'Ball of Desires' my dad talked about?"

A smile broke across his face and he chuckled. "Oh no, far from it. I would rather call this, the 'Ball of Humility.' He can do no magic in there. It is a land devoid of anyone to rule over or conquer. Indeed, look at the cave on the far mountain."

Something moved, then exited the cave. A big cat sniffed the air. I giggled. "Oh, now that's mean! But he deserves it."

Josh shook his head. "It's not to punish him. The cat will never be able to catch him, but he won't know that. He'll spend what's left of his life running from danger. It's his last chance for repentance, I hope he takes it. Sometimes only total helplessness can break through some people's pride."

He turned and entered his house; we followed. The inside appeared like many I'd seen. Fairly sparse, but with a kitchen, a fireplace, and a single bed in a corner. A table sat in the center. Upon the mantle of the fireplace, however, lay a broken ball. Fragments of glass jutted up here and there from a dark base. Josh set Rodan's ball next to it.

Nathan stared at the broken ball. "Is that the 'Ball of Desires'?"

"What's left of it."

I had to admit. Seeing it brought what sounded like a surreal story to life. But in hindsight, the story sounded pretty tame compared to what had happened to us on this trip.

We sat at the table and Josh poured us some tea.

"Thank you." I took a sip. "Um, very good. Tastes like Joel's tea."

"It should. I'm using his tea leaves."

"You know Joel?" I knew I shouldn't be surprised. *This guy gets around.*

"Yes. He told me he gets these leaves from a planet in a distant galaxy."

An uncontrolled heaving of air exploded from my lungs, and I spewed tea over the table. "He gets them from where?" Joel really did get around! I glanced at Nathan whose mouth hung open.

Josh winced as he grabbed a cloth to wipe tea off the table. "Oh, he didn't tell you about that, did he. I've probably said too much. Well, the tea is...heavenly. He promised to keep me in stock."

Why did it seem everyone else knew all the secrets while I struggled in the dark? But I knew he wouldn't say anything more about Joel, so I turned my questions toward him. "So you're the Josh my dad has mentioned in his stories."

Nathan added, "If so, you are much more powerful now. According to Father, you had a lot to learn."

Josh laughed. "I was eighteen when your father left town to go rescue damsels in distress. I did have a lot to learn then."

Nathan leaned closer. "How did you become so powerful, then?"

Josh's smile faded. "Not without suffering and pain." He stared at the wall as if lost in thought. "It's a long story for another time, and involves wizard's secrets. But I wouldn't be here if not for your father."

How often had I heard that? I bowed my head. "But Dad's in a lot of trouble now, as well as our mother."

Josh nodded. "I know, he's been keeping me updated."

I stared at him. "Have you been talking to him?"

He winked at me. "Yes. Not too many people know about it, but I did learn one spell before he left town that allows us to talk over great distances when we need to. Like a message courier but quicker."

Nathan leaned forward. "Is he all right? Can you speak to him now? Can we speak to him?"

"One question at a time, please." He stroked his beard. "Last I heard, he is alive, though he did indicate Beltrid had put him through some bad experiences. No, we can't speak to him now. I wait for him to contact me because Beltrid could pick up on our contact, so your father has to be careful, and it has to be quick. But..."

"But what?" I didn't like how his eyes stared out the window.

"It has been three days since our last contact. I've not heard from him since. It's possible Beltrid may have found out and cut it off."

My gut twisted. "Or he's dead."

"Don't say that!" Nathan pushed into my face. "He can't be dead. I won't accept it until I see it for myself."

"Nathan's right," Josh said. "But we do need to get you two ready for the steam house. It is critical that you go in prepared for what you will encounter."

We both stared at him. "We're ready. What do we need to know?"

"For starters, you will need to take off the ring and the bracelet before you enter. You must go in with no such protections, or the steam house will react to their presence as a lack of faith and bad results will follow."

I swallowed. "All right. But the ring won't come off, nor this bracelet. And what protection does the bracelet give?"

"They'll come off when it's time. The bracelet, I'm not at liberty to say."

"What? You have restrictions too?"

"No, but a promise to Joel that I wouldn't reveal it before he did."

I sighed. "It's very frustrating to be given this and not told how to use it or what it's for."

"It will be evident in time. When you are in the steam house, you must focus your attention on simple obedience. That will bring about the humility needed to come out of there with a blessing."

"Obedience?" Nathan asked. "Obedience to what?"

"To whatever you encounter in there. The keys to finding joy through it are faith, hope, and love. In short, humility is watered by obedience to those three virtues."

Josh sipped his tea. "I learned that the hard way."

I smiled. "I recall the story."

A thought occurred to me. "And what about Dad's parents, our grandparents, are they alive? Is Dad's brother Jake still living around here?"

"Yes, Jake cares for them. They live in town. As a matter of fact, we should get over to their place. We'll also need to see the priest before you enter the steam house." He downed the last of his tea and rose. "Oh, and here's your mother." He held out the bag.

I took it and unwrapped it. The crystal bore no fractures or signs of breaking. Amma still stood, her arms out, frozen in place. A sigh escaped my lips and my muscles relaxed. It would be easier to focus on the steam house without having to worry about her. Did she know all that had happened, or would she would return as from a long dream? I wrapped it up and stuffed it back in my pack.

We set off down the path to town.

One nice thing about taking the rest of the trip with a powerful wizard, Beltrid tried no more tricks on us. At least, I assumed that's why he didn't do anything else.

We entered Reol. No wall encircled it, just a simple village that happened to be on a main road cutting through these parts. A group of houses had been built around a church, along with merchants offering their services and wares along the streets. But no big market place stood out to my eyes.

Wooden beams enclosed most houses. Thatched roofs held aloft chimneys from which smoke drifted lazily here and there. Occasionally a bigger and nicer house of the more well-to-do would catch my attention. At the center of town stood the church building. A dome rose over the roofs and, on top of that, a cross stood guard over the village.

Josh took us down a side-street. After passing three houses, we came across a little cabin. A small but tidy lawn surrounded it; a dirt path led from the street to the porch. Josh stepped up to the door and knocked.

The door swung open. A man, a little younger than Dad, stood at the threshold. "Hi Josh. Who are your friends?"

"Jake, meet Kaylee and Nathan, Sisko's kids."

His eyes widened and a smile spread across his face. "Amazing!" He peered around us. "Where's Sisko?"

Josh sighed. "That will take some explaining. I'll tell you later."

Jake stared at Josh as if processing his words. His head bobbed. "Well, come in." He waved us to enter.

As he turned, I couldn't help thinking about his missing leg as a child. Dad's first miracle healed him of that condition, and now I couldn't tell he'd ever had a problem.

Jake bounded inside. "Mother, Father, you'll never guess who's here!"

We stepped inside. The small house had been kept clean and clutter-free. Against one wall, two beds stood. Upon those beds, Grandma and Grandpa rested. Their bony arms, covered in loose skin, moved to shift them into a sitting position. Flesh sagged on their faces, and gray hair grew on their heads, though Grandpa didn't have a lot left.

"These are Sisko's kids, Kaylee and Nathan."

Their faces lit up, and they asked for us to come closer. I bent over Grandma, and she planted a soft kiss on my cheek and hugged me. Grandpa did the same. Then Grandma asked, "Where's my son, Sisko?"

I glanced at Josh. If Jake didn't know anything, they wouldn't either. If we had our way, he would be here soon. "He's delayed a little, Grandma.

He'll be along later."

She smiled. "I can die a happy woman now. I've seen my grandchildren." She stared at Jake. "Have they gone into the steam house?"

Josh stepped toward her. "No ma'am, not yet. But they will."

She relaxed, smiled again, and stared at Nathan and me.

Then I saw Uncle Seth sitting in a chair by the table. "Uncle Seth, I'm glad you're safe!"

"I'm glad you made it too. You had me worried there for a while." He stood and hugged us both.

Josh motioned for Seth, Jake, Nathan, and I to follow him outside. Once out, he said, "Jake, we need to set up a time to speak to Father Jonah. I'll take care of that. Kaylee and Nathan will stay here with you. Tomorrow they will go into the steam house, and if they are successful, Sisko will come out with them."

Jake's brow wrinkled. "He will?"

"Long story, but he is being held captive. If Kaylee and Nathan come out better instead of worse, he will be freed. So we need Father to bless them and give them any help he can. A lot rides on their success, more than just their own individual futures."

Jake nodded and stared at us. "I understand. I'll go get food prepared and places for them to bed down." Jake returned to the house.

I wondered about something. "Josh?"

"Yes?"

"As much as Beltrid has harassed us, why hasn't he done anything to Dad's family here?"

He smiled. "When Sisko left town, I promised I would protect his family as well as I could. He knew popularity often brought the wrong kind of attention. It's one of the reasons he has stayed away so long, to keep his parents and Jake from being targets.

"Beltrid did cause your grandparents to become bedridden and sick, but I kept him from killing them. So he focused on you. I guess he figured you were more vulnerable."

"And perhaps their sickness or death would be less effective, since Dad would not likely know about it, except maybe through you."

He nodded. "I'll be back, hopefully with Father Jonah." He stepped onto the street and headed toward the parish.

Seth raised a hand. "I'll go with you. It'll be good to get out."

I sat down on the porch. "Well Brother, you've been quiet. What's going on in that head of yours?"

He sat next to me and rested his elbows on his thighs. "Too much, I'm afraid. I'm eager to get this over with, but scared to death at the same time."

"I know what you mean." I placed my arm around his shoulders and squeezed. "But we'll get through his. We have to."

He nodded. "Yeah, for Father's sake, we have to. But that's why this is so terrifying. If my own life was all I risked, that would be bad enough. But if I don't pass this test, he remains Beltrid's prisoner forever. How can I live with myself if that happens?"

"It's Beltrid who shouldn't be able to live with himself. But that's a demon for you. All you can do is your best." Why did my words ring hollow in my own ears even if true? Because I felt the weight of the impending guilt too. "I mean, we know we aren't perfect, and God knows that too. But what's in the heart, that's the key. And Brother, I've seen a bit of it, and you have a good heart."

"I wish I felt as certain."

"You're right. It is a heavy weight. But He wouldn't send us in there if we couldn't do it." I hoped that would be true. I decided to change the subject. "Let's go inside and talk to our grandparents. We have a lot of catching up to do."

He smiled. We rose and entered the house.

35

"Kaylee, Nathan! Can you come outside for a moment?" Josh's voice rang from the yard.

I patted Jake's hand. "We'll be back in a moment, Uncle."

We exited the house and found Seth, Josh, and Father Jonah standing close to the street. Father Jonah's long flowing black robe and hat waved with the gusts of wind.

Josh pointed at us. "Father Jonah, this is Kaylee and Nathan. Sisko's children I told you about. They will enter the steam house in the morning."

He blinked and drew close. He circled as he examined us. He pulled closer and sniffed. Then he put a hand on our foreheads and focused into the sky. He held that position for several moments. I glanced at Nathan; his eyes stared questioningly at Father Jonah.

Then he prayed a blessing upon us that by entering the steam house, we would not only find what we sought for, but even more, what we needed to live our lives in tune with God and His creation.

Then he grinned at us. "I'm so happy to meet you both."

I smiled back, then realized with his unusual introduction, I had not properly asked for a blessing. But being he had already given one, it seemed silly to ask for another. "We're very glad to meet you as well." We both bowed.

He stared at Nathan. "Your biggest temptation will be to allow your anger to run away with you. You must think about what you are doing. Don't react; think it through, then act."

Nathan nodded. "Yes, Father."

He hugged Nathan. "You'll do fine. Don't worry!"

Nathan returned a weak smile.

Then the priest turned to me. "And you, young lady, have already

197

dealt with your biggest fear, but beware of not listening to your heart. Your father had a gift for that. The steam house saw that and is partly why it granted him the ring."

"I know, Father. I do sometimes have trouble separating my own desires from God's voice in my heart."

"You've already taken a step in the right direction. Love frees you to listen. When you can focus on others instead of yourself, you hear what God wants for them. That's why your father ended up losing the gift of the ring. He stopped loving as he should and focused on himself. He could no longer hear God clearly in his heart."

I nodded. "Thank you, Father. I'll remember your words."

He reached out and grabbed both our shoulders. "And remember, above all, be obedient to what God shows you in there. Do that, and you will not fail."

He hugged me, and I felt confidence flow through me. Somehow this would work out, though I couldn't say how.

Father Jonah left, and we returned to the house. Dinner consisted of bread and cabbage soup—the traditional meal before entering the steam house.

Our grandparents told us many stories of Dad's childhood. Most we had not heard before. Several caused us to laugh. Some we exclaimed, "Aw," while others we said, "Yep, that's Dad all right."

We talked fairly late, but they grew tired and we had to get some sleep for the task the next morning. After bedding down, I felt chills crawling down my skin. I didn't feel cold; I was scared. My whole life came down to what happened in this steam house. Failure loomed beyond its doors, coupled with guilt and disaster.

"God, help me save Dad, I can't do this alone." I whispered.

A hand reached out and touched me. I jerked and turned my head. Joel knelt over me.

He sat on a chair. "You're not alone."

The chills disappeared. I gazed into his eyes; they watered. "Why are you crying?"

He smiled weakly. "Sympathy tears."

I liked that. I cuddled down and drifted toward sleep. A last thought echoed in my mind before dreams overtook me: after tomorrow, life will never be the same. Of that much, I was sure.

The next morning I awoke to a busy house. Jake and Josh scurried around, getting breakfast ready and helping Grandma and Grandpa out of bed and dressed. Nathan still lay in his bed, uncharacteristically.

I shook him. "Hey, get up sleepy."

He waved his hand at me. "Be quiet. I can sleep as late as I want."

I sighed. "Nathan, that's not going to stop the inevitable."

He rolled over. "I know." He closed his eyes. "But I can pretend for a while longer, can't I?"

Josh leaned over us. "Nope, get up or I'll cast a spell on you."

Nathan flung his eyes open and smiled. "Can you turn me into a frog or something? Then I won't have to do this."

He laughed. "No. Instead, I'll send you straight into the steam house, quick as a wink."

"I'm up, I'm up!" He sat up and yawned. "Where's breakfast? I get a last meal, don't I?"

I laughed. "Get him some hay. He eats like a horse anyway, may as well feed him like one."

Nathan bopped me on the back of the head.

I rolled over onto him and we wrestled. I pinned him down after a few moves. "Do you say 'uncle'?"

"Uncle, get this crazy girl off me!"

"That'll do." We both laughed as we helped each other up. Not so much because of the corny pun, but the release of built-up tension felt good. Plus, it could be the last time we would have that much fun for all we knew.

We washed up and ate breakfast. They gave me a special pair of pants and blouse for wearing in the steam house. Usually, they said, women used the steam house on separate days than the men, but since Nathan would be with me, I needed more modesty. Nathan, however, received as his sole clothing a towel wrapped around his waist, firmly fastened in place.

After some final words of encouragement from Seth, Jake, and Josh, they helped Grandma and Grandpa up, and we left the house.

As we entered the yard, several kids jumped up and down excitedly. They danced down the street. "Here they come! Here they come!"

I peered down the road, shielding my eyes from the sun. A crowd of people lined the dirt path. "What's going on?"

Jake cleared his throat. "My brother is somewhat of a hometown hero. As stories of his miracles drifted back into town, his status as a legend multiplied. So naturally, as word that his children would enter the steam house spread, many dropped everything and rushed to see the outcome."

"Great. If we fail, it will be spread over the whole land."

Nathan frowned. "This is hard enough without having an audience."

The crowd grew as we approached the steam house. The whole town appeared to have turned out. Kids pointed at us. I even saw one young man selling rings among the crowds. Several wore them on their fingers. I couldn't imagine how he had obtained them on such short notice.

The people parted as we approached; the steam house slid into view. A hush fell over the crowd. The steam house appeared simple enough. An octagonal building constructed of wood, now weathered and in need of painting. A sign hung over the doorway. Faded blue lettering against a white background read, "Steamy Realities Steam House: Sweats out both body and soul. Warning: Only the pure of soul should enter. We are not liable for negative results."

The last part didn't sound too comforting. I guess it wasn't meant to be. Pure or not, I would have to enter.

Joel broke through the crowd and approached me. He held out his hand. "Time to give me the ring and bracelet."

I felt weird. The protection of the ring did provide some comfort. I would feel naked without it. But that's how it is entering into a place of judgment—a naked soul for all to see.

I pulled on the ring and it slid off my finger. It had encircled my finger for such a short amount of time, yet I knew this would be a rare event. It released Dad only twice: when he violated it and when he gave it to me. I handed it to Joel. Would it return to me again?

The bracelet likewise now snapped open with ease. I still had no idea what it did or why I had been given it. I might never know if I failed today.

I placed it into Joel's hand as well. He stared at me. Sadness dripped from his eyes. He pulled me to him and hugged tightly for a few seconds.

I whispered into his ear, "You know something bad will happen."

He pulled back. "Me? No, I don't know anything."

"You're a terrible liar."

He closed his eyes tight. "I'll be praying for you." He turned and pushed his way back into the crowd. I would receive no comfort from him now—only an abiding sense of dread.

I breathed deep to keep my sense of terror submerged and turned to Nathan.

His jaw had set; his eyes stared firmly into mine. "Let's do this."

I grabbed him and squeezed tight. "I love you, Brother. Whatever happens, I love you."

He squeezed back and smiled. "I love you too."

I took a deep breath and faced the steam house. I held Nathan's hand tightly for support and stepped forward. Cheers erupted from the crowd as we opened the door and entered the unknown.

36

The heat hit me in the face and I gasped. The door closed behind us. I surveyed the interior: a wooden bench ran the circumference of the eight-sided building. In the middle, a set of volcanic rocks had been piled over a fire, which lapped at them with gusto.

I spotted one man sitting by the door. Other than him and us, no one else used the building.

He rose. "You're Sisko's children?"

I nodded.

"If you need more steam, take this ladle…" He grabbed a wooden ladle sitting in a bucket of water by the door. "And slowly pour the water out as you rotate it in a circle." He poured it onto the rocks, and steam sizzled upwards. "That's all there is to it. When you think you've been in here long enough, then come out. Good luck to you both." He shook our hands and then exited. The door slammed shut behind him.

I sat down on the bench. I hadn't been in a steam house before, but this one appeared much as I expected. I wondered why this one possessed such unusual qualities.

"Nathan?"

"Yes."

"Be sure to tell me…, well, on second thought, maybe I don't want to know."

"What?"

"You know, Dad said you can see others changing but not yourself until you get out."

He nodded. "Yeah, I don't think I want to know either. But if you're curious, so far, so good." He smiled.

A moment passed. "Well?" he said.

201

"You said you didn't want to know." I winked at him. "But you're doing all right too."

He rose and strolled around the building. His arms dripped with moisture; his chest revealed years of hard work.

He paused and focused on me. "Maybe we should think good thoughts. It might help."

I nodded. "My favorite thought is riding a winged horse again."

He stared at the ceiling and shook his head. "You're not helping me! That's one of my scarier thoughts. No, my favorite thought is Crystal. Before I knew Beltrid controlled her, I felt complete. I had so wanted to marry her."

"I'm sure you'll find her again, and maybe then it can happen for real."

He smiled. "I hope so."

As Nathan continued to stroll around the building, I wondered what we waited for. Maybe we had been in long enough and we could leave? Nathan hadn't changed yet.

He sat for a while, stared around the building while kicking his feet, drumming on the bench. He arose, grabbed some water in the ladle, and poured it over the rocks. A cloud of steam rose thick. I wondered if he had put too much water on because the cloud expanded thicker than it should have.

Then I froze. As the steam cloud thinned, Beltrid's figure loomed before us. In one hand, he held Dad firmly behind the neck.

I jumped up. "Dad!"

Nathan spun around and then backed up to where I stood. "What do you want? I thought we wouldn't be seeing you again."

Beltrid smiled. "I didn't mention this exception? How forgetful of me. As to what I want, it has always been the ring. Come to find out, this one doesn't have it anymore. What a pity."

He drew near to us. I felt defenseless. No sword, nothing but the bare clothing on me. "How can you be in here? The steam house reveals flaws of the soul, and I imagine you have plenty."

"I'm already a demon, what more can the steam house do to me?" He stared at my hand. "And I see you didn't bring the ring into the steam house. That means you are free to give it to me."

Dad raised his head and his eyes met mine. "Don't do it, Kaylee." Beltrid slapped him across the face and blood slung from his nose. "Quiet, slave!"

I gritted my teeth. I so wanted to slap him back, but I knew the outcome of that. "What do you want with it anyway? It would not perform miracles for you or any of your slaves."

Beltrid let out a long, hard laugh. "Miracles? Is that why you think I want it? To force God to grant me miracles?" He fixed his eyes on Dad.

"None of you know the true history of this ring, do you?"

Dad gave no indication he had heard. But Beltrid had revealed enough information that I knew this ring operated on more than a simple vow. It existed before the day it appeared on Dad's hand. The mystery of the ring flowed deeper than we knew.

I cleared my throat. "I can't give it to you. Another has possession of it at the moment."

His faced reddened and he screamed, "Who? Joel?"

I remained silent. He stomped around as if deciding what to do. Then he spun around and lifted Dad into the air like a kitten. He spat upon the ground. "I'll at least make sure that on this earth, none of you will be able to wear it again!" He drew out a short sword from his belt.

A knot formed in my stomach. "No, don't kill him!"

He grinned. "Will you give me the ring? I'll spare his life if you do. When you exit the steam house, accept it from Joel but don't put it on. Put it in your pocket and give it to me later."

My gut twisted. How could I give it to him? I considered promising it to him so Dad could be freed, but refuse once we had left the steam house. But what would the steam house do to me for lying in it? I certainly wouldn't keep the ring, and Beltrid wouldn't release Dad because I had come out worse than when I entered.

For a moment, I felt as if I had no choice. Either I promised him the ring and fulfilled that promise, or I refused and Dad would die. But Beltrid had made a promise too.

I focused on the demon. "You are bound to your word. If we leave the steam house without changing for the worst, you promised to release him." I straightened my back. "I cannot give you the ring. I will not."

His lips drooped for a second before rising into a smile. His red eyes beamed. "Yes, I am true to my word, but I never promised in what condition he would be released. You want him back? You can have him!" He swung the sword through the air and plunged it into Dad's chest. Dad's eyes widened for a second as a huff of air escaped his mouth, and then he slumped over in Beltrid's hand.

My legs wobbled under me; my eyes refused to blink and my breathing stopped. I reached my hand out. "Dad!"

Beltrid laughed, his eyes boring into mine. Visions of him laughing in the dream flooded over me; thoughts of running away battered against my mind. Beltrid flung Dad's limp body onto the hot rocks.

"No!" My legs gave way, and I dropped to my knees. Nathan's wide eyes stared at Dad's body. I couldn't believe what had just happened either. We had entered this steam house to save him. Now he lay dead, and I felt I would join him if I could. I felt tears forging trails through the sweat on my cheeks.

His laughing continued. My face flushed as I gritted my teeth. I would end this now! I had no idea what I could do against a demon, but I didn't care. I didn't care that his power had nearly killed me the last time when I wielded a sword. All I knew is he would pay, and I would do everything in my power to destroy him. I screamed something between a wail and an attack cry and flung myself toward Beltrid.

Before I could reach him, a blow from my side shoved me off my feet. Nathan's arms wrapped around me and I grunted as we crashed onto the floor. Beltrid laughed, but Nathan whispered into my ear, "Kaylee, he knows the steam house will make you into a beast or something for letting your hate fly. Already, your skin is turning color."

"What does it matter now? Dad's dead!" I slammed my hand onto the ground; a sickening guilt rose into my voice. "We failed to save him."

Nathan closed his eyes. "I know. Father's dead." He lifted his head and fixed his eyes on me. "But he also wanted to make sure Beltrid didn't get the ring. Beltrid doesn't want you to have it. If you wear it again, he will have lost. But only if you control yourself."

I calmed down. Nathan was right. Beltrid killed Dad in front of me, in the steam house, specifically to destroy me so that I couldn't have the ring. Besides, I knew a physical assault against him would prove pointless and give him opportunity to kill me as well. I squeezed Nathan's shoulder. "Thanks for saving me."

He glanced at Beltrid and then back. "No problem. I owe you a few anyway."

We stood. Beltrid no longer laughed. "I killed your father!" he declared. "What are you going to do about it?"

I stared him in the eyes. *Listen to your heart* were the priest's words. And from my heart burst forth the answer of how to battle a demon and win. "What am I going to do? I'll tell you what I'm going to do. I'm going to walk out of this steam house, accept the ring back, and go help as many people and do as many miracles as it will allow me to do in my lifetime."

I narrowed my eyes. "Your kind isn't destroyed with hate and swords, but with love and humility."

He stomped his feet and growled. "Then I'll see you in Hell one day."

"Don't count on it."

He let out a piercing scream and raised his hands as if casting a spell. Nothing happened. His eyes darted around and he gritted his teeth. He raised his hands again. Still he failed to vanish out of the steam house. He growled.

Nathan twitched a smile upon his lips. "What's the matter? Having magic trouble?"

Beltrid sped to the door and yanked, but it wouldn't open for him. He growled as he frantically beat upon it, but the flimsy, wooden door responded to his attempts as if it was encased in iron.

Then I smelled something. It surprised me, because Dad's burning flesh should have been producing a horrible smell. Instead, I smelled something akin to incense, only much sweeter and richer.

I turned to check Dad's body; my mouth dropped open. Nathan had noticed it too. His body emitted clouds of heavenly steam purer than anything I had ever smelled.

It developed cracks, and shards of light burst forth from it. The more it cracked, the more the light filled the steam house.

Beltrid screamed a horrifying sound, like a dying animal, only worse. I covered my ears as it rang loud and solid. The light from Dad's body shot through Beltrid; he fell to the floor writhing, his eyes wide in terror. Then Dad's whole body burst into flames, yet they didn't devour him. Beltrid gradually faded from view along with his tortured and screaming growl until Nathan and I stood alone in the steam house, shaking.

However, that didn't last long. Nathan wrapped me in his arms and squeezed. After a moment, we sat on the bench, allowing our minds and bodies to digest what had just happened. Dad's body still puffed out whiffs of sweat steam, and light poured from him. Everywhere the light hit me, a pure joy cascaded and grew throughout me. I wanted to sit there forever and soak it in. Pure contentment and joy and humility and love, all rolled into a piercing light that warmed my soul. I shouldn't feel such overwhelming joy while staring upon my dad's dead body, but this is what life is about, what we reach out for so much in this world yet will not find except in His reality. Dad had found it.

"Nathan, do you feel that joy?"

"Yes. It's the most wonderful thing I've ever felt or tasted in my life."

"Remember Dad's story about when he died?"

He nodded. "Paradise."

"It's the divine light. By killing Dad in the steam house, Beltrid allowed its fire to reveal what lay hidden in his soul, the divine light and joy of paradise that he carried with him. Beltrid couldn't endure it."

Another voice penetrated the steam. "That's right."

I spun my head toward the sound. "Dad?"

A spiritual body filled with light floated above us, but clearly with Dad's features. "The great thing about this steam house revealing spiritual realities, you can see me before I depart." He sank to the floor.

Nathan reached out and grabbed Dad's hand. "Depart? Where?"

"Where else? Paradise. My time is up—I won't have the choice to return this time. But you have both made me very proud."

"Father…" Nathan stared at the ground and swallowed. "I never had the chance to say how sorry I was for not believing you." His eyes met Dad's. "Can you forgive me?"

A smile spread across Dad's face. "There's never been a moment you weren't already forgiven, Son. Being your father has been a constant joy, even among the difficulties."

Tears mixed with sweat over Nathan's cheeks. "Thank you."

I reached out and grabbed Dad's other hand. It was strange feeling such pure joy, yet sadness at the same time.

He smiled and a peace filled his eyes as I had never seen. "Please tell your mother that I eagerly await the day she'll join me in Paradise." He grabbed us both around the shoulders and hugged us tight. "Don't cry too long. We'll all be together again some day. But I have to go now. Paradise awaits and I can't put it off any longer."

"Bye, Dad. I love you." I cried happy tears even amidst the sad.

Nathan wiped his eyes. "I love you too."

"I love you both and I'll continue to pray for you." He vanished through the ceiling. His body on the rocks no longer emitted the light, but the fragrance of paradise hung heavy upon him.

I felt something in my hand. I spread my fingers to reveal a key resting in my palm; a heart-shaped, crystal protrusion extended from the metal stem. I held it up so Nathan could see. "Love. Dad gave us the key for love." Who else could have had any more?

Nathan grinned.

A golden glow still surrounded Dad's body. We found extra towels by the water bucket and pulled him off the heated rocks. After he cooled enough to handle, the glow disappeared as well. I put my arms under his, and Nathan grabbed his feet.

We stared at each other.

"Well, time to face the crowd," I said.

Nathan wore a silly grin on his face.

"What?"

"You said you didn't want me to tell you." He winked.

I paused, realizing he meant the steam house had changed me in some way. At least he didn't act like it was a bad thing. I pushed the door open, and we exited with a puff of steaming air.

Gasps filled the air as we exited the steam house carrying Dad's body. We laid him on the ground. Seth, Jake, and Josh rushed over—Jake fell upon his body and wailed. My heart broke, and I knew they believed we had failed. And in one sense, we had. We had come to save Dad, but he died. Yet we did save him in a way we didn't expect.

Seth and Josh turned to me with wet eyes. Despite the joy resonating in my heart, I couldn't help but cry with them. They didn't have the advantage of talking with him before he left, to experience his joy and peace.

I noticed Grandma and Grandpa sitting by a storefront. They couldn't move without help and I could tell they wanted to be with their son. I briefly thought about healing them before remembering I didn't have the ring on. And despite not wearing it, I clearly felt God didn't want me to do that. Had the steam house sharpened my spiritual senses? Or maybe Dad had prayed secretly for me in that regard before he left. In any case, I knew to leave them in God's hands.

I motioned for Nathan to follow me. We helped Grandma and Grandpa up and supported them as they stepped toward their son's body. Tears traveled through wrinkles until they found their way onto the ground. The crowd parted for them, and we let them down upon Sisko's body so they could grieve.

We stood back a ways. Though I felt sadness knowing I wouldn't see him again this side of eternity, I couldn't forget the joy of Paradise I had felt from him, and the peace on his face as he left us.

In one sense, his death felt like a tragedy. In another, it was the perfect ending to an amazing life that would never be duplicated again. To die for one's faith in God, to defeat evil, and end up in Paradise—what better way to go?

Josh stepped beside me. His eyes widened for a moment as he checked me over, then focused on my face. "Kaylee, did Beltrid kill him?"

I nodded.

"And what happened to Beltrid? Did he get away?"

I shook my head. "Dad's death sent him into the abyss. The steam house revealed the glory of Paradise in his soul. Beltrid couldn't handle it."

Josh stared at Dad's body. "I imagine not. Amazing." He returned to grieve with the family.

I felt a hand on my shoulder. I turned to see Joel standing beside me.

He still had tears in his eyes. "I cried because I knew what you would have to go through, not for your father. I knew it would be difficult for you."

"It was very difficult. I would have lost everything if it hadn't been for Nathan."

He raised an eyebrow. "But what did you gain?"

I realized I hadn't considered what had happened to us in there. I checked my body; It appeared normal. Wait, no! It really was normal again! My skin and muscles had turned back to their former color and size.

He held a polished mirror to me. "I guess you might want to check in this?"

I received it and stared into Joel's eyes. Images of my dream flashed across my mind, but I knew Beltrid couldn't do anything now. I peered into the surface. My face had returned to its former beauty. I touched my nose and mouth, as the latter crested into a smile.

"Now you're as beautiful on the outside as you are on the inside." Then he held up the ring.

I felt a rush of excitement flash over me as I reached out my hand. He slid it onto my finger.

Warmth spread over my hand and up my arm until its energy enveloped me.

He grinned. "Now we still have you for a while longer."

I pulled on the ring; it didn't budge. "Guess so. But Beltrid said something about this ring having a history. We had assumed he wanted the ring to control God."

"We knew you would find out eventually." He sighed. "The ring on your finger was forged in the divine fire of heaven. But like anything that God makes, it can be corrupted. Beltrid wanted the ring so he could place it upon someone bent to evil. Nathan was his target until we stopped him. If your father had continued using the ring in his selfish condition, he could have performed supernatural events, but for evil purposes."

"But what about all the talk that God ultimately controls the ring?"

"He does. But evil exists in the world and in Satan. As long as they exist, good can be corrupted for its use. When the time comes, then God will eradicate all evil. Now, for the sake of those who will unite to Him, He allows it."

I fixed my eyes on him. "Why didn't you ever tell this to Dad? Or me? We didn't know the full risk of the curse."

Joel frowned. "Did Adam and Eve know the full consequences of eating from the tree? No, God simply told them not to eat from it, or they would die. They couldn't understand what that meant."

"Yeah, and see what happened to them!"

Joel sighed. "You're not seeing the point. They failed to trust Him. We knew Sisko's heart. Even when he failed, he didn't fall into the curse because he trusted God."

I wrinkled my brow. "But he said he had been cursed."

"He touched it, yes. But because he kept his love and faith in God, he didn't fall. He refused to allow evil to use him, for twenty years he held the ring and did nothing with it."

I paused to think. "That's because he didn't know he could."

"Exactly."

My eyes jerked to meet his. "But I do. Doesn't that make me a greater risk?"

He smiled. "To some degree, yes. But we don't have to worry about that now. You have it, and your heart is united to Him. Beltrid has been vanquished and evil's dominion has taken a heavy blow today."

"But what about the bracelet?" I pointed to the metal gleaming in Joel's hand.

He glanced over at Nathan. "Perhaps you had better check out your brother first."

I raised an eyebrow. What did he mean? I examined Nathan up and down. He appeared normal enough. Then the sun glinted off something on his left wrist.

I tapped Nathan on the shoulder. He had been lost in his own thoughts as he watched the family cry around Dad's body along with the villagers sending up their laments. He jerked and turned to me. "What?"

"What did the steam house do to you?"

He looked himself over. "I don't know. I seem normal enough. I must not be bad or good."

I lifted his arm up and pointed to the bracelet. "This wasn't there before."

He glanced at it. "Oh, that. Yeah, it appeared when I exited the steam house. But so far, nothing's happened. It's shiny though."

"Have you tried to take it off?"

He shook his head and pulled on the bracelet. No matter how he tried, he couldn't unsnap it from his wrist. "It seems to be stuck."

Joel pointed at it. "Look at the design."

I examined it and gasped. It bore an engraved image of a winged horse, just like mine. I turned to Joel. "What does this mean?"

"Put yours on."

I took the bracelet from him. I stared at Nathan and he stared back, wonder in his eyes.

I snapped the bracelet onto my wrist. Nothing happened.

Joel nodded to Nathan. "To activate it, you must say, 'Upwards.'"

Nathan wrinkled his brow. "Activate it?"

I chuckled. "You didn't think the steam house would give you a bracelet just for good looks did you?"

He shrugged. "All right, here it goes." He cleared his throat. "Upwards."

Brightness grew around him until a solid light shone. Some of the people where we stood spun around and stepped back. As the light died, a beautiful, white, winged horse stood where he had been.

I stopped breathing. His beauty captivated and entranced me. Several who noticed gasped and stared.

Kaylee? Why are you looking at me that way?

I heard his words in my head! "Nathan, you're...a winged horse now."

No way. He turned his head and examined his body. *Oh my, I don't know what to say.*

I rubbed his neck. His silky hair sent chills down my arm.

Oh, now that feels good. More, more.

Joel cleared his throat. "Kaylee, as long as you wear your bracelet, he will remain a winged horse. Once you take it off, he will revert to his human form. However, his bracelet, like your ring, will not come off."

I stared at Joel. "You mean, we're united in a fashion?"

He grinned. "Exactly. The steam house revealed that you need each other. His mission is to help you fulfill the calling of the ring, so it has become part of his responsibility as well."

Kaylee, ask him, can I walk away if I don't want this mission? I relayed the question to Joel.

Joel's face fell. "Yes, he could reject it. Once outside a five mile radius of your presence, the link would no longer work and he would revert back to his human form, but..."

Nathan neighed. *But what?*

Joel met Nathan's eyes as if he had heard. Maybe he had. "If you walk away from your mission to aid Kaylee with the ring's calling before you are released by the bracelet, over a period of years, you'll discover that you cannot get around as well as you can now. Eventually others would have to carry you where you want to go. You would go from being able to fly to being dependent upon someone else to get about."

Nathan's head sank as if he considered what he had heard.

Joel stared me in the eyes. "And Kaylee, all the rules about using the ring apply to Nathan. You cannot use his gift for selfish purposes, or you will be cursed and the bracelet will release him. The ring will guide you. But he is free to use his gift as he wills, though he may be judged in how he uses it as anyone else would."

"I understand."

Nathan faced me. *God knows I need this, so who am I to say no? But I only ask this one thing: that we find Crystal and make sure she's all right as soon as possible.*

I smiled. "You already know the answer to that, Brother. Of course we'll search for her."

One more thing, make sure you know where I'm at before you take that off. If I'm flying around—

He cocked his head to one side. *Fly? I can fly!*

He spread his wings and leaped into the air. Air swooshed around me with each beat. He rose into the sky, blazing white in the sunlight. He circled around overhead, then dived toward us. I instinctively ducked as he pulled out and shot back toward the clouds. He circled a few low puffs of clouds a couple of times before he glided to the ground and landed at a run, stopping before me.

That was indescribable! I think I like this change.

I chuckled. "But you were terrified when we fell from the sky-island."

He spread his wings. *I can't fall off of these.*

I held up my wrist. "Are you ready?" He nodded, and I unsnapped the bracelet. Nathan reverted to his human form in a blaze of light. A few people had seen it and talked among themselves. But our family had remained focused on Dad's body.

I needed a necklace to keep my bracelet with me. Dad had one on his neck with his wedding ring on it.

Then I remembered. "Nathan, to the house! We can free Amma!"

He realized what I referred to and we shot down the street. Seth pounded after us.

We burst through the door and grabbed my pack. I took the key out of my pants pocket, pulled Amma out, and placed the key into the crystal's remaining hole. Then I broke it off—the ball throbbed with light.

Seth flung the door open and stood at the threshold. He noticed the crystal ball on the ground. "Did you—"

I nodded and focused on the crystal.

It glowed, and a stream of light floated up from it like steam rising. It twirled and swirled in varying colors until it formed the shape of a body. Then Amma materialized into it and fell over into our arms.

She jumped back and froze for a couple seconds. Her arms had been raised as if fending off an unknown danger.

The fear on her face turned to confusion. "Where am I?"

"Amma!" I flung my arms around her and squeezed. Nathan enveloped her as well. We had saved her, and it felt great to hold onto that reality after seeing Dad leave.

She stared over my shoulder. "Seth? What are you doing here? Last thing I recall is waking up outside and encountering a strange man." She examined her surroundings. "And this isn't even my house. Where am I?"

Nathan rubbed her shoulder. "It's a long story. But the short answer is, you are in Reol, Father's hometown, at his parent's house."

"And where is Sisko? Did he go to town?"

I could tell none of this had registered yet. "Amma, that's part of the long story. I'm afraid you've been frozen in a crystal prison for a few weeks."

She stared at me like I talked nonsense.

Seth hugged her. "Welcome back, Sis."

We related to her the story of our trip to Reol and the events in the steam house as briefly as we could. Upon hearing Dad's fate, she hung her head and her shoulders shook. But her face lit up as we related his joy and conveyed his message to her. We led her to his body outside the steam house.

She stood over him; her eyes glistened wet with sorrow but remained firm with joy. "He talked so frequently about Paradise, I know he's in total bliss now." She leaned over to him. "This is the second time you've done this to me. You better stay there this time. I don't want to go through this again."

I imagined Dad sitting in Paradise, watching us through a window against a set of trees. The image caused me to chuckle. I waved at the sky in case he could see. I knew he would enjoy that.

The funeral expressed Dad's life and joy beautifully, and people from miles around attended to pay their respects. Many had been helped at one time or another by Dad and many related their story to us.

Father Jonah ended the funeral with words of comfort, commending him to God. We buried him at the village cemetery next to others of his family.

Seth stayed and visited with us for a few more days before journeying back to his house.

Once Amma found out we would be traveling most of the time, and she would be by herself, she opted to stay in Reol with Sisko's brother and help him take care of his parents. Nathan and I felt good about that too, knowing Josh would be watching over her.

We told her we would go back and move what we could of our belongings for her use. It would take more than a month, but at least now we knew the way and what to avoid.

With Rodan and Beltrid no longer a threat, it should go smoothly. Well, it should, yes. But one never knew either.

I did inherit Dad's necklace. I snapped the bracelet around it to hang upon my breast.

The bracelet had bound Nathan and me together. Not like a husband and wife, but definitely more than a sister or brother. We shared a melding that could only be described as spiritual, but with an amazingly physical difference. I depended upon him, and he upon me. The steam house had seen we needed to work together.

After spending time with Josh at his place again, we stood upon the grass in front of his house.

I pulled the bracelet out. "You ready to fly?"

Nathan grinned. "Let's do it."

I took the bracelet off the necklace and placed it on my wrist. Nathan said, "Upwards," blazed into a flame of light, and appeared from it a winged horse.

I patted his thighs. "My, Nathan, what muscular thighs you have."

All the better to kick you with if you don't get on.

I laughed, then jumped upon his back. "Giddy-up!"

He turned his head and fixed his eye on me. *Hey, I'm not some ignorant horse you can command.*

I winced. "Sorry. I got carried away. Can we go now? Please?"

He neighed and jumped into the air. His wings extended and flapped, shoving us higher into the sky. I waved at Josh.

He waved back. "Return and visit sometime."

"We will."

I leaned down and wrapped my arms around Nathan's neck. I watched the land roll beneath us as his wings beat out a steady rhythm. "This is wonderful. I loved you before, Brother, but now you're also my favorite horse in the whole world!"

I can tell you, being a winged horse is a whole lot better than trying to ride one.

"To each his own." I felt like I could sleep up here. Clouds swooshed inches above my head. I stuck my arm up and watched as eddies of white moisture trailed behind us. I giggled.

Then I felt a nudge in my heart.

I scanned the ground, and a house below beckoned to me. "Nathan, someone down there needs me."

You know, I could keep going.

"Nathan, I need you and you need me. And being bound to me, you are bound to the ring indirectly. It's our calling."

He neighed and bobbed his head up and down. *Of course. I only wanted to make sure we're a team. Let's do this.*

I held on, and he dived toward the ground. I wasn't just my brother's keeper, we were each other's, and everyone else's. This could prove to be some adventure.

After serving as a minister in two churches, marrying a life-long partner in 1982, helping to give birth and raise three wonderful children, and work his way up to an experienced bookkeeper and now financial officer for a Texas city, what would be the next challenge for R. L. Copple? He discovered in 2005 a passion for writing fantasy and space opera. Since October of 2005, R. L. Copple has published numerous short stories and flash fictions at magazines such as Dragons, Knights, and Angels, Everyday Fiction, Digital Dragon, and Resident Aliens—a complete list can be discovered at his website: www.rlcopple.com/published.php.

He has written more than seven novels and saw a novella and novel published by Double-Edged Publishing, and now *Reality's Dawn* and *Reality's Ascent* are being published at Splashdown Books, to be followed by the third and final book, *Reality's Glory*. Be sure to follow blog.rlcopple.com for the latest updates.

The Reality Chronicles
by R.L. Copple

Reality's Dawn
Reality's Ascent
Reality's Glory

Coming in April 2011
from Splashdown Books:

The Crystal Portal
by Travis Perry and Mike Lynch

And Yeshua said,
"His ears will be a sign to you."

A time-travelling warrior elf on a manhunt for an evil genius. A state-of-the-art robot from New Los Angeles. And a carpenter's son from first-century Israel. Entering the Portal to the Crystal World, they join forces with a princess of Sapphire City to defy their power-mad adversary.

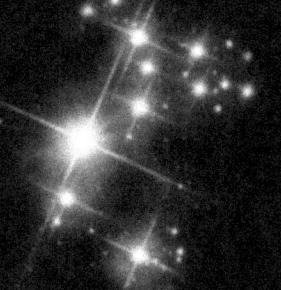

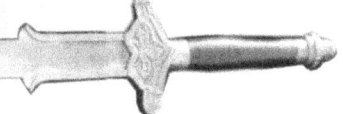

Sequel to
The Duke's Handmaid

nor íron bars a cage

~ caprice hokstad ~

In a last-ditch effort to find his missing son, Duke Vahn sends his most trusted servant to pose as a runaway slave in the hostile country of Ganluc. Meanwhile, the challenge he faces at home is no less daunting. This beautiful story is full of images: leadership by serving, ungrudging chivalry, and faithful romance.

Book Two of the Ascendancy Trilogy

www.ingramcontent.com/pod-product-compliance
Lightning Source LLC
Chambersburg PA
CBHW060917180626
46817CB00004B/1304